THE SUMMER JOB

Also By Adam Cesare

Tribesmen

Video Night

The First One You Expect

Exponential

Mercy House

Zero Lives Remaining

The Con Season

Collections

Bone Meal Broth

Collaborations

All-Night Terror (w/ Matt Serafini)

Jackpot (w/ Shane McKenzie, David Bernstein, Kristopher Rufty)

Bottom Feeders (w/ Cameron Pierce)

Crawling Darkness (w/ Cameron Pierce)

This edition copyright © Adam Cesare, 2017

Editing for 2014 edition by Don D'Auria

Cover by Fredrick Richardson

Interior Layout by Scott Cole

Black T-Shirt Books Logo by Chris Enterline

All rights reserved.

This book is a work of fiction. Names, characters, places, and incidents are either products of the author's imagination or are used fictitiously. Any resemblance to actual events, locales, or persons, living or dead, is entirely coincidental. No part of this publication may be reproduced or transmitted in any form or by any means, electronic or mechanical, without written permission from the author.

THE SUMMER JOB

by Adam Cesare

Prologue

For the first time in twenty-six years, Hugh Mayland was winning the war against his wife.

The battle took a turn as they crested the ridge to look out over the town nestled in the woods. Hannah lifted her hands up to her mouth in awe of the beauty surrounding them, leaning back into her husband's chest.

Not only had the trip to America been Hugh's idea, but so had driving across Western Massachusetts instead of dipping down through Connecticut into New York.

This skirmish had been one of culture and landscapes: pastoral vistas versus urban/suburban sprawl. They'd started out in Boston, with the intent of staying for a few days before continuing down the coast and ending up on the beaches of Florida.

But Boston bored Hugh.

"It's not London, it's barely even Leeds," he'd said.

"Maybe that's not it. Maybe it's your hatred of everything the slightest bit modern," Hannah said, adding, "And young people."

That last part rankled him, probably because it was true.

There wasn't a moment that didn't go by where Hugh wasn't rolling his eyes at a college student. In Boston, there was no escaping them. The little pricks used their iPhones to cut through the subdued natural light of the Isabella Stuart Gardner Museum, take pictures of themselves sitting on John Harvard's lap, tweet their thoughts on a local production of Beckett's *Endgame* while it was still being performed.

They were a waste of years and money, and Hugh wanted to be away from them.

The ageist angle was not the way to approach this situation, though. He would have to convince her in another way.

"Look at the *Fodors*. They list McDonald's under the cuisine section in every guide we've got. Every city in the world is now identical. Why even bother traveling?"

"I feel a proposition coming up," Hannah said, moving the hair out of her eyes, looking girlish even if the hair was going gray in spots.

"Let's see the parts of the country that humans haven't fucked up yet."

Gone were the days of proper English gentlemen, but Hugh still used profanity sparingly. If you didn't hold back, why should anyone take your fucks seriously?

The war he waged with his wife wasn't Hugh's idea. Not that it was Hannah's either. Some permutation of the struggle existed in every marriage. Theirs was not unique, but it was often one-sided.

It in no way diminished the love that he and Hannah felt for each other.

Hugh's gruffness was always upended by Hannah's patience and forethought, as if the natural ebb-and-flow of their life together mirrored the plot of those American sitcoms that Hugh detested so much. The studio audience laughed at Hugh's failings, clapped when Hannah was proven right, and then let out a coo of acceptance as the couple reconciled.

After all these years, three grown children, two affairs (one apiece, each over a decade ago), Hugh could finally bask in the glory of victory.

And it was all thanks to a little town in Western Massachusetts, nestled in the hills of the Berkshires, a handful of miles east of where the Commonwealth backs into upstate New York. Mission, where there were so few people, but what people there were seemed exemplary.

"We've seen a handful of sunsets. How many were better than this, do you think?" Hannah asked. She was poking fun at Hugh's propensity for listing his experiences. The best movie of the year, the best fish and chips he ever ate, his top five most re-readable books.

"There are none that can compare," he said, pulling her close. He put his lips to the back of her neck, stopping right at the point that the downy hair brushed against them. Not really kissing, just waiting and breathing.

They watched the sunset together in silence, Hugh's hands resting on Hannah's hips as a chill set in, cutting through the heat of the day and making everything perfect.

The tops of the trees seemed to glow, with the sun dropping right into the valley on the horizon, like a coin into a slot. The sky did a magic show of purples, blues and different gradations of gold.

There was no way of telling, looking out over the woods and the few rooftops of the small town, what century they were in. Even in London's most historic districts there were reminders of modernity: satellite dishes, electric billboards, etc.

If Hugh inhaled deeply, he could catch the chemical scent of their bug repellent, but he didn't let that hint of modern comfort ruin the experience.

"What's that?" Hannah asked, breaking Hugh out of his stupor.

She pointed to the treetops at the base of the next hill, a thin pillar of smoke snaking through the branches.

"Campers," Hugh said, his jaw automatically beginning to set, his mood ruined by the possibility of boisterous Americans.

Hannah hugged his arm tighter, trying to wrest him back into the last rays of the sunset. There was no sun left, though. One moment it was day. The next it was night.

What Hannah did next surprised him. It seemed to surprise her as she was doing it. She kissed Hugh deeply, reaching up to kneed the back of his neck with her fingertips.

He stared at her, mouth agape and lips moist.

"Don't let anything bring you away from this," she said. It was as if she'd read his mind. Although he couldn't remember her ever saying those exact words, it was not the first time that she'd ever dipped into his subconscious to extract a thorn.

"Nothing could," he said, taking her hands away from his face and kissing her to reciprocate.

She smiled. Her face was hard to make out in the sudden darkness, but the picture of it stuck there behind his eyelids, the impression of a familiar room after you've turned off the lights.

"In fact, why don't we go say hello?" he asked her.

Now it was Hannah's turn to look surprised.

"Who knows? Maybe they'll be some charming young people."

♦

Hugh led Hannah through the woods, following the music and the glow of the fire until they reached the camp.

The site was lived-in. Not the impromptu clutter laid down by a group of weekend warriors, the kind of folks that pitch a tent, warm a can of baked beans over the fire and declare themselves campers.

No, this was more like a modernist *Swiss Family Robinson*. There was music as they approached, under which Hugh could detect the steady hum of a generator. The music was rock, but not overly aggressive. The kind of thing that you might have heard pouring out of East End clubs a few decades ago, back when even the punks only wanted to get high and sleep together.

These campers were kids, but not the kind that had ruined Boston for Hugh. These were country folk and even their in-party mode was softened by the laconic, well-intentioned mood of the countryside.

At least that was what Hugh projected on them in the first few moments of watching. For a time Hugh and Hannah went unnoticed, observing a few candid moments of young people at play.

They were young, but not teens, not all of them. Most were well into their twenties, unwinding after a hard day's work, no doubt.

Their clothes were nondescript: no designer names, no vulgar images. The guys wore jeans and T-shirts, skirts and monochromatic tops for the girls.

Hugh and Hannah watched the group talk, joke, and drink. The two smokers among them were discreet, segregating themselves to the outskirts of the congregation.

Towering above the party, jacked up as high as it could get off the ground, was a caravan.

Or a trailer as the Yanks called them.

It hadn't moved in a while. If the bald tires weren't a dead giveaway, the old Airstream was surrounded on all sides by saplings and full-grown trees.

"Hey there," a voice came from the left of the small rabble. They'd been spotted.

"Don't look like that," the same voice called. "You got this look like we caught you peeking over the fence at our orgy." The owner of the voice parted the crowd, older than the other partygoers by at least a decade. He was tall and heroin-skinny with a scraggly beard, a length and style right at the border between homeless and chic.

"We saw the fire," Hugh said, stammering.

"Are you British? Is Smokey the Bear outsourcing now?" The kids laughed around the bearded stranger. His voice bounced around the forest around them, the music had been turned down. When did that happen?

For the first time since they'd been in the States, Hugh was aware of the difference in accent.

"We didn't mean to intrude," Hannah spoke up. There was an apparent embarrassment in her voice and a hint of something else that Hugh picked up on. Fear?

"I'm just kidding, y'all, meant no offense," the tall man said. "My name's Davey. I'm the den mother around here." The kids offered this a light chuckle. "Join us. Please."

And they did.

The Londoners had drinks in their hands so fast that Hugh could barely process the movement. Hannah lifted her cup to her mouth but didn't drink. She pitched an eyebrow at Hugh, who offered her a slight shrug and drank deeply from his own red Solo cup.

Citrus and berry and vodka and apple and turpentine with an undercurrent of something licorice-y that didn't fit at all. Gin? It was terrible. It was the kind of drink that a high school student would mix if they were given free rein to raid the liquor cabinet and refrigerator.

The music was back. Hugh couldn't tell if it was louder than before, or just seemed so because they were at the heart of the party now, not off at the outskirts. It was louder and meaner, but something about that pleased Hugh.

Hannah took a draught of her own cup, leaning against Hugh for support, backing her ass into his hand. He gave it a quick pinch.

Hugh looked around. This wasn't the stilted cocktail party the couple was used to attending. Davey was nowhere to be seen, but the young people seemed to double up, filling in the negative space and intensifying their dancing, carousing and joking. The kids weren't mushing Hugh and Hannah together uncomfortably, but they didn't keep their distance either.

Every so often a large kid with a beard would hoot and the crowd would part. He would then throw another armful of kindling on the fire. The flames flared up, sending a gush of smoke into the air and washing the citrus-hooch taste out of Hugh's mouth.

They hadn't learned anyone's name, and Hugh didn't particularly mind. Hannah was knocking her empty plastic cup against her lower teeth, a sophomoric clacking that Hugh couldn't help but smile at. A mousey girl cut through the party and filled it from a plastic milk jug.

"Thank you," Hannah said, but the girl just bowed and shot off in another direction, ready to refill someone else's drink.

"I like it here," Hannah said, laughing. Around them the chitchat and joking had discreetly morphed into dancing, a dance that pointed out the lone inequity of the party: the guys outnumbered the girls.

As the bonfire flared, the bearded kid dusted off his hands on his overalls and plucked the mousey drink girl from the crowd. He gently took the jug from her, returning the cap and placing it at the base of the tree. Then he took her tiny hands in his massive ones and twirled her around, the way a groomsman might dance with the flower girl at a wedding reception.

Hugh could see the blemish now, the large jagged scar running up the mousey girl's left arm, so prominent that it looked like it had been built up with dark wax. The girl so innocent and beautiful immediately became an object of pity and (if he was being honest with himself) disgust.

The bearded boy twirled her around, eyes off the scar, oblivious to it.

Around them the dancing was less saccharine, the guys with their hands in girls' back pockets, most doubling up in an attempt to offset the lack of female partners. Light, flirtatious kisses were traded, with deeper more adult ones creeping up along the shadows, behind the trees.

Hannah rubbed Hugh's palms and he looked down to find his feet moving without him. He was dancing, the citrus-smoke burn in his nostrils like an alcoholic lozenge. Hannah guided his hands up and down, grinding like a woman born two decades later.

Her mouth was moist and sour. Her tongue darted along his teeth and a millisecond later was gone. "Hannah," he said, wishing he could double his arms around her, constrict her like a snake in a loving embrace.

He looked up and the spell was broken. They were being watched. It wasn't obvious, but the kids were sending too many sideways glances their way, some of them flat-out staring.

Hannah followed Hugh's eye line and noticed it too, separating from where she was pressed against him, looking embarrassed that she'd been caught dancing with and loving her husband in public.

The eyes sobered Hugh. This wasn't their place. This wasn't their time.

"Let's ask them to point us back in the direction of town," Hugh said, "It's late."

Hannah gave his hand a short squeeze that let him know she was on board.

Taking a step towards the rest of the partygoers, Hugh's world drunkenly rocked and tipped. The music was noticeably louder than before.

He made his way towards the bearded young man. The boy had taken a rest from tending the flames and had retired against a tree stump, the mousey girl on his knee like a sexually aware ventriloquist's doll.

In Hugh's imagination her scar pulsed and throbbed like an artery. He had to will himself to stop looking at it.

"Excuse me," Hugh said, his own voice coming out too loud, cutting through the song.

The bearded boy looked up.

"Could you tell us how to get back to Mission? To the hotel?"

The boy stared back at Hugh. The young girl on his lap was pushing her fingers into his beard, making curly Qs of hair around her fingers. In the firelight their pale skin looked orange.

Her scar looked black.

"You head south, which is the path in between those two clotheslines. Leads to a break in the woods that faces the post office, one block up from the hotel. You keep on that trail and you can't miss it. The trail disappears after a while. But by then you should see lights."

The directions didn't come from the bearded boy, who still hadn't done anything except stare up at Hugh and creep his hand farther up the mousey girl's thigh. The voice came from behind them, Davey had reappeared.

Hugh and Hannah weren't the stars of the show anymore. All attention was on Davey. Behind him, the door to the trailer was open, a sliver of electric light peeking out.

The music had gone low enough that Hugh could hear the pop and crackle of the fire, the up and down of his own breathing.

"I don't know that you should leave yet. If you wait an hour or so and some of the kids can walk you back, make sure you don't get lost. Stay and dance a bit more. You were doing all right, *chap*."

Davey wavered above them, close enough that if he fell down, he'd land on top of them. The lids of his eyes looked heavy, like either he'd just woken up from a nap or he was drunker than either Hugh or Hannah.

The tall man breathed in deep, giving a nod and closing his eyes at the same time, looking about ready to pass out. The motion was too subtle for a secret communiqué, surely.

The music was back up, sparks buffeted Hugh's jacket as another log was thrown on the fire, and Hannah gripped his hand tighter.

She wasn't the only one touching him now, though, Hugh looked down to see the mousey girl's small fingers trying to work their way between him and his wife's hands.

"Stay and dance with me," the mouse said up to Hugh. She placed a small hand on Hannah's hip and pushed his wife towards the bearded boy.

Hugh looked up for help, for Davey, who was the only other adult present, but he was gone.

There wasn't just dancing, but singing now. It was a low hum of voices, the kind of sing along where no one seems to know the words, just the tune.

The small girl in the knit white dress and the scar had almost succeeded in unknotting Hugh and Hannah's fingers when the bearded boy grabbed Hannah by the wrist and gave a swift tug, separating husband and wife.

Something was going on here. They were somehow being taken advantage of, but what does one do in a situation like this? Hugh could feel the dismay climbing up his spine, encroaching upon the polite smile he'd plastered to his face.

The bearded boy had his arm around Hannah's waist, was twirling her around the same way he had the young girl. Hannah's feet moved in time, keeping up with the dance, but her pained, blank expression told Hugh a different story. She was trying to calculate a way out, same as he was.

"We've really got to get going," he said to the mousey girl in the white dress as she swung herself back and forth, a fist made around each of Hugh's thumbs.

She could have been holding his hands, but she was playing up her size, showing just how big his thumbs looked in her tiny grip. This close, Hugh could see through her Lolita act, could see the dark lines under her eyes, the kind that told him she was at least in her twenties. She'd had time to earn that scar.

The girl didn't acknowledge his request to leave, just kept dancing and smiling her half-childish, half-suggestive smile. Hugh glanced behind her to check on Hannah, craning his neck to see past the rest of the partygoers.

The bearded boy swung an elbow out at another young man, a motion that served both as a dance move and to keep the smaller boy from trying to cut in between him and Hannah. He was territorial. He'd taken a stranger's wife in hand and he wasn't letting her go.

Hugh shook his thumbs free of the girl's grip, her fingernails scraping his skin raw.

"Hey," she said, pouting like a favorite toy had been taken away.

With the bearded boy occupied with Hannah, no one had been feeding the flames, but still the bonfire raged higher. Tendrils of fire licked the low-hanging branches, threatening to ignite the whole dry forest.

Hugh jostled his way to Hannah, taking the outside track, trying to keep on the far side of the bonfire, not wanting to feel the heat any more than he already could. He still wore his jacket, but he didn't need it. His lower back was drenched in sweat.

"Excuse me," Hugh said, physically parting two youths that didn't want to let him pass. With every step the mood became more antagonistic and Hannah seemed to be swept farther out of reach, still in the pantomime of dance with the bearded boy, but Hugh could see that her feet were no longer touching the ground.

The boy had his hand on her ass, was picking her up by the pelvis, his large hand like a bicycle seat.

"Put her down now," Hugh shouted. That changed everything.

Every eye was on him, every shit-eating smile turned towards him. He was painfully aware of the sweat dribbling down his chin, the noxious lemon-booze stink oozing out of his mouth.

Like magic, the bearded boy began to lower Hannah. When her feet were just a few inches from the ground he released his grip on her ass, letting her slip down to the ground.

At first Hugh thought she'd passed out, the drinks and the exhaustion of the day conspiring to black her out.

But then he saw the bearded boy's other hand. His arm was slick up to the elbow, oily black in the firelight. He held a small knife, blood dripping down the handle.

"What have you done?" Hugh screamed, trying to close the distance between them, trying to run to where Hannah lay, but finding himself glued in place by the rest of the boys and girls.

Hugh bucked against them, throwing wild, helpless punches. He caught the mousey girl in the mouth with the back of his left hand, feeling her teeth mash against her plump lips. Their young muscles held him firm, giving up a bit of elasticity but redoubling their hold as he struck out.

The music was switched off now. The only sound was the crack of the firelight and the shuffle of shoes against dirt as Hugh's captors repositioned themselves. Twigs snapped as the ones that weren't holding him pressed in, forming a circle that stopped at Hannah's body.

The bearded boy's eyes gleamed in the firelight as he held his bloody hand out in front of Hugh's face. He didn't smile, even when everyone around him did. For the bearded boy this was a serious matter.

"Christ, Jesus Christ!" Hugh said. He was not a religious man, but it was the only exclamation that fit. The words did nothing to abate the bearded boy's approach.

Raising the knife, the boy placed one fat thumb against the flat of the blade and scraped away the blood. Hugh could see the metallic gleam of the knife, see the semi-coagulated accretion on the boy's thumb.

Sheathing the knife in his jeans pocket, the bearded boy raised the bloody thumb and kissed it lightly. The kiss left a small dot of red in the middle of the boy's mouth. He made a mark in the air with the thumb and made some sounds deep in his throat.

All around them the boys and girls made a similar sound, a primal amen to echo the boy.

The boy was going to paint the blood on Hugh. "Fuck you," he shouted and wriggled against them. Fingers crawled out of the darkness, calloused palms covered over his ears, pinning his head in place.

The boy pressed Hannah's warm blood to one cheek and then the other. Hugh tried his best to scream but they held his jaw shut. The boy finished up by pressing his thumb to Hugh's forehead, leaving a fat, warm droplet like it was Ash Wednesday in hell.

Taking a step back, the boy lowered his hands to his sides and waited.

"Toss him to the flames," Hugh heard Davey's voice boom. Whether Davey's long, lanky body was lost somewhere behind him or beyond the crowd that held him down, Hugh couldn't tell.

The hands hoisted him up onto his back and into the air. In the instant before facing treetops, Hugh grabbed one last look at Hannah. She lay with her back against the brambles and dead leaves that coated the forest floor, her eyes half open, legs splayed in the firelight. She looked like a child's abandoned toy.

Beneath him, his pallbearers laughed and joked and flirted. They swung him sideways, pointing his head forward, a compass for the flames. Behind him fingers stretched forward to support his head. They all wanted to lay hands on the crowd-surfing rock star.

Upside down, the flames of the bonfire didn't look like they were stretching to heaven, but instead like they were pressing up against the sky, their propulsive force trying to send all of the woods down deeper into the earth.

"Don't do this," Hugh said. It was too late, though. The kids at his feet were heaving him up and over, flipping him end over end onto the flames.

Hugh Mayland's head bounced off a knot on one of the larger logs, dulling his mind as he inhaled the smoke of his own flesh but not dulling the pain.

Part One:

Reason to Believe

Chapter One

Her name was Silverfish.

At least that was her name in high school, back when she'd bleached her hair platinum blonde, shaped it into a Mohawk and dated a guy who liked to be called Rott.

He spelled it with two T's.

She had cooled down on that stuff in college, cut down on the video games and eased off the punk rock act a little. Not too much—she'd still spit in your drink if you said anything untoward about The Misfits. Only the Danzig-era Misfits, though.

Her name was Claire and she waited tables. She did it professionally, now that she was out of school.

At least she did when there were patrons, which was rare on a Wednesday afternoon shift.

The Mohawk was gone and nowadays her hair was more red than it was anything else. She was a natural redhead, kinda. That was what most people call the color, but it was really more of a chestnut brown with a hint of red.

Guys that like redheads took to her, but that wasn't anything to be proud of.

Claire kept a stripe of platinum shooting out of her crown, where she could brush over it if need-be. She bleached the roots weekly, preserving the last vestige of Silverfish in a sea of Claire.

The more we try to change about our lives, the harder some things cling. Usually the most embarrassing aspects.

Just as she began to finish this thought, the service bell dinged from the kitchen.

The bell usually signaled that an order was up. But there couldn't have been an order because there was not a single patron interested in eating.

There was Tommy and Dale at the bar, but neither of them had been able to keep down solid food since before the Sox won it all in '04.

"The bell is a privilege, not a right. Don't make me take it away," she said, bellying up to the service window. Window boxed there, his tattooed arms resting under the heat lamps, was Mickey.

Mickey was not the kind of guy you wanted touching your food. Claire knew this because they'd been dating for the last four years. Move your amps? Sure. Score you weed with the bouncer he went to high school with? Definitely. Rearrange the crispy chicken on your Crispy Chicken Caesar Salad? No, thank you.

"Want to hit the Middle East tonight?" Mickey asked, the sweat from his forearms fogging up the stainless steel countertops.

"I thought it was that place in Allston tonight. For your own show?"

"That manager is a prick. Plus I think he's a fucking Nazi. We're not playing there again. Not gonna send the foot traffic their way." This was a circuitous, indignant way of saying that Mickey's band had been fired.

Mickey was not only the jewel of the kitchen staff at the non-franchise Applebee's-level joint Sunrise Cantina, but he was also the bass player for The Nun Puppets.

For close to a decade The Nun Puppets had been kicking around Boston, Cambridge and Allston. Occasionally they'd catch a club gig where they could play their own stuff, but they made most of their money playing covers at the bars in the South End.

They weren't terrible on the nights they actually played, but most nights ended with Mickey and his drunken bandmates arguing with management because they wouldn't play the set list they agreed to. For the Nun Puppets, covering "Jack and Diane" was an unlivable sin, but plagiarizing Black Flag was a God-given right.

Mickey hit the bell again. "Well, Middle East or not?" he asked.

She looked at him, the way she got to see him sometimes when she had an abnormally clear head. Or when he was being a particularly abrasive asshole.

His black pompadour had sagged in the heat of the kitchen, and the droplets of sweat on his brow were getting caught in the crags of his face. He was older than her, five years older. He had acne scars and bad tattoos. He owned a motorcycle cut, but no bike.

Mickey seemed like a good idea during her junior year, but so did a liberal arts degree.

"I think I'm going to stay in tonight. You have fun," she said, leaning into the window and giving him a peck on the cheek. She felt the muscles of his face stiffening into a frown under her lips. His sweat tasted like pot smoke and fryer oil.

Mickey gave a nearly inaudible sigh and dragged his forearms off the countertops. This was the start of a pout session that would probably last into next week.

The rest of her shift was two orders of nachos, a plate of jalapeño poppers, six dirty pitchers of beer and too many hurt, furrowed glances from Mickey to count.

♦

Claire stripped her Sunrise Cantina T-shirt off and pulled her own blouse from the backpack. She stood behind the service door, only mildly aware that anyone who walked past the alleyway was getting a free show. After she'd slipped civilian clothes over her black bra and pale skin, she tossed her bag into the back room of the restaurant and hit the streets.

It was the last week of May: that magic tipping point when traveling in Boston once again became enjoyable. In the last week of May the streets were cleared of students and it was possible to move all the way into a T car.

The sun was struggling to find a foothold in the clouds, but it was warm enough to indicate that the seasons were changing. Instead of catching a train, Claire decided to walk.

She cut across the Commons diagonally, moving away from downtown and towards Back Bay. If nothing else, the park offered fantastic people watching. College kids played various intramural sports; the adults went about their business, trying not to make eye contact with the musicians playing for change; and the drunks peeled off their clothes and lay out in the sun, basking themselves like chemically dependent lizards.

The park was so enjoyable that she was one block beyond it before her thoughts circled back to what she needed to do about Mickey. She turned down Newbury, hoping that the window shopping and deluge of irredeemable assholes would keep her mind off the subject.

It didn't.

Before she hit Copley, she'd realized that the end of Mickey and Silverfish had been a long time coming.

He acted like a child. He had always been like that, but when their relationship was beginning these qualities were somehow endearing.

For the first two years Mickey's exuberance for his music (and for Silverfish) was unstoppable, maybe a bit doe eyed, but still infectious. He was an artist, an artist who surprised her with cheap presents and talked about their sunglass-bright future.

But the bulb had dimmed. Maybe that wasn't it. Not so much dimmed, but maybe it had been pointed in the wrong direction the whole time and Claire was just now realizing it.

The Nun Puppets weren't excruciating, but they would never be famous. The members were never quitting their nine-to-fives. Eleven-to-six in Mickey's case, with three unsanctioned smoke breaks.

"Do you have a moment for women's rights?" A voice asked, pulling her out of her thoughts.

Shit. She'd run into one of those college kids with a vest and a clipboard who looked to shake down passersby for charitable donations. Usually she was better at avoiding them, but she'd drifted too close to this one while deep in internal strife.

"Sorry, another time," Claire said, keeping her eyes down. *Don't look at them, don't engage them*, she told herself.

"Wait a second," the voice called back, but Claire kept ahead. *This one was really desperate*, Claire had time to think before a hand clamped down on her shoulder and tugged her around.

"What the fuck is your prob—" Claire screamed and stopped herself. "Allison?"

"Ta-da!" Allison said, seemingly oblivious to the fact they had now created quite a scene out in front of Marc Jacobs.

"What are you doing?" Claire almost added "outside of the apartment" but thought better of it at the last moment. Anything that kept her roommate from sitting around all day and creating more dirty dishes was a gift that ought to be cherished.

"I got my old job back!" Allison waved a hand from the top of her dirty blonde ringlets to the soles of her Kate Spades, showing off her Planned Parenthood vest and accompanying clipboard.

"Job" was probably an overgenerous term to use, but Claire couldn't talk from inside her glass house that reeked of curly fries.

Allison kept her hand outstretched, waiting a moment for Claire to acknowledge this clearly earth-shattering moment.

"Congratulations!" Claire contorted her face into something like joy, at least enough in the ballpark to get Allison to buy it. Allison bought most things.

Allison had been Claire's roommate and best girlfriend since freshman year. She'd worked for various organizations in college as a way to boost her resume. She didn't need the money.

The most precise way of describing Allison would be that she was, and still is, a bright, beautiful, perky, lovable fucking asshole.

If the computer in the housing office had not placed Claire and Allison together freshman year, they never would have been friends. They probably never would have spoken to each other. But the computer had, thus fusing the pair into something that CBS would turn into an edgy version of *The Odd Couple*, but in real life more closely resembled a whirling ball of love and hate.

"What are you doing on the Newb?" Allison asked, turning Newbury Street into "the Newb". This was one of her trademark maneuvers: abbreviating words that didn't have or need abbreviations.

"Just walking home from work. I needed the fresh air."

"Is everything okay? What's wrong, babykins?" Allison had her hand on Claire's shoulder, already trying to tangle her up in some kind of calming BFF embrace.

"Nothing's wrong. I'm fine. You should get back to work," Claire said. As insensitive as Allison could be as a roommate, she was hypersensitive to drama. Despite being a leggy, gorgeous blonde, she was an absolute pig, rooting for truffles when it came to gossip.

"I'm not going anywhere until you tell me," Allison took a step closer to the curb and put her clipboard face down on the hood of someone's Beamer. She stood with her arms crossed and stared at Claire.

Allison was going to find out sooner or later. "Mickey and I are breaking up."

"Omigod! Excellent!"

"Jesus, at least feel conflicted about it," Claire said, looking down at her shoes, comparing her Converse high-tops to Allison's tasteful heels.

"Why should I? The guy's a loser. How did it happen? Did it happen just now? Tell me everything. Did he cry?"

"Not now," Claire said.

"Oh honey, did you cry?" Allison was wrapped around her now, trying her damnedest to push out a sympathetic tear of her own. People were starting to stare, Allison's blue-vested coworkers included.

"Cut it out, will you." Claire squirmed out of Allison's grip, the taller girl's breasts smooshing into her face as she struggled.

"Not until you tell me, tell me!" Allison laughed and held on to Claire tighter. Allie was a girl of contradictions. Her dialect was the lowest of vapid daddy's-credit-card slang, but she was still willing to engage in a tickle fight in the middle of a busy sidewalk, free of embarrassment.

"I will, I will," she said. The blonde loosened her grip and Claire slipped out, taking a defensive step back.

"So," Allison said, expectantly.

"You've got work to do." Claire pointed back to the other girl with the donations clipboard. These charities and organizations all used the same trick: have the volunteers work in pairs so they were harder to ignore.

"Hey, Kim," Allison yelled at the other girl, beckoning her over. She was young, maybe eighteen or nineteen, a freshman at BU or Northeastern. As she came closer Claire could see that her clothes under the vest had that distinct white suburban Rastafarian look to them: Berklee. She'd bet her life on it.

"Kim, I'm going to cut out early today. You can go back home now."

"But we've still got another hour of canvassing and everyone's just getting out of work. It's the most traffic we've had all day," Kim said. Her earnestness was deafening.

Allison leaned in close to the girl and lowered her voice.

"Look, I've been at this longer than you. Nobody donates. They'll talk awhile because they think you're cute, they'll make excuses about being hard up for cash or not having their checkbook on them, but I've only ever had, like, five people give me actual money. A girl like you, you'll get a lot of business cards, but no money. Go home, Kim."

"Okay." The girl's lip trembled. She looked a second away from melting into sobs. Claire was trying to hold back her smile by focusing on her guilt in the matter.

Allison brushed a reassuring hand against Kim's shoulder and picked up her own clipboard. She turned to Claire. "Let's get going," she said.

They turned, but a squeak came from behind them.

"Allison," Kim said. "How do I get home?"

Allison laughed and started giving directions to the lost little girl.

At least Claire's thoughts were away from Mickey for the moment, because all she could think about was how badly she missed college. Kim was going to have the time of her life, and she didn't even know it yet. Claire envied her.

After Allison had scooted the girl on her way she turned back around.

"Let's go get shitfaced."

Chapter Two

Claire woke up drunk, but not sick. Not yet, at least.

"Fuck." She took a deep sniff and the acrylic smell of the carpet made her gag. She rolled over on the floor, realizing that she'd been kicked out of the bed.

Grabbing on to the comforter, Claire clawed her way up. Allison was sprawled on the bed, sheets wrapped around her legs, breathing loudly through her mouth. She was naked, her large breasts sunny side up in the late-morning light.

They only had the one bed and Allison had it to herself on most nights. Claire slept over at Mickey's a lot. That was one more thing they'd have to figure out once she pulled the trigger and kicked Mickey to the curb.

Claire dressed for work to the soundtrack of Allison's mouth breathing.

She fished her keys out from yesterday's dirty pants and was startled when a voice broke the silence.

"Go get 'em, tiger." Allison had one eye peeked open, and most likely spoke without realizing the *Spider-Man* reference.

"What? Put a shirt on," Claire said.

"You're on the market now. Or about to be, correct? I'm just trying my best to get my name on that rebound spot."

"In your dreams."

"Yeah, my wet dreams," Allison said. Her joking sometimes toed the line into full-on repression.

"Don't you also have a job to get to?"

Allison's flirty composure evaporated. She scrambled to the edge of the bed, flipping over the alarm clock and jumping out of bed.

"I am so not used to this yet! But don't think you're off the hook," Allison said, flicking an accusatory finger at Claire. Allison wiggled into her T-shirt and Planned Parenthood vest, no bra. "Dump that fucker or don't bother coming home."

"Don't worry about me. Get going," Claire said, watching Allison bounce out the bedroom door, one shoe on and the other in the process.

The front door slammed and the apartment held the deserted calm of a tornado-ravaged Midwestern town. Claire continued getting ready, brushing her teeth and checking her phone.

There were three emails and ten text messages from Mickey. The correspondence was a story unto itself, with peaks and valleys, exuberance and manic depression.

The exchange started with, *What u up to?*
Continued with, *Sure ur not coming to mid estat?*
Bottomed out twenty minutes later with, *R u pissed at me!?!*
Rebounded into, *U know I love u so much.*
Relapsed into, *Fuk you then!*
The final message was time stamped 3 a.m. *U goNNa B @ Wk tomo? GOODNight.*

This was going to be a rough day and Claire wasn't even out of the apartment yet.

♦

The sirens were in THX Surround Sound. They bounced between the tall buildings and courtyards of Boylston Street as Claire walked to work. She took the long way there to think over the decision, to breathe some fresh air as she pinpointed how she was going to word it.

The emergency vehicles seemed to move with her, and then finally streamed past her. As she got closer to the edge of the park, Claire could see that the flashes were red, white and blue, belonging to emergency vehicles off all types.

Her first thought was an electrical fire at the Park Street T stop. The trains of the Green Line seemed to spend more time aflame than they did running. But as she got closer, she could tell that this was a street-level emergency.

Smoke billowed up from one of the side streets, tall enough that the stench of burning plastic was wafting over the park. The pillar was dense and black, inky in the center with gray edges that gave each separate puff its own unique shape.

The smoke was coming from Sunrise Cantina.

Claire's job was on fire.

Firefighters and looky-loos crowded the mouth of the street.

Sunrise was nestled in one of the few areas of urban grit that still clung to downtown Boston. It was plenty safe to walk around, still an area that tourists could move around comfortably, but it did retain a good number of colorful characters with neck tattoos and rowdy homeless guys.

Claire quickened her step, parting the crowd of onlookers the best that she could.

"Hey, girlie!" It was Dale, one of the drunks from the bar. Tommy stood next to his buddy, bleary-eyed and sipping from his coffee cup too deeply, letting Claire know that there was probably more Jameson's than Dunkin Donuts inside.

"We were worried," Tommy said, eyes still fixed on the flurry of activity around them. "We thought you were a crispy critter."

If Dale and Tommy were from anywhere else, you'd have thought they were lovers. A sociologist would describe their relationship as homosocial. They would also have some choice descriptors for the sociologist, too.

Dale and Tommy were improbable holdovers from a time when most of the neighborhood looked just like them: drunk, heavily accented, mildly racist and too proud.

"What's happening!" Claire grabbed hold of Dale's shoulder, getting jostled by passing rescue workers as they parted the crowd.

"Fahkn' bah's burning down," Dale replied.

"Yeah, it's been going since about eleven. That's when we been here since," Tommy added, taking a belt of his coffee. It was good to know that Sunrise was such a fixture in the pair's life that they arrived a half hour before the doors open.

"Have you seen Mickey?"

"Who?" Dale said. He had only been half listening, distracted by the commotion. The crowd undulated as the police tried to push the line back, wedging Claire between Tommy and Dale. She had never been this close to them before and had never noticed how terrible they smelled or how murky and smudged the silver of Tommy's Patriots jacket was.

"The cook! My boyfriend with all the tattoos," Claire said, not realizing how frustrated and scared she was until she heard it in her voice.

Tommy rubbed a freckled hand against his temple. "Shit, I haven't seen that guy all morning."

"Get out of my way," Claire said and pressed against the two old men, using them to get a boost through the rest of the crowd. The people were packed tightly, as though they were watching a parade or a concert, not a fire in a major commercial district of the city.

"Officer," she yelled to a cop who was threading police tape over a wooden barricade. He ignored her. She dipped her head under the barricade and was suddenly a whole lot less crowded standing where she wasn't supposed to be.

The firefighters had broken out the restaurant's glass storefront and were blasting water into the dining room. A cool mist speckled Claire's face and, when she wiped it away, her hand came back dirty.

"Lady, you can't be here." The cop who wouldn't answer her before now had his hand clamped over her shoulder.

"I work there," Claire said. It seemed like the right answer as she formed the words, but she realized how ridiculous the sentiment was as soon as she saw the cop's reaction.

"Not right now. I'm thinking that you have the day off." He rubbed his salt-and-pepper mustache.

"I need to know if my friends are all right," she said, shaking away from his grip. "My boyfriend is the cook." This was the second time in five minutes that she'd been forced into labeling Mickey as her boyfriend, probably not psychologically conducive to their in-progress break-up.

The cop glanced down at her chest. He was either checking out her tits or noticing that she was wearing her Sunrise Cantina T-shirt. With Boston cops, it could have been both.

"This is going to sound weird, ma'am," he said and hiked up his belt, sucking in his gut. "Is your name Claire?"

"Yeah, why?"

"You should come with me. Your boyfriend's been yelling for you since we got here. He's pretty fucked up."

"What happened?" Images of Mickey burnt to a cinder filled her mind. Her sense memory gave her a whiff of a well-done hamburger crackling on the Sunrise stoves. She began to retch as the nerves twisted around her anger. What kind of cop would use the term "fucked up" to describe a burn victim?

Seeming to read her mind, the cop raised a hand to stop her from bubbling over. "Calm down. He's fine. What I mean to say is that he's drunk."

The cop led her over to an ambulance. Both of the vehicle's back doors were open, Mickey sat on the bumper wrapped in a blanket, sucking on a tube of oxygen. He pressed the plastic mask so hard over his face that it was beginning to leave marks.

Mickey caught sight of her and dropped the mask. He had black marks running into each nostril from where he'd been huffing smoke. Claire's mind raced to piece together what had happened. Had Mickey, thinking she had been on time for work, run into a burning building to try and save her?

"Silverfish," he said, poking a few fingers out from under the blanket and waving her over. Claire was about to be embarrassed by hearing her high school name spoken aloud, but she caught herself. *I should just be happy that he's okay.*

"Where were you last night? Why didn't you call? I was so worried," Mickey said, his speech slurred. "Did you get my messages?"

"Yeah, I got them this morning. Sometimes I need to be alone," Claire said, now conscious of the cop and several paramedics that were listening in on their conversation.

"I love—" He couldn't get the words out before a coughing fit turned into a puking fit. Claire was happy that she'd worn close-toed shoes as the vomit speckled her Converse.

As Mickey swiveled to hold on to the ambulance banister, the blanket dropped away and Claire could see it.

She turned to the cop. "Why is he handcuffed?"

"Because we're pretty sure that your boyfriend burned the place down on purpose."

"Not true," Mickey said, babbling and coughing. "My fire was under control when I went to sleep, but when I woke up there was smoke all over." He spit a glob onto the asphalt. "I was so scared."

Claire looked at Mickey, then back at the cop. They both looked like they were waiting for her to say something.

"Fucking pathetic," she said.

Chapter Three

"What are you doing?" Claire asked.

Allison was sitting on the end of the bed, Claire's laptop on her knees. She didn't respond.

Claire sat up and rubbed her eyes. She tweezed the sleep out with her pinky and thumb, and then rolled it into sandy globules.

"Helping you out with the job search," Allison answered after a few more seconds.

"I just checked everything yesterday, made some inquiries. Nothing looks promising."

"No, you checked everything in Boston. I'm widening the net," Allison said. She was fully dressed, blue Planned Parenthood vest and all. "Waking up earlier than you and going to work is beginning to freak me out."

Claire reached to the floor next to the bed, fishing her phone from her jeans pocket. The time was 11:25, a new unemployment oversleeping record. "You're already late for work," Claire said.

"I know, but this is more important." Allison clacked the keyboard. "How does Ben & Jerry's sound?"

"Delicious."

"No. How does working for them sound?"

"The one on Newbury?"

"The headquarters. In Vermont."

Allison giggled, but it was too quick and told Claire that she wasn't one hundred percent joking about the job.

"There's nothing else in the state?"

"Waitressing jobs are totally out of the question?"

Claire gave her a blank stare that said "better dead than Red and better Red than a waitress again." Waitressing was no longer an option that Claire could stand.

"Everything else requires experience. You've got to hit the bricks, show employers that winning smile," Allison said. "Maybe a little of that rocker chick cleavage too."

Claire shot her a rocker chick bird.

"Or there's always the oldest profession."

"You'd let me get a foothold in your market share?" Claire's quip fell flat. Allison was already over the exchange, ignoring her and hunched over the laptop.

"How does Mission, Massachusetts, sound?" Allison said.

"Where the fuck is Mission?"

"It's right…" Allison paused and Claire listened to her make a few frantic keystrokes, looking up its location. "It's Western Mass., only a two-hour drive," she said.

"With or without traffic?"

"That doesn't matter. It's a position as seasonal staff at a hotel, you get room and board with the gig," Allison read.

"So, it's two hours without traffic then." Claire pulled a pillow over from the other side of the bed and pressed it against her eyes, trying to drown out the sunlight and Allison's help. It didn't help.

"I don't know. This sounds pretty good," Allison's voice was muffled but still audible. Claire ran her tongue over her teeth: fuzzy with whiskey and whatever she'd been mixing it with. Coffee? Gross. Claire felt the bed shift and the blankets pinching her thigh as Allison crawled up beside her.

"Is Mission in the Berkshires?" Claire asked, breathing her own hot exhalation in as it bounced off the pillowcase and back into her mouth.

"Close enough, by the looks of it."

Claire removed the pillow from her ears, feeling the blood return to her cheeks. She knew that she had the fabric design stippled into her face.

"You're trying to get me to move out? Trying to get rid of me?" Claire tried to sound like she was kidding, but the kidding part of their conversation seemed to be at an end. Now that she was fully awake, she didn't feel like it anymore.

She'd been sleeping a lot since the fire. Drinking and sleeping. Despite what she told Allison, she hadn't been looking too hard for work.

"Oh honey. Never." Allison pushed the open laptop onto Claire's knees to free up her own hands. Claire waved off the hug before it could reach her.

"Let me take a look at this."

"I've got to go to work," Allison said. "I'm not kicking you out, but a little time away from the city couldn't hurt and you don't want to go home, do you?"

Claire thought of New York and shuddered.

"Then this one looks semi-promising," Allison continued. "Keep an open mind. Besides, who is more hospitable than you?"

Claire pulled the screen towards her and read:

Come join our Family. The Brant Hotel is looking for a dedicated, hard-working and personable guest liaison to join our staff for the summer. Hospitality experience is encouraged but not required. Serious inquiries only, please. No solicitation.

At the bottom of the post was a phone number and address. "Give them a call, at the very least."

Claire nodded at her and heard the front door close. She highlighted, copied and pasted the address into Google maps and watched green fill the screen. This job would definitely get her out of the city.

Allison had been right. It wasn't the Berkshires, not exactly. The closest outcropping of humanity seemed to be Springfield, but Mission was far enough away that it wasn't Springfield's suburbs. It was the sticks.

Claire checked the timestamp on the post: almost three days old. They'd probably had several responses by now and the chances were slim to none that the position was still open. She felt for her phone under the comforter.

Was she really going to call them right this minute? No more investigation into the business, only the faintest idea of what a guest liaison could be? Yes, she was. She dialed the number and hit send, using the laptop to type *Brant Hotel Mission MA* into the search bar as the phone started ringing in her ear.

The website was about what she'd expected, a few pictures of a quaint hotel. The white siding and potted plants on the steps made it look more like a private residence. The website was so simple in design that it bordered on antique (*Sign our Guestbook!* a banner at the bottom of the page implored).

"Hello, Brant Hotel, how can I help you today?"

The voice on the other end of the line surprised Claire, as if she hadn't expected anyone to pick up. Now she was going to have to ask about the job, possibly set up an interview.

"Hello? Is there anyone there?" The woman on the line kept her voice cheery, ready to help whatever tongue-tied schmuck was wasting her time.

"Hi. Sorry, my cell phone was having problems, I'm here now." Claire started off this relationship with a lie.

"That's fine, sweetheart. How can I help you?"

"My name's Claire Foster and I'm calling in regards to your ad on Craigslist for the guest liaison position. Has it been filled?"

"Hello, Claire," the woman said, giving Claire a picture of a matronly old woman with a soft smile, someone that fit with the bed-and-breakfast images on her laptop screen. "If I'm not mistaken, I think you're the first person to reach out about it. Are you interested?"

The question somehow threw Claire. Was she? "Yes, very much so. I was just looking up the hotel online and it looks quite beautiful."

"Well, thank you for saying so. We've been in this location for over thirty years, watched the town grow up around us. That's why we need the extra help over the summer. We get busier than the small year-round staff can handle. Do you have hospitality experience?"

"Um," Claire said, damning herself for using the ugly placeholder during what was beginning to feel like a job interview. "I have six years of experience in the service industry, as a waitress."

"Waitressing is tough work. You should be well prepared for what you'd be doing here at the hotel."

"If you don't mind me asking, what exactly is that?"

The woman on the line laughed, at what Claire couldn't tell, but it didn't seem to be at her, which was good. "I told Daisy that nobody'd know what the heck 'guest liaison' meant. You'd help with the front desk, check in guests and sometimes help out with cleaning the rooms if Daisy should ever get too overwhelmed. Does that sound okay?"

"Sounds great," Claire said, a little worried about the fact that Brant had casually inserted housekeeping into the list of duties. "Should I send over my resume?"

"I don't know if that's necessary. Do you have a college degree?"

"Yes, I have a B.A. in English from Boston University."

"Wow, I don't know how competitive our pay is going to be. It's a sixty-dollar per diem that includes board and meals."

Not bad, and it's out of here. She looked up at the red-and-white pennant over the bed. *Time to move on.*

The woman took advantage of Claire's silence to add something else. "You sound great, but we're going to need to see you in person to get a better idea that you'll fit in here. Are you still in Boston?"

"Yes. Are you located near any lines of the commuter rail?"

"Sadly, we're not. Would you still be able to make it out?"

"I don't think it should be a problem. When should I stop in?"

"Would sometime this week be possible?"

Claire thought of Allison's car, the one that Claire constantly ridiculed her for having in the city.

"That should be no problem."

"Great. We'll see you when you get here."

"Wait," Claire said, not wanting the woman to hang up on her. "Sorry for not asking earlier, but who am I speaking with?"

The woman on the other end of the line made a sound halfway between a cough and a laugh. Claire wasn't sure if it was meant to be a silly-me or a silly-you. "Well my name is Victoria Brant, Ms. Brant, and this is The Brant Hotel. We can't wait to meet you, Claire."

Claire smiled at that, realized that she couldn't be seen and then spoke. "I'll see you soon."

But Brant was gone.

Chapter Four

Allison drove a black 2010 Hyundai Elantra, a used car that wasn't a used car because it had only been driven around on test drives at the dealership. Claire knew this much about the car because she knew this much about virtually all of Allison's possessions.

Allison told about each one in detail. Same with the netbook that she got with the student discount even though she hadn't been a student for nearly two years. Same with the bundle of panties that she had gotten after a particularly enticing Groupon from Victoria's Secret. She'd made Claire get some, too.

The Elantra nosed in and out of traffic like a mouse, Allison's feet jumpy on the pedals. Just because you own a car in the city doesn't make you a city driver.

Seldom used, Allison's car was reserved for the occasional trip to the Natick Mall or weekend jaunts into Brookline to load up on cheap wine and over-priced food at Trader Joe's. It wasn't exactly a workhorse. Allison paid their landlord two hundred and twenty-five dollars to park it behind the apartment. It used to be an even two fifty, but she got time off for good behavior.

"Suck my dick, you fucking asshole!" Allison screamed, passing on the left and screaming at a driver who had the gall to honk.

They weren't even to I-90 and already Claire was regretting so many parts of this plan. Allison had prodded her to pack a small overnight bag, a change of panties, travel deodorant and a fresh T-shirt in a plastic Shaw's bag.

After the interview they were going to spend the night somewhere in the Berkshires. As inane as they were, sometimes the stories from Allison's life would pop into Claire's mind, word-perfect.

"I've never been to the boonies," Allison had said yesterday while packing her own bag. "But I dated a guy sophomore year that took that skiing class, you know, the one that takes bus trips every other week. Yuck. I always thought he was doing it to fill his schedule with empty space, stretch his four years into five. But maybe he actually enjoyed skiing."

Allison spoke from the driver's seat, her voice doubling for a moment in Claire's ears, scaring the piss out of her.

"What?" Claire asked. Allison was always more than happy to repeat herself if you missed anything.

"I asked if you wanted to put on some music."

She didn't really, but if she didn't, then Allison would put on her own. The thought of auto-tuned vocals or faux soft rock country sent shivers up Silverfish's spine.

Claire picked her butt up off of the Elantra's passenger seat, getting enough slack in her jeans to fish her iPod out of her front pocket. The iPod was old, a hundred and sixty gigs but only a quarter full because Claire had lost a bunch of her music the last time her computer had crapped out.

On her last computer, Claire had named a playlist *Allison* and stocked it with music that wouldn't totally alienate her friend. No deep cuts, but instead the radio-friendly stuff. Nirvana, some Baroness instrumentals, and Ramones tracks that were safe enough for a Kidz Bop cover (although the thought of a choir of children covering "The KKK Took My Baby Away" made her giggle). These songs were comforting, but more importantly they kept the Chris Brown at bay.

Claire plugged in the aux jack and the iPod spooled up. She started off slow. Bobby Bare Jr. covering a Pixies song. By the end Allison was tapping her finger in time against the steering wheel.

"Not bad. I like it," Allison said. It was hard to tell if she was genuine or just being nice. It wasn't that Allison was a great liar, just that everything she said carried this aura of insincerity that called the veracity of every statement she made into suspicion.

Claire just *mmm-hmm*'d and nodded. She ran her tongue along the inside of her lower lip. You couldn't tell by looking at her now, but in high school she'd had a piercing there. There was still a tiny dot of callused skin there she could feel. Or at least Claire liked to imagine that's what she was probing, not just the contours of her flesh.

She still had other piercings and they seemed to glow hot under her clothes as she thought about them.

They passed Exit 13 to Natick. This was the farthest west Claire had ever been on 90, and she'd also bet that it was the farthest that Allison and the Elantra had been too.

"So," Allison said, starting with one of her most beloved nonwords, "did you look up anything about this place? What are people saying about it on Yelp?"

"I didn't check," Claire said. The people on Yelp were no help at all. The biggest bunch of poseur assholes on the internet, in Silverfish's estimation. That was some kind of achievement when you considered the internet as a whole.

Allison wrote Yelp reviews all the time.

"Their website was nice, if you don't mind a little clipart," Claire said. Allison laughed a bit.

"As long as there was a big banner at the bottom of the page asking you to sign their guestbook, or maybe an option for tabs or no tabs, the place sounds like a gem."

"There was!"

The two girls laughed, Claire sitting a little more forward in her seat, reminded why she'd stuck it out with Allison so long. They were good together.

Who else would have driven her out to the middle of nowhere? Nobody besides her mom, and that would have been a road trip with no survivors.

Allison yawned. "I'm beat. Do you want to drive for a bit?"

Claire had gotten her driver's license late in high school and had less than six months of driving experience before moving up to Boston, where no one in their right mind had a car. Her driving made Allison look like Ryan Gosling in that movie where he kept his shirt on. Allison knew this, liked to play with her about it. It could have been a bitchy power play, could have been big sister needling. Again, it was hard to tell with Allison.

"Yeah." Claire called her bluff. "Pull in at the next rest stop. You buy me some Roy Rogers, I'll drive the rest of the way."

"Deal. You're def getting held to that."

Claire had a theory that the abbreviation of definitely stemmed from everyone's inability to spell it correctly. It always got spellchecked into defiantly.

♦

Allison had picked all the skin off of her chicken.

After Claire ate the skin, they hit the road.

Claire was good at tuning Allison out when she wanted to, which was lucky because Claire needed all of her concentration to keep the Elantra in the middle of the lane. Driving made her anxious. Before college, there were a lot of things that made her anxious: what she was wearing, what people thought of her, how to keep her grades a few points above a C, but these days it was only driving.

Her body and brain associated driving with high school. The self-consciousness of her formative years came rushing back the second she touched the wheel, made her semi-sick, made her feel like a bout of acne was ready to bubble up under her chin.

Listening to Allison's constant chatter, the concerns of a barely employed college grad, was soothing in the same way that some people put on tapes of whale sounds or lit Yankee Candles.

"Get out your phone and plug in the address. I think we're getting close."

Claire chanced a quick glance over at Allison. Her phone was already out.

Dense woods surrounded them and pressed closer as the roads got smaller. Over the last hour traffic slowed to just a couple of cars, all of them speeding past Claire, all of them more confident drivers who knew where they were headed. Claire clicked on her lights. It wasn't dark yet. She was just anticipating sunset.

"Next exit," Allison said. It was less an exit, more of a delicate bend off the main road. As they took the turn the world got darker, a combination of taller, closer trees and the coming sunset.

"It's beautiful out here," Claire said. She didn't really mean it, but she needed something to say to keep her hands steady on the wheel and to get Allison talking again. Allison's drone was white noise that she'd gotten used to while driving to the point where now she needed it.

"It's okay. It's not, like, Northern Cali or anything, but it's pretty. Shit. Did you pack bug spray?"

"No," Claire said, leaving off the "Why the hell would I pack bug spray?"

Allison shrugged, already on to the next thing. "You know who came from out here?" She didn't wait for Claire's answer. "Meghan Laheri. You remember her from Towers?"

Meghan had lived on their floor freshman year. "Yeah. Do you still talk?"

"Hell no. But I see her on Facebook all the time. She's getting married. Believe it?"

Claire wasn't friends with Meghan on Facebook, even though she was much closer to her during school than Allison was. Claire had a policy of not friending anyone who didn't friend her first.

"Isn't she a little young?" Despite her best efforts, Claire was interested now. She listened to Allison instead of the radio.

"Well, I know lots of girls from school who are getting married. All the religious-types mostly, but some normal ones too."

Come to think about it, Claire had gotten a few notifications about engagements as well. Were other girls really that much ahead of her in the game of life? Would she have even considered marrying Mickey if he'd asked? Probably not.

"I can see that look you've got," Allison said. "Meghan Laheri is probably only getting married because she got knocked up. She was always such a dunt."

Claire scrunched up her face, looked over at her friend. "A dunt?"

"Yeah, she was a dumb cun—" Allison couldn't get the rest of the slur out. "Jesus!"

There were people in the road.

Claire hooked the wheel, the Elantra skidding perpendicular to the double yellow lines, the force of the turn feeling like it was going to flip the car over. Gravel dinged the side of the car and dust blocked out the dusk.

When the car finally stopped, Claire wiped the hair out of her eyes and then turned to check on Allison.

"Little mother fuckers," Allison whispered, looking out the passenger's side window.

Claire had to lean forward against the wheel to get a better look at them.

A group of kids, their ages ranging from early high school all the way up to around Claire and Allison's age. They stood on the side of the road for a minute, staring back at the car.

What were they doing crossing the street in the middle of nowhere? Claire put the car into reverse, backed up into the right lane, and stopped about twenty feet from the kids.

The whirr of power windows sounded.

"What are you assholes doing? We could have killed you!" Allison yelled at the strange kids and then paused, leaning a bit more out the window, waiting for their response. Not a creature of subtlety, Allison never asked rhetorical questions.

The group stood still for a moment. There were eight or nine of them, but it was hard for Claire to get a count because some were standing so far off the road that they were practically in the woods.

Their clothes were plain. Not modern, but not old-timey. They could have been the fresh-faced, costumed ensemble of an off-Broadway play.

The eldest-looking of the boys—not the tallest, but the eldest—stepped forward and raised his hand. "Sorry about that, we didn't see you coming. Is everyone okay?" he said.

He was handsome and spoke with an unmistakable earnestness. He would have gone far if he'd not stuck around here. Claire was already making up a history for the guy, the way she sometimes did while people watching. Maybe he was a farm boy. She wondered if they had farms in Mission. They'd certainly passed by enough on the way here.

Behind the boy who'd spoken, several of the younger kids smiled. It was impossible to tell if the expressions were meant to be friendly or mischievous. Claire could never tell with teenagers because she had recent first-hand knowledge that ninety-nine percent of the time kids were up to no good.

Allison didn't roll up the window, but said nothing.

The boy spoke again, "Is the car all right? Do you need a push into town?"

Claire could see that Allison had recovered from the shock of the boy's civility, was about to unleash on him. Claire stopped her.

"No, we're fine. Thank you though," Claire yelled back.

The boy nodded, about-faced to the rest of his group and they disappeared into the woods.

Claire used the master controls on her side of the car to roll Allison's window back up.

"They almost run us off the road and you end up thanking them? Great job," Allison said as Claire put the car in drive and continued down the road into Mission.

Chapter Five

Mission wasn't what she was expecting. Its Main Street was not Main Street U.S.A. but instead a gas station, a small post office, a general store, and The Brant Hotel. That was it.

To the south, beyond this bustling commercial hub, Claire could see houses. Well, she couldn't see the houses themselves, it was too dark for that, but she could see their lighted windows floating a good half mile away in the dark of the woods. The windows were not only raised because some were on the second story, but because the houses were built on the light incline of a hill.

"Looks happenin'," Allison said, breaking the silence.

The hotel itself was more like a large three-story house, situated to the north, opposite both the general store and the gas station. The streetlight outside the hotel, one of the two on the block, bounced off the white façade of the building and made the gold leaf of the sign glitter. The effect was inviting, a beacon in the dark for the weary traveler.

Claire brought the car closer to the hotel and inspected the sign. It was white and green, matching the building. Under the name of the hotel was a carving of a jumping rabbit, painted over in the same gold leaf as the lettering.

"Parking in the rear?" Claire motioned to the long driveway on the side of the building.

"Because I winter here for the skiing?" Allison said. "Like I know."

Claire didn't answer. Three hours in a car with Allison and one near miss was enough to piss on anybody's parade.

Gravel crunched as she pulled the car around the back of The Brant. Claire pulled up the emergency break and shut off the engine. Allison unbuckled her belt and turned around in her seat.

"Creepy," she said, staring into the woods that backed up to the hotel. The red of the Elantra's brake lights made the shadows blacker.

Claire wouldn't have found it "creepy" without Allison's suggestion—her childhood home had backed up against the woods, but now she couldn't stop looking.

Allison popped open the passenger side door and got out.

"Hey," Claire got her attention and tossed her the car keys, then got out on her side.

The small parking lot had five cars, including the Elantra. The Brant was neither deserted nor bustling.

On the other side of the car, Allison stretched. She touched her toes and made a sound halfway between an orgasmic moan and the mew of a kitten. It was obnoxious, but it was why all the boys loved Allison Pomero.

Not that all the boys snubbed Claire, quite the opposite. Claire's piercings, the wisps of tattoos that you could catch when she wore a tank top, if her tips had been any indication, there were guys who went in for that.

Claire envied Allison's Banana Republic good looks and wholesomeness, but there were times that Claire was positive that Allison felt the same about her. Claire was probably more Hot Topic than anything else, but fuck that store. The babbling brook of jealousy they shared helped to keep their friendship strong.

"Let's get going," Allison said, cracking her knuckles with her hands to the sky, belly button peeking out.

The pathway back to the front of the building was a lighted terrace overlooking a garden. Bags of top soil were balanced over the railing. Claire guessed they were part of the beautification process for the busy summer season.

Claire glanced at her phone. It was 8:05. Low signal out here in the boonies, but enough. No new texts. That was good. Maybe Mickey had given up.

"Cute," Allison said, running a finger along the shutters that lined the terrace. Her constant need to talk dampened down by the long day. Now she only dripped adjectives.

The windows and shutters were green, freshly painted. White siding with green trim. The Brant was a classy joint.

They entered the lobby, the tinkle of sleigh bells heralding their arrival.

"Nice," Allison said, but she didn't keep it to one word this time. "Totally presh. If you fuck up your interview, you mind if I take the position? You can drive yourself back to Boston."

It didn't sound like a joke to Claire, but she forced herself to giggle just to keep the game going.

They were alone in the atrium, drifting towards the front desk with their heads on a swivel. The lobby smelled great. Claire guessed the smell was potpourri mixed with the freshly stained and polished hardwood floors.

Allison's heels clicked and then went soft as they passed onto the rug in front of the desk. The rug was green-and-white fabric with gold thread tracing the shape of the jumping rabbit from the sign. They had a theme going here.

The front desk was oiled wood, old but well cared for.

Claire glanced down at the registry. There was no computer at the desk, only an old-fashion guestbook. Names, phone numbers, dates, number of nights. It was quaint, but under the front cover was a credit card swiper. Claire frowned. The machine ruined the back-in-time illusion.

There was movement somewhere down the hall. Allison dinged the bell on the desk and Claire gave her a look.

"What? Isn't that what it's for?"

The bell still ringing, a smiling older woman turned down the hallway and started walking towards them.

The woman's back was stock straight, her dress floral and conservative. She had a few years on Claire's mom, but she wasn't old. Middle sixties, probably. The smile might have been real, might not have.

"Hello, I'm Claire Foster. Are you Ms. Brant?" Claire didn't wait for her to answer, willing to gamble that this was her. "We spoke on the phone about the position."

"Of course, dear, I remember. It's nice to put a face to the name."

Ms. Brant took her hand, not really shaking it, just holding it for a brief second and giving it a soft squeeze. She flicked her eyes over to Allison.

"Hi, I'm Allison. I'm just Claire's ride. Lovely bed and breakfast you've got here."

"We're a fully functioning hotel, not a bed and breakfast, but it's nice to meet you." Allison didn't get a hand squeeze, but at least she didn't look like she was expecting one.

Brant turned back to Claire and spoke. The woman had thick glasses that made her eyes seem larger. The glasses could have made her look like a bug-eyed old woman, but instead they gave her a kind of cartoon power.

"I thought we might start with a tour, Claire, just to let you know where everything is, but it is getting close to bedtime for me."

A little before 8:30 was bedtime? Claire thought, but didn't push it. "I'm so sorry about that, we would have been here earlier if I had known."

"Not to worry, I know how silly it sounds to be turning in so early. Maybe the best way for you to experience what we do here would be to stay the night. I can have my best girl show you around before you turn in. Quietly, of course. We do have guests."

Claire watched as Allison tensed up.

"Staying the night, would that be okay?" Claire asked, unsure whether to direct the question to her friend who'd driven her there or to her prospective employer.

She caught Allison nod in her peripheral vision.

"More than okay, it would be essential for your understanding of what staying at The Brant is all about. Luckily we have two rooms ready, one for each of you."

"That's too much, we can stay in the same room," Claire said, glancing at Allison, looking for some kind of direction.

"Yeah, that would be totally no problem. I've just got to call in to work, tell them that I'm probably going to need tomorrow off," Allison said, flashing her phone at them both and backing out the front door.

"Your friend is very pretty. She is just a friend, I assume."

Claire stared at her for a moment, getting the implication, but not one hundred percent sure how to answer.

"She's my roommate, has been helping me a lot lately since I broke up with my boyfriend."

"Then I don't see a reason that you two can't stay in the same room, if that's what you want."

Claire took a mental note that the new boss was a little conservative and attempted to change the subject. *Was this still an interview?*

"How long have you owned the hotel?"

"It's over thirty years at this point, close to forty, actually. The hotel changed the economy of Mission. I like to tell people that I turned a one-horse town into a five-horse town, at the very minimum." Brant chuckled, folksy and practiced, but still enough warmth to ring sincere.

Claire felt her phone buzz in her back pocket, a text message. If Brant heard or cared, she didn't show it. The text was most likely from Allison, some inventive profanity and spelling. Allison was not pissed about having to stay here for the night. She was upset by a decision being made for her. They'd had a plan: to stay somewhere halfway between here and Boston. Allison liked to stick to the plans that she'd made.

"During the off-season we keep a staff of only four, a skeleton crew of locals, but during the summer we hire on a few more. This year it will only be you and one of the local boys as a part-time handyman. It's not that business will be slow, we don't expect that, but," Brant paused for effect, "the economy. Obamacare."

Claire nodded like that made a shred of sense to her, not endorsing the statement but not condemning it.

Allison re-entered the lobby. "All set with work. I can stay the night."

"Excellent. Let me call Daisy to give you that tour," Brant said and glided behind the front desk, her dress billowing behind her. "But first, please sign in here. You won't be charged for the room, of course, but you still should sign. Keeps everything consistent and official." The older woman smiled and twisted the ledger towards Claire, offering her a gold pen on a red ribbon.

Brant picked up the wall phone behind the desk and dialed a couple of numbers, too few to be anything other than an extension within the hotel.

Claire filled in her information, aware of both her terrible handwriting and Brant's eyes on her. When she was done she stepped out of the way and offered the pen to Allison.

"That's okay. We only need one of you." Brant cradled the phone against her shoulder and snapped the ledger shut with one hand, catching the ribbon in its pages and yanking the pen out of Allison's hand.

"Hello, Daisy?" she spoke into the phone. "Can you come

down to the lobby please? Two guests need to be shown to their room. No reservation." She paused, listening to the other end of the line for a moment, listening to Daisy. "The new girl."

"And friend," Allison added, smiling at Claire.
"And friend," Brant echoed, smiling but not really at all.

Chapter Six

Claire and Allison had the covers pulled up over their heads and they were laughing like it was 1993 and they were having a sleepover. The tops of their heads made the blanket into a teepee above them. The air inside their makeshift fort was warm with exhalation and the sweat from the day's drive. They whispered, unsure if they shared walls with any of The Brant Hotel's handful of guests.

Like any young girls, their whispers had a target. The whole conversation was bitchy and mean and they never would have said any of it to their faces, but Ms. Brant was a mess and Daisy was even worse.

Shortly after being dialed up by Ms. Brant, Daisy was downstairs and ready for action. She was older than Claire, but not by much, thirty. Thirty-two, tops. Regardless of her age, Claire had dropped ecstasy at warehouse raves with less energy and natural enthusiasm.

Daisy was pop radio turned to max volume.

When you live on a college campus, you get used to a certain level of strained passion, go-get-'em charm that rarely charms anyone but the yokels and their grandmother, but Daisy put every campus tour guide to shame.

Claire and Allison had followed after Daisy as she beamed and blasted her way through the hallways of The Brant.

"Built in 1978, The Brant has served as a beacon of Western Massachusetts tourism for nearly forty years," Allison said, affecting and exaggerating Daisy's slight lisp. The lisp wasn't a serious speech impediment, but even the gentle joking was uncomfortable enough to get them both laughing again.

The blue-and-white quilt around them glowed as Allison flicked on her lighter.

"What are you doing?" Claire asked, forgetting to whisper.

"Smoking a cigarette," Allison said, still giggling.

Claire pulled the blankets off their heads, mussing Allison's hair and letting in the cool air of the hotel room.

"You can't do that in here. I specifically remember Daisy telling you that. 'If it blackens your lungs, what do you think it will do to the vintage cotton drapes?'"

"Yeah, well, fuck the drapes and fuck Miss Mayberry 1991," Allison said. She gave a meaner laugh this time, the kind that couldn't have come without practice all throughout high school. Claire often wondered if they would have been friends in high school. Not in a million years.

Allison lifted a cigarette to her lips and began to light it. Claire caught her wrist and pulled it down.

"Don't—I mean—it seems like I've already got the job, whatever that means, but please don't ruin it over something stupid like this. They're going to be able to smell the smoke in the morning."

"You're right." Allison said, leaving out anything close to an "I'm sorry." Allison Pomero didn't do sorry.

"Let's go outside. Quietly, so we don't wake the lordly lady of the manor."

Allison laughed. She was back with Claire, inching away from the abyss of asshole-ry.

♦

A little after midnight, they snuck out of the hotel without event. It had been years since the two friends had held a conversation that lasted hours, but tonight was different.

"You're really going to live here for three months? You don't even have a cousin to marry out here," Allison said.

On their tour, Daisy had told her all about the lodging she could expect as a guest liaison. She talked about the job just like Brant had, as if Claire had already begun working.

In Daisy's words, the living situation was "Just like a hotel, only you have to clean up after yourself."

"It's not that bad. Most of the people that come through will be from Boston," Claire said. "It's not like I'll be completely shut off. They've got to have internet somewhere. How else did they get that spiffy website?"

Allison ignored the joke. Brant's outdated website no longer amused her. "Do you think they'll fire you when they find out that you can't make a bed?"

"Not true," Claire said.

"That you've never successfully loaded a dryer?"

"I've told you a thousand times that the dryer in our building doesn't work, that's why I always have to run it again," Claire said, laughing.

She laughed to shake the feeling that this cigarette break was a goodbye, at least for the summer. It was a shame that the last day she would see her friend for a few months was also the day that Allison seemed the most tolerable, the most worthy of being called a friend.

Allison pushed her chin up to the night sky and aimed a puff of smoke towards the amber flood light above their heads. The light overlooked the parking lot and the two stood under it, listening to the stillness of night in a small town.

There were the occasional sounds of animals in the woods, the tiny thud of moths crashing against the flood lights, but beyond that it was silent.

"I don't mean to make fun of it. It seems like a great job and I think it will be good for you," Allison said.

Allison knelt and stubbed the butt against the exposed brick of The Brant's foundation. She flicked it towards the dumpsters that backed up against the woods. The cigarette wasn't completely out and Claire watched the faint glow.

"Thanks. You going to have another one or are we done out here?"

"'Breakfast will be served at 8:30, please be in the dining room no later than 8:15,'" Allison repeated Ms. Brant's last words to them. Her Daisy impression was in the ballpark, but her Brant needed work.

"One cig more, then. Give me one of those," Claire said, holding two fingers out for a cigarette.

"Should I enable you like that?" Allison said, smiling.

"If I'm in for a few months of clean living up here, I'm going to need a smoke for luck."

"True. I didn't think of that. No parties. That will be good for you as well."

"For my liver and its self-esteem, at the very least," Claire said and reached into the pack of Newports. Newports. Even Allison's cigarettes were Connecticut assholes.

Claire leaned in to let Allison light it for her. She pulled a breath in, but felt the end of her nose glow red hot for a moment as Allison jumped back.

"Jesus Christ!" Claire shouted, holding her nose and looking up at her friend. The flame snapped back into the lighter, taking the orange out of Allison's cheeks.

Allison clapped one hand on Claire's shoulder and used the other to motion to the woods behind Claire. She then took a step toward the hotel, directing her body toward the service door and pulling Claire with her.

"There's someone in the woods. Right there," Allison whispered, eyes fixed on the tree line.

They both stood still, tensing, letting the other know that they were ready to run in an instant, making sure that they would escape together. No girl left behind.

Claire searched the darkness for movement. If there was someone there and they did intend to do them harm, they would have to cover about fifteen yards of parking lot before reaching the back of the hotel.

There was the snapping of branches that quickly became otherworldly loud as the blood pumped in Claire's ears.

"I am so sorry," a male voice called out from inside the woods.

Hands raised, a young man walked onto the gravel driveway, stopping a few feet before the asphalt of the parking lot started. It was the boy they had spoken to on their way into town. The guy who was with that group of kids, the ones that Claire had almost smeared across the road with the Elantra. The older one. Upon further inspection, he'd also been the handsome one.

"I'm here for the dumpsters," he said and then allowed himself a beat. "Not to do anything ungentlemanly to you two ladies." He tried to exaggerate the friendliness in his voice, let them know he was harmless enough to make a goofy joke.

"Here for the dumpster? At one in the morning?" Allison said, her voice thick with the kind of "likely story buddy" they taught you at girls-only self-defense class.

"I'm serious. The hotel doesn't recycle. I come and get the bottles," he said. "Turn them in for beer money," he added, like that would be the detail that proved it.

"Isn't it, like, a little late for dumpster diving?" Allison kept at it, trying to vet this guy's story.

"Let's just say that the woman who runs the hotel doesn't exactly like it when I do this," he said. "She claims the bottles are her property and that I wake the guests." While he was talking, he took a few steps into the lot, his trajectory aimed at the dumpsters, not the girls. He kept his hands out in front of him, though, just in case they didn't see where he was headed.

"You hear that? He's stealing from the hotel," Allison said. She gave Claire a pat on the butt. "Quick, go stop him."

Claire couldn't tell if the tingle in her cheeks was from the blush or from coming down off of the adrenaline high.

"I'm Tobin, by the way," he said.

Claire had met a Tobin once at an undergrad party that had gotten sloppy. He'd tried to go down on her in the coatroom, but had thrown up on the host's floor instead.

That loser had been skeletal skinny and had beaten her at *Settlers of Catan*. This guy, the Tobin of Mission, Massachusetts, was tall and slightly muscular. He was the kind of guy she could picture hoisting bales of hay. Shirtless.

Tobin flipped open the plastic lid of the dumpster and backed his face away. Claire presumed he was trying to avoid the smell. "Are you girls guests at the hotel? Staying in town long?" He wiped his hands, reached into the back pocket of his jeans and pulled out a white garbage bag.

Claire took a step towards him so she didn't have to talk quite as loud, worried about waking up the guests. Or Brant or Daisy. She was unsure which woman she'd rather risk pissing off.

"I'm going to be working here for the summer. Guest liaison."

"Is that anything like a maid?" Tobin waved the bag in the air like a bullwhip, opening it up with two flicks of the wrist. The tendons in his forearms were taut like guitar strings, moving rhythmically with delicate strength.

"I'm guessing it's exactly like a maid." Claire said, realizing how close she was to this strange, hot guy. She was near enough to smell warm, early summer trash. When did the situation change so drastically? How did she get so comfortable?

Tobin shot her a pretty smile at that and then pressed his belly up to the edge and hooked himself over the lip of the dumpster.

"He's adorbs," Allison whispered, sidling up beside her. "But be careful around the locals. You don't know where they've been." It was a good thing that Tobin was rooting through bottles and spoiled food, or else he would have heard.

Tobin smacked both feet back against the asphalt and tossed a wine bottle and Budweiser can into the bag. "Where are you from originally?" He didn't wait for an answer, but flipped his torso back into the bin and kept searching for recyclables.

"Boston," Allison said. That was an oversimplification, Claire would have said New York for herself and Connecticut for Allison, but Boston worked. They'd been there for almost a decade. When did it become their home?

When Tobin came back up for air, he had a few more treasures. He threw them into his bag with a clang and Claire jumped at the sound. She understood why Brant didn't like him doing this. The noise he was making was definitely enough to wake the guests with windows facing the parking lot.

"Before I forget," Allison said, closer to him now than Claire was. "I'm Allison and this is Claire."

"It's nice to meet you both," Tobin said, offering a cute little salute that said, "I'd like to shake your hand, but I'm covered in last Tuesday's breakfast buffet."

Allison kept the conversation going, not letting him jump back into the dumpster by sheer force of flirtation. "Hey, Tobin. You look like the guy to ask."

"Ask what?"

"If someone is only in Mission for one night, what is the one attraction they have to hit?"

"Chamber of commerce-type stuff?" he asked. He looked about ready to put his thumbs in his front pockets, but then remembered the grime he was covered in.

"Yeah," Allison said. "Or locals-only hotspots. Whatever you feel are the highlights. There's not, like, a *Zagat* for Mission."

"You'd need to drive about an hour for anything with a brochure," Tobin said. "There's the Norman Rockwell Museum in Stockbridge."

"Do we look like we want to go to the Norman Rockwell Museum?" she asked. Claire could see the sex falling out of her lips in rivulets. "Besides, I asked, 'What is there to do in Mission?' Not Stockbridge."

"Nothing," he said. "But there's always a party somewhere out in the woods."

Allison turned to Claire, done with her one-on-one session with Tobin, reporting in with her intel. "There you go. Now you know what you'll be doing on the weekends."

They talked with him for a little while longer, then watched his ass as he disappeared back into the woods.

Chapter Seven

Claire had set the alarm on her phone so that it would vibrate before it rang.

Although she'd slept soundly, she woke with the first buzz beneath her pillow and switched it off before the unpleasant chirp of the alarm could sound.

Sitting up, she looked at the room for the first time in the sunlight. According to Daisy, it was one of only three rooms in The Brant that came equipped with two twin beds instead of one king size.

These rooms were usually rented out to parents who were traveling with their children. The children slept in the twin beds while mommy and daddy shacked up in one of the rooms down the hall. "Shacked up" was Claire's term, not Daisy's.

The décor was tasteful, not at all what the pictures on the website had led her to expect. There were no doilies on the nightstands, for one thing, just smooth oak. Not only that, but the blue-and-white quilt that looked so uncomfortable was merely decorative. There were modern fleece blankets and linen sheets underneath.

The room lacked the antiseptic smell of a Holiday Inn or Motel 6. Claire liked that. There were small touches that let you know the furniture hadn't been mass produced, like the small golden rabbits etched into the knobs of the dresser drawers. She doubted that there was a warehouse somewhere with a thousand of those knobs.

As her mind returned from the edge of sleep, as she stopped apprizing the uniqueness of the furniture (something she'd never do with a clear head), she realized that the bed across the room was empty.

The sheets were tousled, but Allison was no longer under them.

Allison often didn't make her bed and she made it a habit not to wake up before noon. It was possible that she'd had trouble sleeping in a strange bed. Claire usually had the same problem.

Claire tossed her legs over the side of the bed and checked the bathroom. Allison wasn't there.

A mental shrug manifested itself as a physical shrug. Allison must have went out for a morning cigarette, was planning on meeting her downstairs at breakfast.

Checking her emails with one hand, Claire pulled down her panties and sat on the toilet.

♦

"Eat, please," Ms. Brant said to Claire while taking a biscuit from the tray Daisy held out. "Don't wait for Daisy or you'll be waiting all summer."

"She's right. Even when I do eat breakfast, it's never much," Daisy said, walking to the middle of the table and setting down the tray within arm's length of Claire. "So much to get done in the mornings, but you'll know all about that."

"I guess I will," Claire said. She picked up her fork and cut her egg. Bits of the egg whites were still gooey and see-through. It would have been great hangover food if she'd had one, but now it mildly repulsed Claire.

The dining room was five circular tables orbiting a long rectangular one. The large table looked like it could seat eight or nine. Alternating green and white tablecloths, with a set of gold rabbit salt and pepper shakers on each table. The effect of the room's size and order was striking and the impression it left was very unlike a bed and breakfast. Brant must have taken great pride in that.

"Is your friend not joining us?" Ms. Brant asked.

"She had left the room before I woke up to come down. She's probably on the phone with work. You'll have to excuse her. She's a workaholic," Claire said, then asked herself why she was still lying. She already had the job, no reason to disseminate lies about Allison.

Daisy interrupted Claire's thoughts with a sound. It was the kind of "stupid-me!" utterance that people make when they realize that they've left the stove on.

"Dang it," she yelled and turned to Brant. "Sorry, Ms. Brant," she said before turning back to Claire. "I was supposed to tell you that

Allie had to head back to the city. She said that she didn't want to wake you," Daisy said, flattening the back of her dress before sitting down beside Claire. "She also wished you luck for the summer, of course, said that she wanted to come stay a weekend at the hotel."

Don't call Allison Allie. I don't even do that, Claire thought. She hated Daisy in that moment for no reason other than that it felt good.

The single buzz of a text message went off in Claire's pocket, but she ignored it.

"That's really strange," Claire said, feeling every word of it, staring into her runny eggs and burnt sausage. It was strange, but not unbelievable. Allison was a flake, ruled by impulses baffling to empathic life forms.

"She seemed like a sweet girl, I look forward to her next visit," Ms. Brant said. "Claire, please let her know that she will stay and eat at a significant discount, should she make the trip."

"I will. Thank you." Claire said. *I'll let her know that as soon as I'm done breaking her fucking shins for leaving me in Mission, Massachusetts, without even saying goodbye.*

Claire took a few breaths through her nose and realized that both women's eyes were on her. She grasped for something to end the silence, diffuse the rage. "The breakfast is great, Ms. Brant. Did you make it, Daisy? You prepare sausage just how I like it."

Claire wondered if it was possible to fake a blush and watched Daisy scrunch up her plain face in embarrassment.

"Not me, no," Daisy said. "I'm afraid we'd have to be calling poison control if any of my cooking made it to a guest's plate. It was Roy, the cook. He's just fabulous."

Ms. Brant cut in, timing her words with Daisy's break. "He's wonderful," she said with small nod. "When you're done with your breakfast, Claire, we'll have a line-up so you can be introduced to the rest of the staff. Roy included. After that, Daisy can explain your duties in greater detail."

The phrase "line-up" reminded Claire of a prison movie.

Claire excused herself and asked Daisy for directions to the bathroom nearest the dining room. She didn't have to go, but she needed a break to check her phone.

The text had been from Allison.

Sorry to ditch u. Have to get back home. Good luck!

It was the most grammatically correct text Allison had ever sent.

Chapter Eight

Allison woke up in pain, but that wasn't the worst part.

Her mouth was gummed shut with blood and she had to work her tongue around the corners of her lips a few times before she could scream.

Where was she? Last thing she could recall, she had gone to the bathroom, looking to flush her mouth out after too many cigarettes, and then what?

Why was she in the woods? What time was it? There were slashes of dim light poking through the branches, but was it dawn or dusk?

These questions were no longer important as soon as she noticed the tooth.

Her front left tooth was missing. Well, not quite missing, but broken so badly that only a gritty stump remained.

She jabbed her tongue into the shard of enamel, tasted a splash of fresh blood welling up, and she began to sob.

Growing up, Allison had nightmares like this: that her teeth were falling out one by one. It got to the point where these dreams were so familiar that her conscious mind would echo through the nightmare. Her own voice would talk over her mind movie, reassuring young Allison and reminding her that it wasn't real.

Ride it out, honey. You're just having a bad dream. Remember what the dentist said, "That's a very common nightmare. But don't worry: your teeth are staying put." The dentist let his hand rest a little too long on your chest when you got to high school. You stopped going back after sophomore year.

Her dreams felt real at the time, but she'd never lost a tooth as an adult, only baby teeth. She'd never had one knocked out or shattered. Turns out that her imaginings had been way off-base. This was so much worse. She'd had nothing to compare it to.

Allison gagged on the taste of her own blood, felt the pulsing ache from her face and mouth and knew that she was awake.

The events of last night came back, not like a flashback in a movie when a character asks "What happened?" and the audience is treated to a soft-focus, third-person version of events. This was someone else's memory thrust into her own mind.

The memories were tactile and disjointed. There was the running faucet, the gold flash, then the crack, the hands, the muffled words, then the blood, then nothing.

Male or female? Familiar or strange? Glasses or no glasses? She played Guess Who, trying to Nancy Drew her way into identifying her attacker. It didn't work. She hadn't seen anything beyond the smack in the head.

She rubbed her thighs, smudging dirt and blood all over her plain white nightgown, the one that Daisy had supplied. "You didn't come prepared to stay, I'm guessing, those bags don't look big enough. I've got all the essentials. They'll fit," Daisy had said before coming back to their room with two matching nightgowns.

The woven cotton pajamas were frilly, ugly and too big, kind of like Daisy herself.

Allison remembered back to last night. They'd gone inside after they were done smoking. Claire hadn't worn her nightgown to bed. Allison didn't intend to either, but had put it on as a joke and found it warm enough to keep on.

She was thankful for it now. The woods were cold, and going to sleep in her panties last night would have made the situation even worse.

Either her eyes were adjusting or the sun was rising because she could see better than she could a few minutes ago.

Inspecting the ground around her bare feet, she could see the long, brown streak where, she assumed, she'd been dragged. If the streak wasn't enough evidence, the back of her ass was slick with mud and dead leaves.

Her upper lip and nose burned, even in the chill of the morning (night?). Did the heat mean that something was broken? She raised a hand, ready to check the injury as gently as possible, but stopped herself.

An idea shot to the front of her mind, a bright, burning road flare of a notion. The burning question she should have been focusing on this whole time. Was her attacker still here?

Allison fixed her attention on the world around her.

Admittedly, this was not her strong suit. Allison's world was ninety-eight percent Allison and two percent the world around Allison. "I don't give head," she'd told her high school boyfriend. "Why? Because I'm too selfish, that's why."

Her mind was a disjointed jumble of images and sounds. She had to will herself to focus.

Most of the trees around her were too skinny to hide an assailant. If there was someone out here with her, they weren't close. If they were coming back, why would they have left her out here on her own?

Maybe they had to set your big ass down and then head back for their chainsaw, she answered.

There were very few times when Allison's own sense of humor failed to amuse her. This was one of them.

Her hand shot to her hip, groping for her phone. The nightgown had no pockets, so she'd stuffed her iPhone into the elastic waistband of her panties before she'd gone to bed. Either her attacker had taken it, or it was somewhere on the forest floor between wherever she was and the hotel.

Thinking of the hotel reminded her to take note of her surroundings. She had to figure out where to run to if she was going to run. The hotel was nowhere in sight. There were no landmarks, just trees and rocks.

She spun a few times, trying to figure out what direction to head in. The sky was bluer now. It was morning, then. That was one mystery solved.

"Jinkies," Allison whispered to herself. Even that much movement hurt her face.

On her third spin, she heard a noise behind her. Without thinking, her legs moved.

The balls of her feet thudded against the ground in front of her as she ran from the sound. She didn't look back to confirm it wasn't a squirrel or deer. Some deep part of her knew it wasn't.

Allison's gait was clumsy, her legs were sore and her eyes seemed to buck against her control as she tried to keep them in front of her.

In high school, she'd worn a special bra to run track. Even

then she'd been all woman. The bra was heavy duty, taped her tits down like a Caucasian Mulan.

The brassiere and her training had worked for her, All-State, baby, but now one massive head injury and almost a decade later, she wasn't burning up the track.

There were sounds of pursuit behind her and she couldn't help her curiosity. She looked.

Who the fuck was this guy?

She was almost disappointed that she didn't recognize her pursuer, as if the sight of Daisy or Tobin or even crazy old Ms. Brant would have fit better. At least a familiar face would have given this insane narrative a little more coherence.

Instead of any of them, it was a burly guy dressed in all white. He was huge and bestial with thick black hair not only on his face, but the backs of his hands as well.

He was big and athletic. His arms pumped back and forth, his mouth fixed in a perfect runner's "O". She could hear him sucking air in and out, the way she wished she could. Efficiently.

Whoever he was, he was going to catch her. That much was certain.

And what would he do when he caught her? Was he going to take the rest of her teeth? Or was it going to be worse? All Allison could remember from self-defense class was to claw her attacker with her car keys and use her knees to aim for his nuts.

She didn't have her car keys.

Ducking low under a branch, she decided that bobbing and weaving was her best bet. She would take the most obfuscated path she could, bounding over rocks, cutting between the closest set trees that she could spot, hopefully causing the beast to get tripped up.

That's what he was—a beast.

Judging from the sounds behind her, he was outpacing her worse than she first estimated. For such a swarthy-looking guy, he was quite a runner.

Snippets of the next hour (or less) of her life flashed through her imagination. She played herself a greatest-hits clip reel of her death. Big calloused European hands tightened around her throat, his beard mashing up against her already broken mouth, that feeling she'd had once off the coast of Martha's Vineyard—drowning.

No! She forced her drunken eyes to fix on a mossy rock and she bent down to it. The nail on her pinky finger bent outward and broke in on itself as she pried the stone out of the earth. It would hurt like hell later, but now all she cared about was prying the rock free.

Pill bugs ran for cover as she lifted it up, leaving a smooth void in the ground.

Dirt and lichen sprinkled her nightgown as she hoisted the rock up even with her breasts. Taking a breath, she turned to face her attacker.

She had a picture-perfect idea of how this should go down. She had to wait until just the right moment, let his momentum draw him to her so she could lower the sharpest edge of the flat rock into his face. It was almost cartoon violence, the way she wanted it to go. In her mind, she would cleave his fucking face in half.

Allison never got the chance because the beast had slowed his approach as soon as he saw her arm herself.

"What do you want?" Allison screamed. Of all the questions she'd asked in the last five minutes, it was the only one she'd spoken aloud.

The beast didn't answer. He just took a step forward, closing the distance between them to about ten feet. She lifted the rock higher in response.

Her hands were beginning to shake. The only sound was their breathing.

The sun was higher now. *What time was dawn these days? Was it seven o'clock? Earlier?*

The beast didn't look particularly menacing. He wore white tennis shoes and had a face like a pizza delivery guy.

He was the kind of delivery guy that Allison thought people tipped twenty percent because they didn't want him visiting their apartment with a few of his buddies. It was only money and Allison had seen too many Lifetime movies. She'd had a very active imagination, especially since she had moved to the big city.

The beast began to circle around her, earning the nickname she'd given him. She expected him to snarl, maybe drool a little, but he didn't. He just stared, sweat beading on his forehead.

Her weapon grew heavier and heavier the more she thought about it. *Why did she stop training with the medicine ball?* Because it was hard, that was why.

She began to pivot with him, raising and lowering the rock,

giving herself micro-rests.

They both stopped moving with the gunshot. The clap was sudden and loud enough that Allison dropped the rock, missing her foot by an inch or two.

In the still after the shot, she could hear animals scurrying around in the underbrush.

"Don't move a muscle, Roy," a voice said. Allison followed the sound to Tobin, coming up behind Roy, the beast. "Unless you want me to blow a hole through your dress whites. I don't want to do that. That would be all kinds of trouble."

Finally, a familiar face, Allison thought, remembering back to all the flirting she'd done with Tobin last night.

The situation still didn't make any sense. Tobin's arrival also didn't help explain the waves of pain radiating back from her nose and upper lip, but her current predicament felt better, infinitely better, than the situation that existed a moment ago.

Tobin had a camouflage hunting vest slung over the plain T-shirt and jeans that he'd been wearing to go dumpster diving. He had a matching hunting cap pulled over his brown hair. Tobin's strange redneck fashion sense made him look like a character in a Nicolas Sparks novel or a character in a movie based on a Nicolas Sparks novel. He was country without being threatening, a Toby Keith song made flesh.

She noticed that Tobin hadn't bothered with those bright orange safety tags hunters usually wore. This told her that he had a dangerous side.

"Hands up and turn around," Tobin said.

Does he mean me? A sickly burst of fear sent a bubble of stomach acid up her esophagus.

She put her hands up, but so did Roy.

Roy looked just as tense as she imagined she did. Sweat had run down his forehead and was now sopping his thick eyebrows.

"I said, turn around," Tobin said.

Roy did.

"Winchester two forty-one. You know this gun, right?" Tobin asked. He kept the butt of the gun flat against his shoulder, but made tiny circles in the air with the barrel, keeping a bead on Roy while he did this.

Roy didn't nod, didn't do anything but look a little more pissed off than he had when he was chasing Allison.

"At this range, if I shot you in the belly, I'd liquefy your organs. It would kill you straight out. Shit. That would be it, wouldn't it? That would be the big deal we were all waiting for. The starting gun."

"Yeah, that's why you wouldn't dare." Roy said. No accent. He was so dark that Allison had expected an accent. Italian or Greek maybe? Like the guys that run diners.

Tobin kind of smiled at this, faking confidence but not completely succeeding. Allison had seen that same look a few times on the boys that had tried to pick her up. Different context, but it was the same feigned swagger.

Tobin took a couple of steps forward and placed the barrel of the gun flush with the palm of one of Roy's upheld hands.

Roy squinted, trying to remain composed.

"Allison, right?" Tobin said, not looking over at her, but addressing her for the first time.

Allison couldn't speak, wasn't really decoding the words.

"Could you just scootch over for me, Allison? Take a few steps to your right."

She did.

Roy started to say something but Tobin shushed him and moved the gun a few inches up.

Tobin lined the circle of the barrel up to the knuckle of Roy's pointer finger and pulled the trigger.

There was that same boom as before, only this time it wasn't followed by silence.

"You fuck," Roy screamed and pulled the hand to his chest, splotches of red already spreading on his white uniform.

"Get out of here before I have to start some real trouble." Tobin said. "And don't go looking for your finger. That shit's vaporized."

Roy did as he was told, skulking off in the direction that he'd chased Allison from. Back to town?

Tobin held out his hand for her, propped the butt of the gun against his hip.

"Are you all right?"

"No, I'm hurt," she was able to say, expecting the words to bring pain, but they didn't. She was too numb.

"Oh sweetheart, it's okay. Let's go get you fixed up," Tobin said.

He put his arm around her, not to seduce her but to comfort

her. He smelled nice.

    After a few steps, he spoke again, "Allison, didn't anyone tell you that there was a war going on?"

Chapter Nine

Disney doesn't call their employees "employees" but instead calls them "cast members". The idea was that all their employees played a part in transporting their customers to Fantasyland, making their dreams come true. In practice, though, the chipperness of most cast members should be read as unhinged by anyone over seven.

Daisy wasn't an employee of The Brant: she was a cast member.

Thankfully, she seemed to be the only one. The rest of the staff was just that—staff. They worked, clocked out, and cashed their checks.

There may have been a countrified sweetness to them, but they did not grovel at the altar of Ms. Brant like Daisy.

It took less than a week for Claire to grow into the world around her. Her ability to assimilate so quickly scared her, but only a little.

Allison had been right. The worst part had been learning to make a bed.

Daisy had trained her in the proper use of the industrial washers, restocking the linen carts, cleaning the guest bathrooms, but she had neglected to demonstrate how she got the sheets so tight and the quilts so smooth. That was one thing Claire had to figure out how to do on her own (with help from a YouTube video entitled *Best tips 2 make a bed*).

By the third day, Claire had memorized the schedule, which, it did not surprise her, featured more cleaning than she'd been told it would. Waking up at five thirty to fold the sheets and load up her cart with miniature shampoo bottles was tough, but it was getting easier.

Around 9:30, Claire would clean rooms. She started at the end of the west wing, third floor, and consulted her chart until she reached an unoccupied room that needed cleaning. After the guest rooms on the second and third floors were done, she was finished for the day.

Not a bad gig, considering that this early in the season she only ever had to clean four rooms. For the rest of the day she'd surf the internet in her room until she'd have to bring the cart out again for turndown service.

In the two-hour span between prep and cleaning, Claire helped the cook with whatever he needed.

Although Daisy would never say it—Claire bet she never even thought a bad word—helping Roy was the shittiest duty at The Brant.

It wasn't that Roy himself was that bad. He may have spoken more in grunts than words, but it didn't come off as rudeness, just a stoic professionalism. He was tall, dark and gross-looking, so maybe it was the Lurch school of manners.

What sucked about this detail was the mess. Claire didn't deal well with being covered in food stuffs. If she was going out with friends and it was ribs for dinner, she'd need a stack of wet naps and would prefer to be seated closest to the restroom.

Roy needed her help handling food. She would crack eggs, tenderize and batter chicken-fried steak, anything that he needed doing. By the time she was ready to wash and head up to the third floor, there was a thick coat of slime on her hands, apron and forearms.

Roy wasn't incapable of these things or above the grime, but he was injured.

The morning Claire had arrived Roy had missed Ms. Brant's line-up because he'd cut half a finger off chopping wood.

By the end of the week, Claire was better at her job but her days were longer. The "rush" hadn't been much of a rush, just a steady increase in occupied rooms until almost all of the second floor rooms were booked, rooms that needed their bathtubs wiped down, their pillows fluffed and their floors vacuumed.

As a waitress, Claire was used to spending time on her feet, but it was the up and down of guest liaison-ing that exhausted her.

It was good though, the increased effort felt like therapy. She was scrubbing extra hard, making sure that she removed all the dead skin from the inside of her soul.

Changing clothes at the end of the day helped, too.

Claire now spent most of her waking hours in her uniform: white tights under a knee-length green dress with a white apron on top and green half-sleeves. Her custom dress took two days to complete, the seamstress adding one final touch: her name embroidered on the apron. *Claire* in green thread on the left breast, over her heart.

Before she'd slipped on the dress for the first time, Claire stood naked in front of the bathroom mirror. Even though guests were asked not to smoke, there was a ceramic ashtray in each room. Claire placed hers on the edge of the sink and then ran her fingers over her skin. There was a small *clink* as she removed each piercing and dropped it into the ashtray.

They were only a few small hoops and studs, but taking them off made her feel lighter, sleeker. *Warning: Small Parts May Present Choking Hazard.*

Without her metal, Claire Foster no longer posed a choking hazard.

She wondered how long it would take for the holes to close completely, wondered if some of them ever would.

The tattoos wouldn't ever come off, but she didn't want them to. Claire didn't regret them. They would be the only thing left of Silverfish once she let the streak in her hair go un-bleached.

Her job title was a misnomer because the only task that Claire didn't do at The Brant was deal directly with the guests. She would still see them from time to time, but she wasn't undergoing this transformation because of them.

It wasn't because Ms. Brant told her to either. Although she seemed conservative in many ways, the old woman hadn't mentioned Claire's appearance.

Claire was doing this for herself, affecting change that she was in charge of.

Starting fresh.

♦

When compared to Claire's drunken post-grad life, everything about working at The Brant was strange. But there was one aspect of her work at the hotel that would have been considered peculiar by anyone's standards.

There was one room on the third floor that Claire didn't clean.

"You don't have to take care of this room. He's my responsibility," Daisy said, covering her mouth, like she was blocking her words from the peephole of Room 31.

"Who?" Claire asked, and found herself being shushed by Daisy.

Daisy took her by the arm and walked her to the end of the hallway before answering.

"Father Hayden lives in that room, poor thing," Daisy said. "I see that he gets everything he needs."

"Who is Father Hayden?"

"He's the town's priest, or was, or still is," Daisy said. For the first time since Claire had arrived, Daisy seemed unsure of herself. Daisy probably never had to give this part of the tour before. It seemed to Claire that she was getting to see something closer to the real Daisy now. She was a woman-girl unrehearsed and insecure, one who was unsure of all her answers, of herself.

"Well, let me back up here. Did you see the church on your ride in?"

"No, I don't think so," Claire said. They may have driven by it, but churches weren't something that Claire kept a constant lookout for. If Daisy had asked her to spot an Arby's, Claire could have given her a more definitive answer.

"That's because it burned to the ground some years ago. Now we only have a lot where a church used to be." Daisy said. She was back in full storyteller mode now, not as sharp as she was as a tour guide, but close. "Father Hayden was still inside when it went up."

Daisy paused and stared at Claire expectantly. Claire realized that this was the point in the story where she was supposed to gasp. Instead she said, "That's terrible," and Daisy continued.

"Third-degree burns all over his body. The flames seared his eyes so he's blind now. His ears are gone, but he can still hear a little, I think. Ms. Brant says he's deaf, but I don't know if that's correct. Poor thing." Daisy seemed to be reveling a little too much in these details, using a strategically placed "poor thing" here and there to free herself from the accusation that she enjoyed describing this freak show. Daisy didn't seem like the kind of girl who hit the movies every weekend, so she had to use real world gore to fill her enjoyable violence quotient.

"The doctors said that he wouldn't survive," she continued. "But Ms. Brant wouldn't believe them, and she was right. She sought out specialists and those doctors brought him back from the edge. She paid for everything too. Kind of gives you a new perspective into your boss, right? She cares so much about Mission and its people."

Claire didn't know how to respond to that, so she just nodded. She didn't want to let her cynicism leak in, but a small, dark, petty area in the back of her mind was giggling, amused at Ms. Brant's impeccable handle on public relations. She's at least gotten Daisy to drink the Kool-Aid.

"After he got better, since he used to live in an apartment attached to the church and that's not there anymore, Ms. Brant lets him live here in thirty-one. Rent free, of course."

"That's really nice of her," Claire said.

"It is. He doesn't have many visitors. It's not that the people in Mission aren't devout. Most of them can't bear to look at him. It does take some getting used to, but I've been taking care of him for years now. I don't mind it, even if it gets messy sometimes."

Somehow even that vague description gave Claire a vivid mental picture. She winced against images of baby-smooth scar tissue and weeping orifices.

It was about fifteen minutes after this conversation that Claire asked Daisy about Tobin, hoping for some small talk to wash away the spooky and awkward topic of Brant's crispy pet priest.

Daisy might have looked less mortified if Claire had tackled her and tugged down her Spanx.

"Why do you need to know about him? When did you even meet him?" Daisy's voice was panicked for the first question and accusatory for the second.

"The first night I was here, Allison had gone out for a smoke and I went with her," Claire said, unsure what she had to be defensive about. Were Tobin and Daisy involved? Mission's well of talent couldn't be that shallow.

Saying Allison's name aloud still hurt. Aside from the occasional quick text, the bitch had dumped her.

Daisy waited for the rest of the story, one hand on her hip, the other leaning against the linen cart.

"He was going through the dumpster for recyclables and telling us about the town."

"I knew he was still doing that. I hear him sometimes," Daisy said, more to herself than to Claire. "That's all, you haven't seen him since?"

"No. Why? What's wrong with him? He seemed nice enough

to me," Claire said, no longer staggered by Daisy's tone. She hadn't transformed so much that she was going to allow herself to be intimidated by someone that so closely resembled one of Strawberry Shortcake's less popular friends.

"Oh, there's nothing wrong with him. He's a warm-blooded American male, as you saw, and I've certainly heard tales to prove it. But he and his friends get into trouble."

Claire remembered what Tobin had said and brought it into play now. She wanted the depth of her knowledge to shock Daisy. "Are you talking about the parties out in the woods?"

If Daisy were in a costume drama, she would have put the back of her hand to her forehead and yelled "The scandal!" before fainting.

It took her a moment, but when she regained her composure she spoke in a deliberate monotone. "He told you about those 'parties'? I'm sure he was really slick. He is the handsome one. But did he tell you what they do at them? It's all drugs and sex and shame. Building bonfires and hooting like animals. They've even tried to get the guests of the hotel once or twice. Ms. Brant says that they are the worst plague that Mission's ever had to endure. And this is a town that survived a catastrophic flu epidemic at the turn of the last century, so that's saying something."

Occasionally Daisy would talk in this hybrid dialect that was half her words, half Ms. Brant's.

"Kids partying in the woods? Doesn't sound like much of a threat to me." Claire tried not to sound so much like she was goading Daisy, but she was too into it at this point.

Daisy looked to both ends of the third-floor hallway, realizing that they were having this conversation out in the open. She put a finger up to her lips and took a key from one of her apron pockets.

"In here," Daisy said, opening the door to room thirty-eight. "We can talk in here without a guest hearing us. I don't know why we didn't do this before."

Claire followed her into the empty room.

"It would be okay *if* this were just a case of kids being kids, but it's not."

"What is it?"

"Well, I don't know too much about it, but I talk with everyone in this town—those kids excluded, of course—and what I hear is that there is a wino that throws those parties. I mean a grown man that lives out in the woods. The kids think it's cool to have some dirty flower child supply them with liquor and who knows what else. Does that sound like a healthy relationship for an adult to have with a group of teenagers?"

Claire thought back to high school and the bums her friend convinced to buy them bottles of Rumple Mintz, her friend's parents who would allow semi-supervised keggers to be thrown in their garages. "No, sounds a bit creepy to me," Claire said. She was tired of hearing about Mission's milquetoast "dark" secrets. She just wanted to finish the day's work and go illegally watch bad TV on her phone. "I didn't know any of this. I was only asking because, well, like you said, he is the handsome one."

Daisy smiled, patted her on the back, and led her back out into the hallway. "He is, but don't let that little devil fool you. You *don't* want anything that David and them are cooking up in those woods. Their activities are an affront to the lord."

Claire nodded emphatically and said that no, indeed, she did not want any part of those illicit activities.

Inside she did, though, and filed the wino's name away.

David.

Silverfish very much wanted a taste of Mission's local nightlife.

Chapter Ten

After the two strange conversations she'd had with Daisy, one about a BBQ'd holy man and the other about a messianic hobo that the town's children idolized, Claire waited for Tobin every night.

The window to her room faced the parking lot, so she kept it open a crack and stayed up listening for any sign that he'd returned to clean out the dumpster. This was how she fell asleep for three nights straight, not reading or watching TV, but sitting in the silence of her hotel room and listening.

It would have struck her as eerily silent had she not known that most of the guests were kept on the floor below her, with most of them housed in the opposite wing.

Claire's room was on the third floor and the only guests that were there with her were the Chopins, a young married couple.

And Father Hayden, who wasn't really a guest. She tried not to think about him.

The Chopins seemed nice enough, but Claire had a hard time trusting anyone her own age whose idea of a good time was vacationing at The Brant. When they weren't taking in the local flavor, they were using Mission as a hub to venture out and explore the rest of Western Massachusetts. She tried to imagine Mickey sweeping her off her feet and depositing her in a suite at The Brant. Would they pour over brochures for wine tastings, local theater and nature walks? In all their years together, they'd never gone on vacation, but something told Claire that it wouldn't look like what the Chopins were enjoying right now.

It was Thursday night, which in her glory days would have been Thirsty Thursday, before she heard him again. He woke her out of a sound half-sleep, and for a moment she'd incorporated the sounds of clinking bottles into a dream.

Instead of her nightgown, she slipped on her T-shirt and jeans. These were the only clothes of her own that she had at the hotel because of the odd circumstances under which she was hired. She made a mental note to go shopping this weekend. Maybe she could catch a ride to the nearest mall so all her clothes didn't have to come from the Mission gift shop.

This was the first time all week she'd worn her jeans. It felt strange to be without her piercings, like she was wearing only part of a Claire costume.

The Brant may have been an old building, but the doors and floorboards were creak-free. Getting downstairs unnoticed was easy. The back door was a fire exit, but it didn't sound. Roy was a smoker, and she'd seen him use it every day while she helped him whisk pancake batter or tenderize meat for chicken-fried steaks.

By the time she got downstairs, Tobin was already into it with the dumpster. His faded jeans fit snug, giving his ass that kind of picturesque, late-'80s music video vibe. The view would have been excellent if her mind hadn't been pumping in the smell of the overripe garbage.

"Hey," she said, not trying to scare him but not altogether unhappy that her greeting made him bang his head on the top of the dumpster. The plastic and metal reverberated through the night, and Claire became acutely aware that she'd probably just woken up Brant, Daisy, and even the poor innocent Chopins. Those two were likely sore from touring the butter churn factory or whateverthefuck.

"Hey. It's Claire Foster from Boston, formerly of Long Island. What are you doing out here?" He spoke with a lack of surprise that turned Claire off. It suggested that he knew that he was the only game in town and that she had no choice but to seek him out. He might have been right, but that didn't mean that she had to like it.

"It's Tobin I-don't-know-his-last-name from Mission, Massachusetts, formerly of Mission, Massachusetts." She waited to hear if that sounded as mean as she wanted it to, but it still came out flirtatious. "I'm thinking of picking up smoking. You got a light?"

"Left my Bic in my other pants."

"That's okay. I don't have any cigarettes anyway."

"Good, they're bad for you." Tobin tossed one last Bud Light bottle into his bag and closed the dumpster with a clatter. "Did you know that every time someone lights someone else's cigarette in a movie, it actually means something different?"

He left the bag on the pavement, leaning against the dumpster, and started walking over to her.

"I did know that actually, but I've had some film studies classes. Where'd you learn it?"

"Read it in a book. Also from watching movies," he said, dusting himself off as he approached. "It's super obvious, you know, not really something that you need to be alerted to if you're watching somewhat closely."

He was right, that was totally amateur hour. How else did you tell the audience two characters were balling under the Hays Code? Fay Wray had to light up because there was no Sasha Grey back then. But Fay could have been Sasha, would have been if that's what the world called for.

"You miss your friend?" Tobin asked, rattling her out of her semi-pornographic thought processes.

"Not really, she ditched me without saying goodbye."

"Is that right?" Tobin suddenly got a troubled look. Troubled or amused, Claire couldn't tell which.

"It's no big deal. She's fine. She's done shit like this before," Claire said. "Why are you so sad? Do you miss her too? The taller, prettier one?" She messed up her face into what she imagined was a picture of childish jealousy. At least that's what she was trying to look like, but she was hopeless at the art of flirtation, so it might have looked like a seizure.

"Allison the prettier one?" Tobin said and waved his hand to show that he thought she had to be kidding. "Taller is objective, but you're way off-base calling her prettier."

"Bigger boobs."

"True, but that's not always a one-to-one ratio," he said, letting his eyes take a momentary dip to check hers out.

"So where are these mythical parties I hear so much about? Daisy says that they are an 'affront to her Lord'. That's an exact quote. I didn't make it up."

"I believe it. There's a lot of people in this town that talk like that. Dwyer, that old guy at the general store? He won't even serve me. Says that it's because of the company that I keep. That means I have to drive up to the highway rest stops to get my Slim Jims and Pepsis."

"In *this* economy?" Claire said, trying for sarcasm. She could tell that the statement perplexed Tobin. "That was something I constantly heard douche bags that didn't tip say. When I was waitressing." She wanted Tobin to know that she was joking.

He laughed more than the joke called for to make up for the awkwardness.

"So where are they?" She held her hands out.

"I don't usually go to the Thursday night ones."

"Ha! I was kidding. There actually are ones on Thursdays? Why don't you go to them? Different crowd?"

"No, there's never a different crowd. I mean, we have special guests sometimes. But Thursday's usually my night to rest," he said and then pointed a finger back at the bag of bottles. "And earn a little beer money."

"I've heard a bit about your special guests. Poaching from the hotel's clientele, eh? Boy does that piss them off, I bet. Ever ruin any young marriages?"

"Only a couple," Tobin said, his tone different now. They'd been straddling the fine line between endearing verbal foreplay and flat out embarrassment and Claire had been the first to cross it.

"Want to go tonight?" Claire said, checking her phone for the time. 12:30, the night was young.

She had him conflicted. He looked down first at his feet, then at her feet. Finally, he spoke, "Do you have anything better for walking in?"

She ran back into the hotel, switched out of her flats and into her work shoes. Her maid shoes were all-white Reebok running shoes. It unnerved her that she was the same shoe size as Daisy.

Chapter Eleven

From even the most freewheeling perspective, getting into a pickup truck with a strange boy after midnight in a new town was not a great idea.

Tobin had parked on the street in front of The Brant instead of pulling into the driveway.

His truck fit him so well that Claire could have described it before seeing it. It was a red late-model Ford that was kept in decent shape but had seen some action.

As she pulled open the passenger side door and stepped up, she got hit with her one and only thrum of panic. *What if he drives off with you and you're never seen again?*

She pushed the thought away. If he was set on doing that, it was probably too late now. Besides, she was the one twisting his arm to take her. If she was going to get Buffalo Bill'd, his reverse psychology was flawless.

They drove for a much shorter time than she anticipated.

"We've got to walk from here," he said, pulling off to the side of the road. "Could you get the flashlight out of the glove box?"

She had no idea why, but she expected there to be a gun in there with it.

There wasn't. There was just a large Maglite and some maps and receipts. Was she so starved for entertainment that her imaginings were desperately trying to slither into reality? Was Mission so boring that it had broken her?

"I hope you don't mind walking through the woods at night."
"Who would?"

He smiled at that, turning that mood back around.
"You're a very adventurous girl," Tobin said. "You're going to fit right

in. We're going to steal you away from Brant like that." He snapped his fingers.

"Is that the way it is, the real reason that Daisy hates you so much? Because it's you versus them?"

"Oh yeah, big time." Tobin opened his door and hopped out.

After he shut off the engine, the only light was a dim streetlamp on the opposite side of the road. Tobin's shadow crossed in front of the hood and he opened her door for her. He took the flashlight from her then offered her a hand down from the truck.

His hands were rough. She'd never felt that before. The tips of Mickey's fingers were calloused, but the palms were smooth and soft, not like Tobin's. It was a nice change.

"We'll have some light," he said, his voice all Ranger Rick, "but you're going to have to watch where you step. You don't want to spend the night in the emergency room because you busted an ankle stepping into a snake hole."

The idea of a "snake hole" worried her more than a broken ankle, but she didn't tell him that.

"How do you know where we're going?" she asked as they walked off the side of the road and into the woods. There was no trail, no indicator of where they were going that she could see.

He pointed to a tree with what looked like a loop of cellophane wrapped around its trunk.

"Even if I ignored that, I could probably make it out to Davey's blindfolded. I've done it blind drunk before."

"Davey? Who is that?" Claire said, not concentrating as much on their conversation as she was on the flashlight beam, trying to keep herself from imagining all the nasty things creeping under the layer of pine needles they crunched under their heels.

"You're saying that Daisy told you about the parties but she didn't tell you about who throws them?" he said, her interest piqued by the sound of a cross-examination.

"Oh, you mean David, the hermit!"

"The hermit?" He said, muttering what sounded to Claire like "bitch" but may also have just been a *tsk*. He took a swipe at a low-hanging branch with the Maglite. The flashlight was heavy and a muscular boy like Tobin could do some damage with it. "The hermit! That's so disrespectful. It's no wonder that everyone in this town hates each other."

His voice had lost that young Marlboro Man cool. Tobin was legitimately upset by how Claire had described Davey or David or whoever. "Don't waste time listening to assholes, especially Daisy," Claire said. She wanted to soothe him, to bring the other Tobin back, so she reached out and placed her hand on his shoulder.

Underneath the thin fabric of his shirt, she could feel that he was muscular, but there was a different kind of hardness there too. "Thanks," he said, gently removing her hand from his back, but keeping hold of it as they walked.

Claire felt the strands of a spider web touch her cheek and she brushed it away as quickly as she could without giving away how badly the sensation creeped her out.

"Am I going to get bit by mosquitoes?" she asked, her words filling some of the emptiness of the woods.

"Maybe one or two on our way, but not once we're there."

She didn't ask why. Citronella, probably. No reason to keep the conversation on the topic of insects.

Taking a quick look down at her feet, she saw that her white shoes were now mottled with dark marks from the walk. They were going to be hell to clean.

"So tell me about David," she asked.

"First of all, he's going to insist that you call him Davey." Tobin's grip tightened as he spoke, their hands warming. "David is," his voice trailed off, either taking a minute to get his thought or spacing out.

"I've never liked my dad," Tobin said, starting up again. "He drives a truck for a living, probably sleeps in town, in his own bed, once or twice a week. He's not here. But for me, for all the other kids who've grown up or are growing up in Mission. David is here."

"How old are you?" She said, getting a sudden pang of fear that Tobin might still be in high school.

"Twenty-two. Why?"

"Just checking. Go on." She felt a great relief wash over her, the feeling accompanied by the distant sound of music. It was not crickets or cicadas or the rest of the music of the forest. It was young people's music.

"Every adult out here," Tobin said, "is so concerned with what's good for the town, that they never pay much attention to what's good for its children."

"Children are the future," Claire said with a smile, feeling old after listening to Tobin speak.

"Yeah," he said, smiling back even wider and picking up his pace, dragging her along. The music was louder now, aggressive and electronic. "And this is where the future is born."

His timing was impeccable. At that moment they crested a hill and there below them was a bright ball of light and sound. The party.

♦

"Don't call me David. Davey, please, I insist."

Tobin had been right about that.

Davey was a tall man, a man tall enough to intimidate, but he was trying to make up for that. He spoke in soothing tones, his hands aflutter. He repeated Claire's name every third statement to remind her that he remembered and cared what her name was.

Just looking at him, it was easy to see why Daisy and Brant hated this man. His dark beard was unwieldy, tufts of hair shooting in every direction. He smelled, too. Not of piss and body odor (which was honestly what Claire had expected. *If it dressed like a hobo and quacked like a hobo.*), but of smoke and herbs.

When Claire was a little girl, her mother had dabbled in New Age mysticism as a hobby. She'd brought Claire along several times to a bookstore in Manhattan that sold supplies for yuppie witches—candles, crystals, herbs.

Davey smelled like a more authentic version of that store. Burning sage and pot smoke seemed to waft off him in waves.

For Daisy and Brant he was the Other, an unsettling reminder that not everyone in the world adorned their homes with golden rabbits and quilts. To Claire he was the most intriguing person, place or thing in Mission, Massachusetts.

Tobin had introduced them and then shifted away from Claire, sidling up next to Davey and whispering in his ear like a Secret Service agent. Tobin was tall, but Davey still had to cock his head downwards to enable Tobin to reach his ear.

"Boston, eh?" Davey said, responding to information that Tobin had shared with him, not Claire. He stretched his arms wide, displaying his wingspan. "My hometown! Well, Cambridge actually, but close enough. I used to teach in Boston."

"Really? Where? I've got friends who teach in the area," she said. It was almost true. She had went to school with people who taught, kept them on their Facebook feed even though they were always sharing the "funny" things their students said and did.

It was insufferable.

"My time as a formal teacher was brief. And long before you and your friends were out of diapers, I'm sure. I was fired for antagonizing the students with art."

Claire smiled and nodded politely, unsure what most of that meant.

"I stood up on my desk and started throwing books at them," Davey said, seeming to answer a question that she'd only thought of asking.

When she talked to Davey, the rest of the party seemed to dissolve into background noise, but now that they'd reached a lull, everything seemed to snap back into focus.

They weren't just partying in the woods—this was a campsite. The silver trailer reflected the bonfire light, lightening up the deep shadows that would have been cast if it weren't there. Above them was a string of dim light bulbs, not Christmas lights, just a handful of full-sized bulbs threaded between the tree branches overhead.

There was a clothesline, what looked like a generator with several car batteries attached by jumper cables, and several tree stumps that had been sanded clean and were now home to stacks of red Solo cups and beer bottles.

If this was Davey's home, it didn't look as if he was often alone.

Claire finished her first beer. She hadn't noticed that she'd killed it so quickly until Davey reached over, placed two fingers on the neck of the bottle and gave a gentle tug to pluck it from her grip.

"We should get you another, Claire," he said. On cue, a tiny girl appeared at his left side holding a pitcher. The girl's height was exaggerated by standing next to Davey and Tobin, but she would have been petite on any scale.

"Are we sure she can handle it?" Davey asked while looking at Claire.

"Oh for sure," Tobin answered, his smile handsome but still devilish in the firelight. Claire told herself that she would be hooking up with him within the week. Not tonight, of course. She'd show some restraint, but definitely within the week.

Tobin bent and retrieved one of the Solo cups from the nearest stump, nudging a big plaid-clad Grizzly-Adams-looking youth out of the way. The bigger boy seemed to growl at being jostled, but relented when he saw that it was Tobin.

Claire got the impression that there was a pecking order at this party, with Tobin near the top.

Holding it up to the light, Tobin peered into the cup to make sure it was dry. His squint and appraisal of the cup was a pantomime that Claire was familiar with: it was exactly the kind of thing she'd done countless times herself. You drink enough cigarette ash and backwash and it teaches you to be careful with your party cups.

Once it passed inspection he handed it to the small girl, Davey's cupbearer.

She poured from the pitcher what looked like orange juice. The smell hit her before the cup was full: floral, boozy, chemical and fruity, every aspect of the scent strong.

"Thank you." Claire took the cup as it was offered. She grazed the small girl's hand as she took the cup, momentarily thrown by the large scar. "My name's Claire. What's yours?"

Addressing her like a child was not Claire's smoothest move of the night. Looking closer at her face, she was probably close to Claire's age.

"This is Eden," Davey said, placing a large hand over Eden's shoulder. "The person, not the place," he added. She guessed that it was the fiftieth time he'd made that joke, but Claire smiled and laughed along with the rest of them. Something about Davey made her want to be good and nice.

Claire lifted her cup, the smell almost overpowering.

"Just a second. Everybody drinks," Tobin said, checking out two more cups and holding them out to be filled. He passed one to Davey. Eden disappeared with the pitcher, off to refill more cups, no doubt.

"He means to say that nobody drinks alone out here in this paradise," Davey said.

"Sounds good to me," Claire said. It was something.

"Poured out for the forgiveness of sins," Davey said, raising his glass. "Go easy on this, but right now, let's fucking drink!"

Although she'd never tasted anything exactly like it, the punch filled Claire with sense memory. Her first weekend in college, Allison had mixed up a pitcher of screwdrivers that was a third plastic-bottle vodka, and two-thirds Florida's Natural. It was a great time, but the novelty had worn off after the sixth week and they hadn't made them since.

When she opened her eyes and lowered the cup, Tobin was closer than he had been. The music seemed louder too and Claire felt her hips begin to sway almost instinctively.

"He likes you," Tobin said in her ear. She could feel the heat of his breath work its way in with the words. She imagined the sweetness of the drink menthol-cooling the inside of her head.

"Who does?" she asked while taking another sip, closing her eyes again.

"David," he said.

"Davey," Claire corrected.

"Believe it or not," Tobin continued, "he doesn't like everyone who comes out here, especially the outsiders. Not everyone gets an invite back."

Claire opened her eyes again and the topography of the party had changed. Davey was nowhere to be found, and all the dancers seemed to have switched positions and styles to account for the change in song.

They were careful about it, but Claire knew that she was being watched, that glances were being thrown her way. Not that she cared, but it was impossible to tell if the girls at the party considered her part of the family or a threat.

"Well, that's nice, but what do *you* think of me? If I am invited back, I'm going to need someone to bring me out here. I'll get lost." She guided his hand around her waist and kept swaying.

"I think you dance well."

The warmth of his body seemed to react with the warmth flowing out from the pit of her stomach. She let him move closer behind her, until the scent of him had folded her up.

Before she could notice, her cup was empty and she was facing him.

From over Tobin's shoulder she could see the open door to Davey's trailer.

Davey's impossibly tall silhouette stood in the doorway, his arm around a full female figure.

This was the last image she could remember from the party.

The rest of her memories were long, chemical kisses from Tobin, the strange hardness of the flesh of his chest and back, and the underbrush cutting up her shins as she stumbled back home to The Brant.

Chapter Twelve

Claire had to pee. Finding the bathroom was proving difficult, though, because by the time she was semiconscious she was already in the hallway, the door closed behind her.

She stood in her panties and T-shirt, her keycard left behind—presumably—in her jean's pocket, locked inside her room.

The hallway pitched and twisted. She was standing inside a funhouse that looked just like the hotel. She did not know for how long she'd lost consciousness, how long she'd been back from the woods, or what time it was.

The window at the end of the hallway told her that it was still dark out, so she guessed that it was around four, but had nothing to back this up.

She saw half the world in a wiry chestnut-red haze until she pushed the hair out of her left eye, the clumsy motion covering her right eye with Silverfish's blonde streak. Her hair had grown out since she'd last bleached it and half the strands were now a brownish-red.

Time and space seemed to run past with long stretches of blackness. When she was finished contemplating her hair she was in the stairwell with no recollection of opening the service door to get there.

She gripped the banister and tried to remember how much she'd drunk, what she'd done with Tobin (was he in her bedroom right now, could she have just knocked and had him let her back in?), whether or not she'd taken anything else, pills or smoke.

Her bare feet slapped against the polished concrete steps and she lost track of what floor she was on or which one she was going to.

Was she going to Daisy for help? That didn't seem smart. In response to this thought, the world swam and a wave of nausea radiated to the tips of her fingers and then back to her brain.

She was going to be sick—no way to fight it.

She vomited during one of the rolling blank spaces that dotted the next few minutes.

She couldn't remember the act itself, but she tasted the puke. Not remembering was a bittersweet sensation since she hated few things more than vomiting, but was sure that she had at least one more episode in the near future.

Now she was somewhere within The Brant that she'd never seen. Either it was a different part of the basement she'd never been in or it was a sub-basement.

Around her were tarps, plastic pool chairs and what looked like umbrellas with the golden Brant rabbit on the edges.

This rabbit got more play than Mickey Mouse.

Mickey hasn't texted in a while, her thoughts traveled off until she tripped over the leg of a chair. She caught herself with her hands, but the ground was rough and sandy, so she'd still drawn blood on her palms.

There was light, not much, but she couldn't remember flicking any switches. It was the blue glow of florescent light ahead of her.

She didn't have to pee now and ran two fingers down the front of her panties to make sure she hadn't had an accident. A puddle of puke on the stairs was bad enough to get her fired, but Claire thought of Ms. Brant slipping on her pee and giggled.

Her underwear was dry. There'd been no accident, but that didn't mean she hadn't removed her panties and squatted in a corner of this basement during one of her blackout moments.

What am I doing here? In some ways she was sleepwalking, but her awareness seemed too acute, the world less dreamlike than she'd imagined it would be if she were asleep. Everything may have been spinning, but there was concreteness to her surroundings, details she wouldn't have invented.

Claire approached the light, crouched lower to the ground now because she wanted to spare her shins any more trauma this night.

The source of the basement's illumination was a door, open just a crack. It was not the kind that opened in or out, but side-to-side on a track. She was reminded of the walk-in fridge in the kitchen, but this wasn't that walk-in fridge. She used that one every morning while she helped Roy prep for the day and, as messed up as she was, she could recognize that she was not in the kitchen.

As she approached, she instinctively wrapped her hands around her bare arms, but then noticed that there was no chill coming from the doorway.

A shadow shifted over the blade of florescent light and she realized for the first time that she was moving towards an inhabited room. This epiphany did not scare her. She didn't care at this point if a coworker caught a glimpse of her in her skivvies, but she did try to approach as stealthily as possible.

Pressing herself against the wall beside the doorway, she listened to the sounds inside. There were footfalls, too many to be coming from one person. *Who could it be?*

She grossed herself out by picturing Roy and Daisy meeting up in the basement, Roy rubbing her crotch with his half-finger and Daisy moaning with a slight lisp. It was revolting and comical, like most of the things Silverfish kept her mind occupied with.

If she took a quick enough peek, she could go unnoticed, as long as neither of them was looking at the sliver of open doorway. She heard a wet smacking sound from inside and cringed. The sound reminded her of the retching she couldn't recall doing, the acid bubbling up her throat, the smell of the vomit still dripping down her sinuses.

Despite feeling the waves of nausea, the pull of curiosity was too much and she looked into the room.

It wasn't two figures but a group of four. The room was much bigger than the walk-in fridge upstairs, with low ceilings but a tiled floor that pitched downwards into a kind of pit. It looked like a high school locker room shower, the kind with no stalls, just one long row of shower heads.

Three of them were cleaning up, wearing black plastic jumpsuits that looked like cheapo HAZMAT attire, complete with surgeon's masks. The fourth figure sat in the middle of the room, a black rubber apron draped over his knees and nearly touching the floor.

The seated man's face was a nightmare.

Nearly hairless, the skin stretched so tight around his jaw that it looked like clingwrap almost at the breaking point. She caught a glimpse of his glassy white eyes and was not concerned that they were looking right into her own because this was Father Hayden, the blind priest.

It took a moment of taking in the details before Claire's addled brain realized *what* they were cleaning.

One of the figures lifted a mop and wrung it out with a yellow plastic bucket, the kind that janitors pushed around schools and office buildings. She watched as the water strained out a coppery red.

She was witnessing the cleanup of a crime scene. The robin's-egg-blue tiles where the mop hadn't passed were covered in oily ponds of blood.

The cleanup crewmember farthest from the door was using a large sponge to wipe down the walls. The graffiti was in thin lines of semi-dried blood, the patterns making no sense at all. Triangles and neat spirals and squiggles, the drawings looked like a difficult math problem.

The third crewmember was tying a knot in a heavy-duty black garbage bag, filled three-quarters of the way. He had two similar bags at his feet. The angles of the bags were organic, the bottoms rounded like half-filled water balloons.

This crewmember was shorter than the rest, the HAZMAT suit tight enough around the breasts and hips to imply the female form underneath. She hefted one of the bags off the ground and started for the door.

In her shock, Claire retreated behind the wall. The world around her became more amorphous as her consciousness faded. No please, not now. She pleaded with herself to stay with it, at least let her find a hiding spot before passing out.

There was a stack of pool chairs beside her and she crawled under the bottom-most one as she heard the metal runners of the door begin to screech behind her.

The sound was too much to handle. She felt the cool of the basement floor against her cheek and then remembered nothing else of that night.

♦

She awoke with coldness still pressing against her face. This time it was in the form of a cool, damp cloth that Daisy had folded over and was mopping over her brow.

"Don't get up," Daisy said, her lisp still carrying that unnatural sweetness, but now very much tinged with a mother-bird attitude.

"What happened?" Claire said.

"I assume, because you smell like a still, that you went out into the woods for a party." Daisy narrowed her eyelids, made her voice a bit deeper.

"Yeah," Claire said, trying to sound ashamed. She wasn't ashamed, and she hadn't meant that. Claire was more interested in how she'd gotten back to Daisy's room.

"You're lucky I woke up later than usual. At around five, I found you. You were lying in front of my door, nearly naked and covered in dirt. I had to rinse you off before putting you to bed."

"Oh." Claire wasn't sure what to say. She felt her own nakedness under the quilt. Neither her shirt nor her panties remained. *Had last night been a hallucination? Was a hallucination that bizarrely specific and detailed even possible?*

It had to be much later than five. Claire tried looking around Daisy's room, but stopped when she reached the window. The sunlight that slashed through the curtains was blinding. It seemed to burn her retinas, boiling the alcohol off her brain in puffs of smoke.

It was already the late morning.

"I told Ms. Brant that you were sick. I told her that it was probably the shrimp Roy had been serving for dinner, so now he's in for it. I hope you appreciate that."

"Thank you, but you didn't have to do that. I don't want him to get in trouble."

"He's in trouble often, every time justified, so he's used to it," Daisy said. "I found the sick you left on the stairs. You would have been fired if Ms. Brant had found it first."

"Thank you."

"Don't thank me. Just make sure that this doesn't happen again. You are expected to be a professional while you're working here."

"I understand. It won't ever happen again," Claire said. She cinched up the quilt and tried sitting upright in Daisy's bed.

"What you need to understand is that them out there." Daisy pointed out her window, motioning to the woods. "They don't care about you. He wants to use up all the youth and beauty you have. He wants to get what he can out of you and then get rid of you."

There was silence in the room. Daisy handed the wet cloth to Claire, then smoothed out the wrinkles in her apron.

"You think I'm exaggerating, but they're not your friends."

"I know," Claire said, unsure if she did, but feeling that this was the only way out of this room. "I've had friends like them before. It never ends the way I want it to." That part wasn't a lie.

"Well, they're not representative of what Mission is about!" Like a switch, Daisy was back in chamber of commerce mode. "Take the rest of the day to get yourself together. I'll take care of your responsibilities today, but only today."

"Thank you."

"We were more alike at your age than you think, Claire."

"Well, I don't know if I'd cover your shift, so you're a kinder person than me." Claire would help her out after this morning, though. Not only to repay a debt, but because Daisy was more human to her now.

"Oh, you'd do the same for me. Besides, the Chopins checked out this morning, so that's two less people I have to look after on your route."

Part Two:

The Congregation

Chapter Thirteen

Terry Chopin died much earlier than he was supposed to.

Victoria Brant watched Roy hit him with the baton, fast and low in the throat. She could hear the crack, knew that the young man's windpipe had been crushed even before Roy realized.

She watched in the pale light as Terry Chopin's desperate, pathetic inhalation slowed then finally stopped as his face turned purple.

The girl did not watch her husband die. She was hooded and unconscious before Roy had dealt the blow.

Killing Terry had been Roy's second mistake of the night and his sweating, red-faced apology told Brant that he knew it. He didn't speak, didn't dare, but Victoria watched as he mouthed "I'm sorry, I'm sorry," over and over while slipping the mask over Terry's head.

As if the burlap bag mattered. The boy was dead.

Roy's first mistake had been in administering the sedative.

It had been in the couple's complementary soufflé, a voucher for which had accompanied their welcome folder.

Terry Chopin, the gentleman that he was, had let his wife eat the lion's share of the desert, and had started awake as Roy entered the room, placing the sack over his wife's face and pulling the drawstring.

As dumb and unreliable as he was, Roy was quick and strong. He'd had the collapsible riot baton fully extended before Victoria's eyes could even register it and in one swift movement had ended Terry's life.

Terry's death had cast a pall over the entire ceremony. Brant did her part, though. She preached with all the fire she could muster, placed her hands on Father Hayden's shoulders, and was sure to make extended eye contact with every one of their parishioners.

Even still, it was the death blow that they were all gathered for, where they derived much of their pleasure, spiritual and earthly. The sight of a thrashing body being made swiftly and permanently still was the reason that many still attended mass. She did not kid herself on this point.

They had the girl, Kendra Chopin, but one death was anti-climatic, especially when the group had been promised two offerings.

If Roy had only laced each of the courses of their meal with a smaller dose of sedative like she'd suggested, but no, that would have taken him a few extra steps. Since his last monumental mistake, the one in which he'd lost half of a finger, Roy's productivity and willingness to follow instructions had taken a nosedive.

It was either that or he wanted an excuse to use the heavy expandable baton that he'd mail-ordered from Canada.

Roy tried his best to make up for it during the ceremony, attempting to pass off Terry's lifeless corpse as unconscious.

After the deathblow had been delivered to Kendra, her blood flowing down towards the drain in the middle of the room, Roy propped Mr. Chopin up on his knees.

Roy said the words, received a half-hearted amen from the congregation and then slashed down with all his might with the mallet, splitting the back of Terry's skull from his topmost vertebra.

The hit may have been ferocious, but the results were unspectacular.

Terry had been dead for too long. His neck only seeped blood. They wanted to feel the warm spray coat their ponchos and, because of Roy, Victoria Brant was unable to deliver that to them.

There was enough blood to go around, though. Roy and the rest of them had rushed forward to daub the fingers of their gloves in Kendra's warm blood.

Victoria did not join them, but stood by and watched as they drew the sacred signs in blood. Doodling on the kill room walls was empty theatrics. It didn't add any kind of power to the ceremony, but Victoria Brant didn't tell them that.

If they wanted to wallow in the spectacle of the event, prolong it by finger-painting like children, she wasn't going to stop them. They were enthusiastic and earnest, and that's what really mattered.

She caught Roy by the shoulder. Behind his blood-spattered goggles, he looked at her with rage in his eyes, as if being interrupted awoke the animal inside him. His face softened when he realized who he was glaring at, his hairy face going from big bad wolf to puppy dog eyes.

"Clean this up when you're through."

He nodded.

Victoria turned and went back upstairs to finish some paperwork. She had a hotel to run.

Chapter Fourteen

Claire worried that she was going insane, so Tobin kissed her tattoos to make it better.

He liked her tattoos and she seemed to like his scars, so they were even.

She ran her fingers around the scars, finding patterns in the hardened lumps on his back and arms. Tobin knew that some of the patterns were there to begin with, while some of them were products of her imagination.

Tobin didn't wait for her to ask, he volunteered a story to go with them. "Remember how I said that I never liked my father. Can you guess why?"

He shrugged his shirt back on before she could answer and buttoned it up. His father had given him some of them, but some of them he'd done himself.

"Tell me again what happened," he said, changing the subject back to what it had been on their drive out to his place. It was more of a shed than anything else, but it was clean and dry and the bed was brand new. She didn't seem to mind it.

He liked it too. Davey had helped him raise the funds to build it and had even poured some of the concrete. The other boys had helped him do the rest. Many of them had construction experience or something close enough to it. Tobin's community had come together to help him build a home and that made him proud.

The only downside of the shed was that it was far enough into the woods that he couldn't get mail delivered, had never even tried because the building was erected in such a legal gray area.

He opened up a P.O. Box at the Mission post office, but never ordered anything juicy. The employees opened his mail before depositing it in the box and made no effort to hide that they were doing it. The message was clear. *We're watching you.* He'd entertained the idea of mailing himself a dead rat, but that seemed childish.

Claire repeated the end of her story for him, about how she'd seen some inexplicable things while she was drunk last Thursday.

"Terrible things," she said. Tobin had no doubt that she'd seen them, but he did wonder how she was allowed to see them.

"I don't even know if they're real. I only remember images and a feeling that they're real. It's like a bad dream times ten," she said. "It was like I was sleepwalking."

"Have you ever been a sleepwalker before?"

"Yeah, actually a lot when I was younger, but it's always been stupid stuff like putting my shoes on and trying to unlock the front door. I grew out of it. The only time I know about in college, Allison caught me putting my clothes hamper in the refrigerator, never anything like this."

"Well, I don't want to tell you that you're crazy, and I really do think that you were sleepwalking, *but*," he said, choosing his words carefully, "I know that Davey has never trusted Ms. Brant. Their fight goes back way before any of us kids had started hanging out with him, but Davey's always warned us about her."

"Warned you about what, specifically?" she asked, leaning up in his small bed. She held a hand out for her shirt and he passed it to her. He withheld it for a moment until she bent far enough forward that he could see the tattoo beside and below her right breast. It was a tiny bat in flight, no bigger than an inch. Without being told, he knew that this had been her first tattoo. It was small enough, hidden enough and juvenile enough.

He loved it and had kissed it twice before they'd started talking.

"Davey warned us that maybe her hold on the town was too strong. That's part of the reason he'd decided to set up camp here and stay as long as he has, because he says he's keeping an eye on her."

Claire looked confused and Tobin wondered if he was laying it on a little too thick, then he wondered what exactly it was he was laying on. What was he putting down the groundwork for? He was so good at following orders that sometimes he scared himself.

"In my dream though, there were multiple people, and blood and the priest," she said. "It wasn't just Brant."

He was silent, not wanting to speak until she pushed this conversation further in one direction or the other. Either she was going to resolve to get out of that hotel (and thereby out of Mission) or she was going to shrug the whole thing off. Tobin wanted to ask her about the priest, but he would wait.

Claire let the wisp of a smile cross her face and Tobin knew that the match had turned in his favor: she would be staying in Mission. "Could it maybe be a weird sex thing?" she asked.

"Could be. Any Ms. Brant sex thing would probably be weird. Too much skin, not enough elasticity," he said.

She chuckled in response, still sounding apprehensive. She hadn't been nervous in bed, but in a way he knew that had been some kind of escape for her. If he'd offered her a drink when she'd gotten in his truck, she'd have taken it.

He waited a beat before redirecting back towards a more serious subject. "Have you seen the priest while you were awake?"

"No, but Daisy told me about him. She told me about his burns and how Ms. Brant lets him stay there for free."

"Did he look as bad as you imagined?"

"Worse."

Tobin stood, pulled on his jeans and buckled his belt. "I bet you could imagine some pretty messed-up shit," he said and poked a finger into her forehead. He left a white mark that filled in red.

"Ow, you prick!" she yelled, but laughed too, not really mad. Tobin already had a good idea of what he could get away with around her.

"What are you going to do?" he asked. "Head back to Boston? You were really loopy that night when I dropped you off. Eden mixes a mean drink."

"I don't think one bad night is going to scare me off. But still, I've had bad dreams, and then there was this."

"I wanted to walk you to your room and put you to bed, but you wouldn't let me."

"Yeah. Put me to bed. I bet," she said. Tobin guessed that the horrors of Ms. Brant's basement were now forgotten. "Want to know the one funny thing that came from that night?"

"Sure," Tobin said. She was slipping on her own jeans now. Playtime was over, he guessed, and stepped into his boots.

"Somewhere between the first-floor stairwell and the basement, I'm ninety-nine percent sure that I peed. That's why I went out in the first place, to take a leak."

"Well, this is a new carpet," Tobin said, hooking a thumb towards the small toilet, the only other room in the shed. "Bathroom's right there if you ever find yourself needing to use it while you're here."

"With that amount of wit, I dare say that you could make it in the big city, young man," Claire said, holding her arms up and standing on his bed. He could see the small skull tattoo under her wrist, stylized and cartoony, but small enough that you might think it was a birthmark at first glance.

He took her hand and twisted it gently, turning her wrist up so he could kiss it. Then he swung her over his shoulder and patted her butt.

"This is not acceptable third-date behavior," she laughed.

"So now we're counting meeting by the dumpsters as a date?" He dropped her down on the bed, the bounce placing considerable strain on his rack raisers. He needed the bed up high or else he would have no place to store his clothes in the small shed.

She jumped to her feet before he could pin her to the bed again. She really was through for the afternoon.

"Just get me back to the hotel before my chaperones get suspicious that I've been gone too long."

"After you," he said. He motioned to the door and spun his key ring around his index finger.

They walked arm and arm to the truck.

"Want to head out to the party tonight? I'd like to see what a Saturday is like," she said. "I promise I'll take it easier on the jungle juice this time."

He didn't expect that she'd want to go back so quickly, and if she did, he thought he was going to have to be the one doing the convincing.

"Jungle juice? I've never heard it called that."

"You don't get out enough, Tobin."

This was true.

"Sure, we can go. I'll pick you up at eleven? Do you mind walking down the driveway and meeting me at the sidewalk in front of Dwyer's General?"

She nodded. "Good idea."

"I don't want to get you in trouble with your boss," he said, then added, "especially if she turns out to be Count Dracula."

Chapter Fifteen

Bert shivered and nestled closer to Jane's chest. He wore a small, pink knit sweater that stayed opened at the bottom so he could go pee without dribbling all over the fabric.

Bert was a two-year-old miniature pinscher. Jane had never once used the pet carrier they'd bought for him during the trip down from Portland. She'd insisted on carrying him the entire drive.

A dog was not a child, but baby steps had to be taken sometimes. Christine had to remind herself of this fact often.

Christine held the door open for Jane and followed her inside the lobby, dragging their heavy rolling suitcase behind her, a duffel thrown on top.

She was only estimating, but she guessed that the bags were much heavier than Bert. Jane was carrying the lighter load.

Relief swept over Christine as she observed that the lobby of The Brant Hotel looked much like it did on the website, better even.

The last time they'd opted to spend a summer vacation south of Maine, Christine and Jane had ended up with a Florida time-share that they no longer owned but were still paying off.

The time-share had been Jane's fault.

Bert had been Jane's fault too, but only Christine had a problem with the dog and it was one she tried to keep secret, so nobody was gaining or losing any blame points there.

Christine followed Jane up to the front desk, her tread heavy as she pictured herself as Jane's live-in servant.

There was a high-pitched mewling sound and for a moment she thought that someone had pulled the fire alarm.

Christine peeked around Jane to see that the woman at the front desk was the source of the unpleasant noise.

The shrieking woman behind the desk was broad and plain, overly made up to compensate for the canvas. Even from a couple yards away, Christine could see that the woman's cheeks sparkled where she had applied makeup intended for girls half her age.

"He's just a wittle-little baby. Oh my, does he ever get confused and think that he's a big dog?" the woman asked Jane, her voice up an octave and demonstrating a strong lisp.

Christine couldn't tell if the lisp was an affectation that came with the woman's baby voice or whether she actually spoke that way.

Either way, Christine had an instant dislike of her.

She was wearing an ugly green-and-white dress that upon further appraisal was a uniform. Over her left tit the name *Daisy* was embroidered in green thread. Christine wondered if Daisy was the girl's name or the tit's. She called hers Larry and Curly.

"He thinks he's big man on campus all the time," Jane said, hugging Bert closer, kissing his tiny snout.

Christine received approximately one-eighth of the amount of kisses that Bert got. Bert didn't even appreciate them, and if Christine ever tried to get that close to him, she'd end up with a bloody lip.

"Hi," Christine said, speaking up and inserting herself into this Daisy/Bert/Jane love-fest. "We're checking in. The last name is Joyce."

"Let me check that right away," Daisy said. Her lisp was no longer as pronounced when she spoke in a more professional voice, but it was still there. She pulled her hand back from Bert's small head, leaving a doggie cowlick between his ears. He didn't look like he appreciated the gesture.

"We have you booked for a seven-night stay, starting tonight. Would two double beds be okay?"

"Not really. I had thought I'd booked a king bed," Christine said. She congratulated herself on pegging Daisy as an asshole before she'd even spoken to her.

Jane always gave her a hard time about prejudging people, but over the last few months she'd learned that as long as she only internalized her snap judgments, she could no longer catch hell for them.

"I'm sorry about that," Daisy said, a plump finger gliding down the grid of the registrar. "Let me see what I have available so we can have this cleared up for you."

Christine saw an opportunity to make things harder for Daisy and she took it.

"Actually, I forgot to ask this on the phone, but does your hotel have a honeymoon suite?"

"We do," Daisy said. The girl looked puzzled. Christine had seen this face a number of times over the last six months. The expression seemed to say, "Two ladies? Married?"

In her peripheral vision, Christine could see Jane shift Bert to her other arm, the way you might adjust the strap on a purse when it didn't really need adjusting.

"If it's not in use, we'll take that then," Christine said. "The increase in rate isn't much of a concern."

"Are you on your honeymoon? You should have told us in advance so we could have the room prepared," Daisy said, looking like she was trying to regain some kind of foothold in the conversation.

"It's been legal here even longer than it has in Maine. You've never had a couple like us in the honeymoon suite?"

"That's not what I meant to imply. What I mean to say is congratulations, of course. But the suite is going to take about an hour before we have it ready."

"Oh, we're in no rush." Christine placed a hand on the desk, leaning in.

These kinds of interactions still made Jane uncomfortable. They might have been newlyweds, but they'd been living with each other for fifteen years. Christine understood why interacting with new people in a strange town might scare her wife, but it didn't scare her. In fact, it felt like her civic duty to explode people's misconceptions, even if she did it by trying to make fools out of small-minded assholes.

"Would it be possible to keep our bags at the front desk while we wait?" Jane asked.

"Sure, if you'll just leave those right here, uh, ma'am." Daisy indicated that Christine should wheel the suitcase to the side of the desk. "I'll go make sure we get that room ready for you as soon as possible."

"Before you go," Christine said, raising her hand from the desk and touching Daisy's fleshy forearm. "Do you have any suggestions about what to do in Mission for an hour or two?"

This seemed to pull Daisy out of her stupor, her eyes brightening. "If this is your first time in the area, taking a walk up and down Main Street may be your best bet. You'll get to sample our historic architecture and get a good idea of where the amenities are located. Of course you could also take a short nature hike, but I wouldn't recommend going too far into the woods. It will be getting dark in a few hours."

♦

"Quaint," Christine said. She didn't mean it to, but the word came out sounding sarcastic. This was her blessing and her curse.

The sidewalk leading away from The Brant Hotel was lined with white flowers, the topsoil under them a rich dark brown, speckled with the occasional white Miracle-Gro grain. The town cared about how it looked.

Christine wrapped an arm around Jane's waist. Bert gave a low growl as she got close, but it was perfunctory, just the sound he made when anyone besides Jane entered his bubble.

"It's not our honeymoon, you know, that was almost a year ago," Jane said.

"I know. It's an early anniversary celebration, then. If you don't want the nicest room in the hotel, I can still check if they've got those double beds available."

Jane smiled. They were only a year apart but Jane would always look ten years younger. She had a girlish face, even as the lines crept in around her eyes and dimples. This close, Christine would be able to spot a hint of gray in her black hair if Jane did not take such pains to dye it every week or so.

The Brant Hotel may have stacked up the lofty expectations presented by the pictures on the website, but the town of Mission was underwhelming. It had none of the artisan shops and cafes that could be found in similarly sized New England towns, just a few store fronts that wouldn't be of interest to anyone besides the locals. There was a general store and gas station opposite the hotel. Christine had a hard time distinguishing where the store ended and the gas station began. It was possible that they were the same thing. There was a neon RX sign in the window of the store. The inclusion of a pharmacy made it three destinations if you were willing to be generous.

A block down from the hotel was a post office, the sign outside labeling it *Mission's Historic Post Office* with no further elaboration on what made the building historic. It was nice, the white façade and columns recently painted, but Christine wasn't going to take the extra step to inquire about its historical significance.

Bert made a kind of crying/whining sound, a favorite of his. In some ways taking care of him was the perfect training for a baby. Jane bent and set him on the ground, taking his lead out of her jacket pocket and clipping it to the back of his sweater.

Most dogs walked or scurried, but Bert pranced.

"What? Do you have to do poops?" Jane asked Bert in the voice she reserved only for him.

In answer, Bert yapped and growled.

"I think he wants a snack," Jane said.

Christine shaded her eyes from the sun, craning her head to see beyond the post office. There was nothing except a small park with a white-and-green gazebo, nice but not going to help fill Bert's belly.

"The general store looks like the only game in town," she said. Jane nodded and Christine took her arm as they walked across the street. It wasn't necessary. There was no traffic at all running through Mission. Main Street was offset from the highway, and the only reason you'd drive it would be if you had business in Mission or the surrounding areas, not if you wanted to get to any of the hundred more exciting small towns in Berkshire County.

Sleigh bells greeted their arrival to the store, the same kind that had been tied to the front door of The Brant. It must have been a town mandate.

The shelves were stocked with rows of groceries, many of which looked like they'd been there for a while. There was no dust, but the sun from the front window had faded some of the packages. Everything looked older in a town like Mission.

"Good afternoon," the man behind the counter said. He had a pharmacist's white coat slung over his plaid button-down, thick glasses over his nose and under that a reddish-gray mustache. They'd stopped at the Norman Rockwell Museum this morning and, upon seeing this guy, Christine was gripped with the sudden terror that they were still there.

"Hello," Jane said. "Do you by any chance have dog treats?"

"Well, I think we might. Let me go look wit'cha," he said. The man rubbed his head, the motion feeling affected and genuine at the same time. It seemed to say, "Bear with me because I'm having a folksy senior moment."

As he talked and gestured, Christine thought of the man in the white coat as an old man, but he was probably right around their own age. The realization saddened her, like looking in a mirror too closely and under the wrong kind of light. Christine was anything but vain, but her mortality was a touchy subject.

The man walked down three aisles before bending to one knee and grabbing a package of Snausages for Jane. It was a cardboard box with a cartoon dog on it. Bert's Snausages always seemed to come in a colorful plastic baggie.

Christine thought of the yappy little fucker eating tainted, ancient Snausages and had to stifle a laugh.

The man made a theatrical groaning sound as he got to his feet. Jane offered him a hand, but he waved it off.

"Nah, thank you, darling. If I don't get my exercise I'll never be able to get up and down when I get old one day."

He was charming, no doubts there.

"Y'both staying at the hotel?" the man asked.

"Yes. We haven't even seen our room yet. They're still making it up," Jane said, putting the box of Snausages under one arm and trying to pick up Bert with her other. His prancing on the store's linoleum flooring was getting too loud to still be considered polite. He wiggled away from her and she left him to walk under his own power. Bert got what he wanted, even if he was usually much more apt to obey Jane.

"You're going to have a great time," the man said, walking them back to the register. "There's been articles calling it the best kept secret of Massachusetts, and I think you're going to see why."

"We look forward to it," Christine said and reached for her wallet. "How much for those?"

"Two fifty, but an even two if I can get yer names. I'm Pat Dwyer. You'll be seeing me around, I bet. Even if you don't come back to the store. I make deliveries to Ms. Brant, whatever she needs."

"That's very sweet of you to knock off the fifty cents. I'm Jane and this is Christine."

Christine noticed how she kept off the last name. Christine hadn't been the one to suggest she take it, either; that had been Jane's idea. And no, they weren't sisters, Pat.

"Pleasure to meet you lovely ladies."

Christine held the door open for Jane, but Bert took this as opening the door for him. He stopped sniffing around the checkout counter and quickened his pace to dance out the store. The smug look on his rat face that seemed to tell Christine, "She's my lady now, what you going to do about it, bitch?"

"One more thing," Pat called back before either of them had a chance to use the door. "Kind of a tip to get the most out of your stay."

"Thanks," Jane said, "and what is the tip?"

"My buddy Roy is the chef over at the hotel. Best cook in town, easy. If you want to have a great stay, the trick is to get in good with him. If you show him that dog of yours, let him play around with him, you'll eat like royalty the whole time you're here."

Christine smiled, not sure what to say to Pat's pro-tip.

"Roy's like a big kid, only he's got a mustache. The guy loves dogs." Pat laughed to himself, something told Christine that he'd practiced this bit before. She grinned and imagined Roy as a simpleton who liked to fuck dogs.

Bert barked from the sidewalk, letting them know that he would like to proceed on their tour of Mission.

Let him have Bert, Christine thought.

Chapter Sixteen

Daisy knocked twice, the way she always did before entering Father Hayden's room.

Ms. Brant called Father Hayden their most powerful weapon against the evils of the outside world. Even though he looked like a sick, defeated man and smelled of his own excrement, Daisy had learned not to doubt Ms. Brant.

The Father was sleeping as she entered, but even in the relative rest of sleep, his breaths sounded like pained moans. She took his water pitcher from his bedside table and brought it into the bathroom. There she rinsed and refilled it, the pitcher cool against her hands.

When she returned, Father Hayden was awake, dead eyes seeming to stare at her for a moment before sweeping the rest of the room.

"It's just Daisy, Father," she said. "No other visitors today."

She held the pitcher with one hand, using the back of her other to caress the smooth skin behind his ear.

Even though he gave a small gasp at her touch, as she kept her hand there it seemed to calm him. This was their secret signal that it was only his caretaker and no-one else. His only other regular visitor was Ms. Brant, and why a great wizard should fear someone as humble and compassionate as Ms. Brant, Daisy would never understand.

Daisy had requested that they try their best to only move him downstairs at regular intervals as not to upset his routine, but the schedule was dictated by Ms. Brant and the celestial calendar. The result of this was that Father Hayden was always agitated in the days following a ceremony, unsure that he wasn't going to be picked up by Roy and moved to his throne downstairs every time someone entered the room.

Using the faint condensation watermark as a guide, Daisy

placed the pitcher back in its spot. She made sure the handle faced the bed to reduce the risk that Father Hayden would spill.

"Feeding time," Daisy said, running a finger down Hayden's throat, over his Adam's apple. This was their signal for mealtime.

The man made a clicking sound in his throat, the scar tissue around his mouth pulling tighter, a bead of drool dropping from the nearly lipless hole in his face.

Daisy untangled the messenger bag from around her shoulders, the strap snagging on her small golden pin. The pin was in the shape of a small golden hare. Ms. Brant had given it to her years ago and she'd had to solder a new clasp on twice.

From beside the bed, she drew Hayden's tray. *Rise and Shine!* was spelled out in yellow letters along the borders of the tray, a smiling sun in the center of the plastic, its face grooved to grip a plate. The tray was built to serve breakfast in bed, but Father Hayden took all his meals this way.

Daisy sat down on the edge of the bed, the extra weight once again making the man irritable. He tried to draw his legs up, but couldn't get his knees past the legs of the tray.

"Don't do that or I can't give you your dinner." She shushed him and spoke to him calmly, even though he couldn't really hear her.

Drawing his three courses out of the bag, she placed all three canisters on the tray, then guided one of Hayden's hands over to it.

Three out of his five fingers were missing nails and all of the tips were smooth and lineless. They were like the hands of a wax figure that had been kept too long in the sun, indefinite and formless.

"Carrots," she said, holding his hand over the first small container. "Berries," she shouted, moving to the second.

He shook free of her grip and found the third, larger Tupperware container on his own.

"Meat," she said as she watched him pry off the lid and dip one finger into the food.

"Here, here," she said, trying to put a plastic spoon into his hand.

It was too late, though. He already had the finger in his mouth. It must have been difficult to suck with no lips because the face he made while eating with his hands collapsed his face in an expression of agony. The melted skin of his non-cheeks drew taut as froth bubbled at the sides of his mouth.

She watched him eat, stopping only occasionally to hack into a napkin, a glob of mucus and food sometimes coming back out through his nostrils instead of his mouth.

After the meat was gone, he calmed down and ate the fruits and vegetables with his spoon.

Before she knew him, Father Hayden used to scare Daisy.

She'd feared not only his grotesque exterior, but also the eternal punishment that could await her because she found him disgusting. She knew, of course, that the Lord knew what was in her heart, which is why she was relieved when she began to enjoy her visits to room thirty-one.

It gave her pleasure to have someone depend on her. There were times when she felt that way while attending to guests, but it was nothing compared to what she got from her relationship with Father Hayden.

Not only was she helping Ms. Brant, but in the process of serving her duty to the hotel she'd gained the companionship of perhaps its most important resident.

"You're looking out for me, aren't you?" Daisy asked him.

Father Hayden looked in her direction for a moment before continuing with his carrot purée. It was a good thing he couldn't see, because the carrots came out of him looking exactly the way they went in. This was a gross observation, but it made her smile, a secret she was in on that Hayden would never get to know.

"No, I forgot. You're looking out for all of us."

His cataracts stared back at her, his throat undulating as he pushed down a mouthful of carrot and berry mixture.

"Well, everyone except the ones in the woods. You've got an eye on them, but for a different reason, right?"

Father Hayden set down the spoon, letting it clatter to the tray and leave a splotch of berries and seeds in the middle of the cartoon sun's face.

"A lesbian couple checked into the hotel today. A *married* lesbian couple. Can you believe it?" She didn't always talk to Father Hayden about hotel gossip, but it was nice to say the things she was thinking aloud sometimes.

"I think Ms. Brant will mark them. Not only because they are flagrantly living in sin, but because things had gone so wrong with the Chopins. That boy's body flopping around like that, it made a mockery of the ceremony. Ms. Brant was so mad at Roy I thought she was going to fire him."

Father Hayden never responded and this time was no different.

"They've got a dog, too. You know how Roy gets with dogs. I told him he could have it," she said, he probably didn't know how Roy got with dogs, or who Roy was, or anything at all. It was nice to talk to someone, though. "I didn't check permission with Ms. Brant. Was that a mistake, you think?"

He gave no response.

"Well, if they're going to end up marked, that means you're going to be going back downstairs sooner rather than later," she said.

She couldn't be sure if he was reacting to this, or had just had enough of sitting up in front of the tray. He screamed the best he could, his half-tongue slapping against the roof of his mouth, then he put both hands under the tray and tried to flip it over.

Daisy caught the edge of it and pressed it back down before he could dump the canisters of puree all over the bedspread.

Sometimes he acted so much like a child that Daisy felt pangs of doubt creep up in the back of her mind. *Could he really be their powerful protector?* She crushed them, though, as she did all doubts.

There was no room for doubt in any part of her life, least of all her faith.

Chapter Seventeen

Eden was beautiful even though her scar was not.

Not all of her beauty came from her youth, but much of it did and she would do anything to be allowed to keep it. She'd asked this favor of Davey on numerous occasions, but each time she asked he simply looked at her and shook his head.

She hated him and loved him when he made that face, as she hated him and loved him during all of her waking hours.

When Eden asked him to guide her towards eternal youth, his expression told her all she needed to know. His half-sad smile reminded her of what he'd said the first time she asked.

"When you ask the impossible, for Him to grant you eternal youth, you are presenting us with a paradox," Davey said, stopping to explain. "That's when something that seems like it can't be true possesses truth.

"When you ask him that, you are exhibiting the wonder and bottomless faith of someone who will always be young, so in a way the very *act of asking* is seeing your wish fulfilled. Do you understand what I'm saying? You will never grow old as long as you believe that he holds the power to stop you from aging."

She had to think about that for a long while, but after she did the answer made perfect sense. It still did not stop the dark marks under her eyes from growing more pronounced with each passing day, though.

Davey's words were often poetic, but she wished that they also had the power to keep the skin of her cheeks elastic and to erase the scar on the back of her arm.

Eden wondered how she could feel so young at night and so old in the afternoon. In the full daylight of her father's fields, miles from the shade of the forest, she could see every imperfection on her body.

It was so bright that she imagined she could see the faults of her face, even without a mirror. Her hair that seemed lustrous and full at night seemed dry and frail in the daytime. She feared that if she touched it in the daylight it would break off her scalp, the way dead grass crumbled underfoot after a freeze.

Her pale eyes that reflected the bonfire so well in Davey's camp seemed dull and cold at home.

Her father had never mentioned her eyes or hair specifically, but she knew that even he could tell that they had lost their luster.

These days her father was reluctant to talk to her at the breakfast table. He'd grown distant from his daughter now that she was no longer his little girl, twenty-six years being the statute of limitations for holding that title.

Eden's father was a busy man, anyway. He worked his land hard, paid his tithe to that old bitch in the hotel, and sang her praises when he was able to feed and clothe the three mouths of his family.

It was no kind of life for a modern man. Eden had felt that her father's existence was meaningless, known it to be true even before she had started talking with Davey.

"I want to kill my father," she'd once said to Davey.

"And what would your mother do?" Davey had asked.

"She'd have the farm. She could hire a farmhand or find a new husband."

"And she'd be okay with you killing your father?"

"No." Eden's face felt flushed. Like she knew that she'd made a mistake by saying this to Davey.

"No, I don't think she would," Davey said. "That's why you'd have to be prepared to kill your mother if you killed your father. Either that or I'd have to end up rescuing you. Your mother might have to die then too. If it were her or me, I'm going to defend myself."

They didn't talk about her parents any more after that.

♦

Eden didn't live in the camper with Davey. Not anymore.

When she wasn't back home with her father and mother, she lived with Jeb.

Jeb spent all his nights in his tent. He didn't go home anymore either.

Jeb had set up the tent a comfortable distance away from the fire pit.

There were still nights that the fire grew too large and Jeb had to collapse the tent to keep it safe from the floating embers. As it was, Eden woke every morning to the pinpoints of light that had been melted into the ceiling of the old tent.

Being with Jeb was like living with a wild animal. Not that he was dangerous, not to Eden, but because of the growling.

His words were growls, his yawns were growls and his sexual come-ons were growls.

Eden was already awake, lying still for forty minutes, when Jeb woke with a growl.

He lifted his arm to scratch at his beard, freeing eighty-five-pound Eden from his fifty-pound arm.

She felt love for everyone in their group. It was a requirement, but somehow she loved Jeb the least.

Jeb tucked his privates back into his denim overalls and pulled the straps up over his shoulders with both thumbs. He unzipped the door to the tent and walked out into the mud of the campsite in his bare feet. Once outside he growled a hello to whoever else was already awake.

After she listened to his heavy footfalls slouch off in the direction of the woods, Eden riffled through their clothes pile. She chose a simple yellow sundress with a greenish stain at one corner and slipped it down over her small breasts.

The fabric felt pleasant sliding over her nipples and the sensation made her think of Davey.

Thinking of Davey made her think of his new girl. The one girl in the camp she refused to love.

That girl, the tall one with the hourglass shape and perfectly even tan, was the one person Eden hated as much as her father.

All the boys wanted the girl. The morning that Tobin had brought her to camp, Eden watched their expressions. Their mouths were practically watering over her blonde hair, breasts impossibly large and high. It made Eden sick to think about.

She rarely left Davey's camper when they ate dinner, but last night she had. Eden was seated on Jeb's lap and she could feel him stiffen underneath her when the girl joined the circle. She had pretended not to notice their stares, seating herself right next to Davey and taking his hand as they said Grace.

During last night's Grace, Eden had prayed for violence. She prayed for the new girl's fiery death, for every act of evil she'd ever witnessed to be visited upon this girl.

You weren't supposed to wish for things like that, not inside of the group. It was one of the rules. They only had a few rules, but they were told to follow them to the letter.

Eden lifted the flap and stepped out into the morning light. A small fire crackled in the pit. Someone had slung their wet socks over the flames to try and dry them. The toes were black with smoke.

There were two people outside. A county boy named Flint slept near the generator. He was curled into the fetal position with his jacket pulled up over his head and arms. It would probably be a few more hours until he was awake.

The other was Davey.

He sat on the steps that led to his camper. There were only two steps, so his knees were up even with his shoulders. He was so tall and skinny that sometimes he looked like a scarecrow.

She could feel his eyes on her as she walked to the Igloo cooler for a drink of water.

"Good morning," he said. She looked over and could see that he was whittling, the shape of the stick in front of him indefinable from where she stood.

"Morning," she said, picking up a cup and filling it with water. The water was cold, a few withered ice cubes clinked at the top of the cup. Yesterday, there was only ice and beer cans in the cooler, this morning they had water. Praise be.

"Come 'ere," he said, waving her over with the pocket knife. "I feel like it's been forever since we had a sit-down."

Craning her neck, she looked around for Jeb.

"He's gone. I'd say for a good thirty minutes," Davey said. There were people, the people of the town, who claimed Davey was a fake. They said that he couldn't see the future or read minds because those weren't gifts that He chose to impart on man. "Does a Jeb shit in the woods?" he asked, smiling at his own joke and waving her over again.

Sliding down to make room, he dusted off a spot on the step for her. She sat, but didn't speak.

"How are things with you and Paul Bunyan?" Davey returned

to whittling as he spoke. She could see the design now. It was a face. She watched as he shaved off flecks of wood. They floated to the ground like summer snow.

"Things are good," she said. What she didn't talk about were the bruises, dark black fingerprints in the flesh of her thighs, the hurt she felt when he was inside her.

"That's good to hear. You're cute together."

It was a strange conversation to have, strange in that it sounded so normal. This was the kind of conversation she would have had with a boy before coming to live in the woods.

Davey pressed the knife into the soft wood and made lips in the stick.

They were full lips. He was carving a woman's face.

If he carves her face, I don't think I could stand it.

"You know that things are always changing, right?"

"Yes."

"Not just between people. Like what happens between me or you or Tobin or Jeb. But, like, cosmically."

"Yes," she said, trying to concentrate now. She felt that she was about to hear something important, and if it was not important, at the very least it would be difficult to understand.

"You also know that things are bound to change between us and the town," he said. He carved eyes now. "You know that that's already started, in a way."

She nodded, her eyes on his knife, on the tender work he was doing. "I'm aware," she said, sounding more like a sullen little girl than she wanted to.

"Good. So if you know that, like you do," he said, starting on the hair, "then you also know that there are some aspects of our lives that'll stay the same, will always stay the same."

Davey would do this often: tell you one thing right before telling you the exact opposite without quite contradicting himself. It was a gift, one of the things that made her believe.

"I guess," she said. "Mountains stay the same. They're always there."

"Even mountains move and crumble. It takes a long time, but they do," he said. He flicked out a chip of wood that landed in his beard. She reached over and brushed it off.

"The things that stay constant are not earthly concerns.

They're ideas and feelings."

She looked away from his hands now and studied his face. When she first met him, she would spend hours looking at his face, trying to tell just what percent of him was bullshitting her at any one time. His beard hadn't been so unwieldy then.

As the months turned to years, she'd stopped looking for the bullshit. She'd seen too much by that point. She'd seen him preach and kill. Watched him grow into the man he was born to be. The challenger. The agitator. She loved him.

"Oh, I understand what you mean now."

He stood, blowing on the carving, sending a fine dust raining down over her.

"That's good that you get the concept," he said, offering her the stick.

She took it, the bark rough against her small hands. It was heavier than she'd expected. The wood was moist and the cuts were green where Davey had gone deep enough.

"Because one of the things that's never going to change is how much I love you. I hope you know that."

She looked down at the carving in the branch. It was her own face staring back at her.

Even though the eyes were still, they seemed to sparkle, the moist wood catching the morning light as it slashed through the trees.

Chapter Eighteen

Roy loved cooking with dog meat, but getting the meat off smaller dogs was frustrating.

This wasn't something that he could have Claire help him with, either, so it would be the first time he'd be filleting without a fingertip.

All his life, the world around Roy had made him aware of his shortcomings. When he was a boy, girls had shied away from his rough looks. In elementary school he'd struggled and he never finished high school.

Roy was dumb and ugly, but—up until last week—he could cook. He could cook well.

Before that fucker had shot his right pointer finger off.

He would kill Tobin. That much was certain—that much Ms. Brant had promised him. It was only a matter of when.

He was going to kill him and eat him. That was one kind of meat he'd never prepared. Whatever Roy was, he wasn't a cannibal, but when he thought of killing Tobin, all his mind could focus on was what to do after. He decided that he would hollow out his chest cavity like a deer and then cook his heart.

Death was too good for the man that had taken his finger, that had left him unable to hold a knife properly.

Over the years he'd honed his skill with a knife to an art form. His hand felt complete with a blade. He could debone any fish, work with any cut of beef, dice and chop any fruit or vegetable. The important thing, he'd learned, was that all your control came from applying pressure with that first knuckle, the one that he didn't have anymore.

He tried working with his left hand, but that didn't work.

In order to hold the knife in his right hand, he had to press harder against the shattered stump of his knuckle. Even through the oxy he'd had Dwyer prescribe (small town general store and pharmacy, no doctor required), pressing the knife handle against his knuckle caused him great pain.

To reduce the pain, he piled gauze on top of his wound. The problem then becoming the thicker he wrapped the dressing on his wound, the more dexterity he lost.

He pressed harder now, trying to separate a lower leg from an elbow. The knife slipped and he ended up cutting a deep gash in his left thumb.

"Damnit!" Roy yelled and tossed the knife across the kitchen. He imagined it sailing through the air like a laser and sticking to the opposite wall with a satisfying *thunk*. The throw had been clumsy, though, so the knife slapped against the wall with the flat of the blade, clattering to the floor and leaving a faint splotch of dog blood.

If Roy hadn't been so comforted by what really awaited him in the afterlife, he would consider this new deformity as his own private hell. Tobin had taken away the one thing he was proud of. The boy had done it so clinically, yet so nonchalantly. Had he known what he was doing when he pulled the trigger?

It seemed unlikely, but something inside Roy told him that he had done it on purpose. There was a cleverness to Tobin that Roy could never hope to aspire to.

After he'd emptied out Tobin's guts and strung up his hide to dry, he would burn down his shed, the one that he'd tried and failed to keep secret from the town. He would burn down that outhouse of a home and cook Tobin's heart over the flames.

Then piss on the embers as he chomped into the heart like an apple.

Roy ran his thumb under the tap, taking it out from under every so often to check if the blood had slowed.

"Screw this," Roy said to himself. The bleeding wouldn't be stopping soon enough, so he grabbed a dishtowel, wrapped it around the cut and watched the edges bloom bright red.

Checking his left coat pocket for his keys, he slid the half-butchered dog into the lunch fridge and locked it.

He didn't need to check his pockets for the baton because he could feel the weight of it tugging at his pocket. The baton had been special ordered from Canada. Roy took it with him everywhere, even though a concealed weapon was no good to get caught with. He thought of his last big mistake, cracking that kid's windpipe with the end of the baton.

To err was human, but to err often seemed to be particularly Roy. When the weight of his accumulated mistakes got too heavy, he needed to escape the kitchen and clear his mind. This practice didn't originate out of a Zen attitude of self-discovery, just the observation that his mistakes would sometimes snowball if he did not allow himself time to cool down.

The way things had been going, Ms. Brant may not allow him to live through many more mistakes.

He needed to calm down.

♦

Roy didn't have a car and it was hard to find a safe, secluded place within walking distance of the hotel.

It's not that Roy didn't have access to a car. He did. At last count, there were thirty-seven that he could still get the engines to turn over.

He didn't dare take any of these cars out for a spin, though. Aside from the obvious trouble it would cause if a state policeman ever pulled him over while he was riding in one, the trouble he would get in with the old woman would be even worse.

No one could make a move in Mission without that move being reported back to Ms. Brant. Even though he could never drive them, he did like to visit them from time to time.

On days like this, when he couldn't get away but *had* to get away, Roy would visit the cars.

Roy was the head caretaker of the car garden. While they were his greatest release, they were also his biggest responsibility.

When a new car came in, he would drive it to the garden at around two in the morning. The garden was two miles from the center of town, far enough from the northern woods that Davey or his kids wouldn't mess with it, hopefully would never find it.

Once at the garden, he would strip the inside of the car down. Fuzzy dice, travel mugs, maps, registration, brochures, and the stuffed animals kids placed on dashboards. Roy would take all of those things and throw them in a large black garbage bag.

Next he would search the car for a GPS. If there was one, he would smash it with a hammer until it couldn't power on, then he would put the pieces in the plastic bag with the other trash.

These days it was getting more difficult because cars were coming with on board computers and geo-locators. Those cars he would have to disassemble until he was sure that there were no electronics left on board. That was always a pain in the ass.

Once he had everything in the bag, he dug a hole and set the bag on fire. Once the fire went out, he pushed the dirt back over the hole.

He had a small tractor to help with this work. He'd asked for a new Caterpillar backhoe, something compact that could still get the job done in a third of the time, but he was told that it wasn't in the budget.

The cars were spread over a few acres of land. Some he parked in the shade of trees, others he half covered with debris after spray painting the roofs and hoods black.

There were no local airports and no flight paths crossing through Mission. It was highly unlikely that the cars would be spotted from a plane or helicopter, but Roy took no chances with his car garden.

In his search for the perfect spot to squirrel away a car, he often had to use the tractor as an impromptu tow truck. When that wouldn't work, he'd have to use an actual truck. There were three in his collection.

He kept two other collections. One was a lockbox full of keys and the other was a stash of license plates. His dream was to one day have a plate from every different state, or at least those in the continental U.S.

He used a bench vise to bend each one in half before burying them all in the same plot of land. There were only eight states represented, too many duplicates for his taste.

Sometimes he felt like a dog, digging holes and dropping in his treasures.

But there was a meditative quality to the act of hiding something away, patting the dirt down the best you possibly could so nobody could ever get your goods.

Roy didn't keep maps of his collection. Paperwork was a liability. The breadth of his collection and his diminished memory meant that he was rediscovering cars every time he visited the garden.

He placed his hands against the black Elantra in front of him. Black was his favorite color for cars. It meant that instead of spray paint, all he had to do was spread a thin layer of dirt and pine needles over the top to reduce the shine of the finish.

Claire's friend had owned this car, but her parents had probably paid for it, he decided.

Claire was fine, but her friend had cost him a finger and got him a massive reaming from Brant.

Well, in actuality it was Daisy who had done both of those things.

He knew she didn't have the guts. Roy knew better than to judge a book by its cover, but it was more than her chubby cheeks and lisp that told him Daisy wasn't a hardened killer.

He'd never say it out loud, but he swore that she got squeamish when she visited the basement. She'd never stood alongside him and the others as they completed the blood sketch. That was a big no-no. Nonbelievers need not apply as far as the ceremonies were concerned.

She'd begged the old lady to be the one to take care of Allison, though. Once she'd given her permission, there was nothing Roy could say or do to stop that train.

He'd armed Daisy with a syringe and a knife. That was his first mistake. Both weapons were too final for Daisy. When she'd gotten cold feet about having to depress the plunger, she'd panicked.

The way she told it, she'd dropped the syringe and alerted the girl, Allison, to her presence, so she picked up the nearest knickknack (a burnished bronze rabbit statue, what else?) from the hallway table and smacked the girl in the mouth with it.

Not content to have fucked up that badly, the silly bitch had then dragged the girl out into the woods to finish the job, before pussing out and running back to the house for help.

"I tried. I tried. I put my hands around her throat, had the knife right above her, but I just couldn't," Daisy had said. It was almost impossible to tell what she was saying through the sobs and the begging. She was covered in spots of blood, having smashed the girl's front teeth in before hefting her down two flights of stairs and out into the woods. "Don't tell Ms. Brant! Please."

She caught him while he was preparing breakfast, already in his chef's whites. He promised that he wouldn't tell on her. Why, he didn't know.

"Thank you! I'll do anything you want." He got the idea that she would blow him if he asked. The idea wasn't particularly compelling, but he'd have that card tucked away for a rainy day.

By the time Roy had reached her, the sun was up and she'd already come to her senses.

She ran faster than he'd imagined she would, and the rest was history.

Roy picked at a long string of cotton gauze that had come loose from his dressings. He didn't dare pull it out though, unsure if the entire pad would come with it. He'd have to wait until he got to a pair of scissors.

Underneath the bandages his finger itched. Dwyer had been able to sew a flap of skin back over the knuckle, shortening his heal time, but it made the wound especially sensitive to movement.

He was leaning against the Elantra and pushed off the car with his left hand, wincing as he reminded himself of the deep cut in his thumb. Sucking on it, he got a mouthful of the grit and dust that he'd coated the car with.

When he looked up from spitting into the dirt, Tobin was there. The boy stood ten yards away, his shoulder against a tree.

Roy felt a rush of fury and surprise so powerful that his vision swam. Before he could think, his right hand was in his pocket, hand around the shaft of the baton. The flesh around his knuckle strained against the sutures as he made a fist.

"Now before you do anything," Tobin said, "please just hear me out and know that I'm awfully sorry about the finger. That's sorry in retrospect, because I know that I was smiling at the time."

"Gonna fucking kill you," Roy said and started to rush for Tobin, flicking out the end of the baton with a satisfying click.

Tobin didn't say anything, just pointed behind Roy in the direction of the Elantra.

Jeb stood behind the trunk of the car. He let his grip on the ax handle loosen and the blade of the ax scraped against the Elantra's bumper with a metal on fiberglass *tink* that sounded louder than it should have.

"Jeb is the only person in Mission bigger and hairier than you," Tobin said. "So why don't we all just chill out?"

Tobin was right. Not only that, but Jeb was half Roy's age. He had all his fingers, too.

No sense of style though. He looked like an Appalachian hillbilly with those overalls and his wild beard. He'd clearly patterned the beard on his messiah, Davey, but the burley youth didn't wear it half as well.

"Say what you've got to say," Roy said, lowering the baton but not collapsing it. He would never collapse it when these fuckers were in swinging distance.

"Well, it's not an apology. I meant what I said about your finger, but that's not why we're here right now." Tobin said. Roy had a hard time focusing on him with Jeb so close behind him. He looked back and the bigger boy had taken a few steps away from the Elantra, coming around Roy from the side so the three of them were no longer standing in a line.

"I am sad about what I'm about to say, but I'm not sorry for it. It's got to be said."

"Just fucking spit it out," Roy said, raising the baton again, taking a step towards Tobin.

"That's far enough," Jeb said. The boy's voice sounded like some kind of prehistoric reptile, thick with smoke and fire and deep as a well.

"Well, you've got to know that you're the most dangerous player on the other side. You do know that, right? And I completely mean that as a compliment," Tobin said. "And don't go saying that someone else in your camp is more 'powerful' than you. I don't mean that fucking medieval wizard Dungeons and Dragons bullshit power that you all think you have. I mean physically dangerous. You're a goddamn beast."

Jeb chuckled at this, the laugh unbelievably childlike when compared with the rest of him.

"The point is?" Roy asked. He felt the sweat of his hands stinging his wounds. It shamed him to be sweating this much. It made him look weak and scared.

"The point is that this is it. This is the start of the war. No more shots across the bow. It's all going to be full-on direct hits from here on out. Got to be that way," Tobin said. He was speaking in clichés, possibly too afraid to say exactly what he meant, but Roy understood him just fine.

It was an understanding that made Roy's balls shrink up into his chest, a tiny animal spray of piss dripping out of him before he could clench it back.

"Stay away!" Roy raised the baton in front of him, pointing the tip at Jeb and giving a few fake swings.

The motions didn't make Jeb budge a centimeter. He stood completely still except for the rise and fall of his hairy chest against his overalls. The ax in his hands looked small in comparison to the rest of him, like a hatchet would look on a normal-sized teenager.

Jesus, Jeb was still a teenager. He was probably still growing.

"Stop that now," Tobin said. "The reason we're talking to you is that we want you to understand, not to make it worse for you, but to make it better. If that's even possible.

"I could have popped you from the woods while you were jerking off over your cars," Tobin continued, "but I didn't. I wanted you to know what was going on."

"Try it then."

"There's not going to be much trying to it, surely you can see that, Roy," Tobin said, reaching his hand behind the tree and coming back with the Winchester, the one that'd taken Roy's finger. "This is a congratulations of sorts."

Jeb scoffed. Most of the boy's interactions all seemed to be variations on menacing breathing.

"Us being here, paying you a visit before anyone else, it means that he thinks you pose a real threat," Tobin said.

"It don't mean that he's afraid of you," Jeb said. It was the most words Roy had ever heard the kid say.

"No, of course it doesn't mean that," Tobin agreed. "It just means that you are tactically significant."

"'He'? You're so far up Davey's ass that you don't even say his name? You kids are pathetic," Roy said. Getting them riled could be part of a plan if he could think straight enough to make one. All he could think about was biting into Tobin's medium-rare heart.

"Watch what you say." Tobin leveled the rifle. "And what you think."

"Like you can read my thoughts? I look like I'm going to fall for that? Fucking pathetic," Roy said, but he wasn't so sure.

"You've made me angry. You've made me regret my decision to be so upfront with you."

They were reaching the end of whatever this was. Roy's arm was getting weak from holding the baton aloft. His finger ached so badly that he wouldn't have been surprised if the stitches had come undone.

At least in a combat sense, the boys were smart. Jeb was closer to Roy, a few of his long strides would put him within axing distance. Tobin was much farther away, Roy was faster and could reach the smaller boy before Jeb could cut him down, but not while Tobin had a gun on him.

"You're weighing the options, but there's only one possible outcome here and you're not going to like it. You need to understand that we're taking care of you first. Any idea what an honor that is?"

Roy spat. Not strictly as an insult, but because if he swallowed the extra saliva in his mouth, then he was going to vomit. Tobin kept talking, ignoring the spit.

"I mean, I don't even think Davey knows Jeb's name and he sees him every day." Tobin laughed and looked to the big boy to let him know he was joking, but Jeb himself was unreadable. He turned his eyes back to Roy. "You're on his radar, such a bright dot that you get a special place in the lineup."

Roy took a slow step toward Tobin, thinking that if he did it slow enough it would go unnoticed. It hadn't. Tobin put a second hand on the gun, steadying the barrel.

"Wait," Roy said, not having to try to make his voice sound frantic. "Don't shoot yet. There's one thing I always wanted to know."

"Yeah? Ask away," Tobin said. He placed his cheek lightly against the stock and looked down the sights.

"You ever get to touch any of those girls that Davey hangs around with, or does he make all you boys blow each other?"

Roy saw it happening better in his mind.

He dove to his right, towards Jeb. The idea was to get close enough to Jeb fast enough that Tobin wouldn't risk taking the shot. At least then he would have some kind of chance, not much, but some if he could get Jeb in the right spots with the baton.

As he ducked and rolled he heard the shot, the bullet punching him in the chest, right above his heart. The bullet might have blown a fist-sized exit wound out the back of his shoulder or got stuck in one of the bones, but it was impossible to tell. Everything was numb.

Jeb hadn't moved to meet him, wasn't stupid enough for that.

Roy tried to balance a few more steps forward after feeling the bite of the bullet, but his legs were falling out from under him. He swung with the baton, knowing he wasn't going to connect but having to try.

The metal bulb on the end of the baton whiffed through the air, twisting Roy onto his back with the momentum.

Only once his back was flat against the ground did Jeb take a step towards him.

The afternoon sun was still intense enough to highlight the dust moats that swam in the corner of Roy's vision, kicked up by his fall and settling onto his staggering failure.

Jeb let the ax fall. Roy heard the blade whizz by his ear, felt the wind rush by as it dug into the ground. Above him, Jeb's furry face cracked a smile.

The fucker's sadistic face was what he needed to see. Roy lashed out with the baton, catching Jeb in the ankle.

Jeb jumped back, holding his foot by the toes and hopping up and down on one leg. It was the least funny Three Stooges bit of all time.

Winding up for the swing had pushed a stream of blood out of the gunshot. Roy felt moisture on the small of his back, unsure whether it was sweat or blood. If it was blood, the exit wound was there and he didn't have much longer to live.

There was a ruffling of leaves apart from Jeb's semi-comical hops as Tobin ran up to the scene.

"This is why I gave you the talk, Roy. You're proving me right," Tobin said. "Such a damn shame you picked the wrong side."

"Fuck you," Roy said, choking. He could taste blood. The vision in his left eye was completely white, and his right was fuzzy. He thrashed out in the direction of Tobin's shadow and didn't hit anything.

There was a sharp slap across his jaw that felt like it came from a gunstock. He couldn't feel anything with his tongue, but he'd definitely lost a tooth.

"Stop being a fucking baby and get that thing from him," he heard Tobin's voice say.

There was a pressure on his right forearm and he tightened his grip on the baton. He tried bucking against the hold, but it was no use. The hand was like concrete.

The next sound he heard was a snap, one of the bones in his arm or wrist popping under the pressure of Jeb's giant hands.

Roy was burning up, rivulets of sweat poured from his forehead. The only thing he could hear beyond the smaller snaps of his fingers was the blood pound of his own heartbeat against his ears.

Cold fingers gripped his scalp but offered no relief from the fever. They were too big to belong to anyone else besides Jeb. Roy felt himself lifted up by his scalp, the sensation a puppy must feel as it's picked up by the scruff.

"You went out a fighter, Roy," Tobin said. Roy was unsure if he could really be hearing him with his ears. "Nobody but us is going to know that, at least for a little while, but the truth remains. You should be proud."

Softer, more distant and earthly, he heard Tobin's voice again, "Do it."

There was the gentle noise of shifting soil as the ax was pried from the ground somewhere near him.

Roy put two fingers on each hand out in front of him and felt the ground. He must have been on his knees then, the earth spread out there before him.

For one short moment, Roy felt like he could see again. What he saw was the forest bathed in afternoon sun. The trees wobbled and then were still again. Then his head fell end over end and his vision went with it, spinning around as his head rolled away from his body.

This was all in his mind, of course. For the last moment of his life, all Roy could see was darkness as the ax bit into his neck.

Not even the comforting fires of hell were visible.

Chapter Nineteen

Christine closed the door, Jane finally asleep after a Benadryl and two glasses of red wine.

Even though they'd barely had time to enjoy it, the honeymoon suite was nice. Christine had never encountered a Jacuzzi tub that didn't smell like mildew, but this one was pristine.

After they came back to the hotel and moved their bags in, they tried out the tub and made love after Bert had gone to sleep on his dog bed in the corner of the room. After that, they'd gone to sleep.

Christine woke up before Jane. No matter how comfortable they were, she'd always had a hard time sleeping in new beds. She'd woken herself up several times during the night, stuck in the same dream she always seemed to have in hotel rooms. Each time she woke was a semiconscious moment of sleep paralysis in which she was convinced that someone else is in the room before lapsing back into the blackness of R.E.M sleep.

Careful not to wake up Jane, she grabbed her duffel bag from the counter, changed in the bathroom, and snuck out into the hotel hallway.

The workout room wasn't terrible, but it couldn't be called a proper gym. There were two treadmills and an elliptical, along with a tower of free weights and a Bowflex for strength training. Christine ran while she watched the local news, the captions almost impossible to read on the snowy TV that hung in front of the treadmills.

Christine returned before Jane was awake to find that the door to their room had been left open. Christine didn't remember doing it, but it was possible that the door hadn't closed behind her. She took a seat on the edge of the bed and flicked on the TV.

The television set was large and bright. She dialed down the volume and channel surfed. The electric hum of the set and the click of the remote was enough to wake Jane out of her slumber.

"Good morning," Jane said, tossing the covers aside and standing.

She was taller than Christine by half a foot, every part of her more slender and inviting. Even after all these years, gravity seemed to work differently on Jane.

"Where's Bert?" Jane said.

She was so enamored with Jane's nudity that Christine had to rethink the question before she could form an answer.

"Is he sleeping in the bathroom?"

Jane pushed her head into the bathroom. "No."

She clapped her hands and called his name, checking the small walled-off foyer that allowed the room to be called a suite.

What followed was an hour of crying and walking around the hotel trying to locate Bert. Jane jostled the box of Snausages, took one into her hand and crushed it.

"What are you doing?" Christine asked.

"He'll be able to smell them better if I crush them up. Dogs can smell food from miles away."

They'd covered most of the ground in the hotel before reaching the front desk.

"Excuse me," Jane said, the older woman behind the desk looked up. Behind the woman's bifocals, her eyes looked red and puffy.

"Can I help you?" the woman said. She didn't wear the uniform that they'd seen Daisy in earlier, but an old-timey floral-pattern dress that was tasteful and fitting.

"My dog somehow got out of our room. Have you seen him or heard anything?"

That wasn't a slip of the tongue. Jane was acutely aware that Bert was *her* dog, not *their* dog.

"What room was that, again?" the woman asked. "I'm sorry to be so preoccupied. Our chef has not shown up for work yet and I'm having a Dickens of a time locating someone to fill in."

"He's a little miniature pinscher. Is there any way that a maid might have come by our room this morning and let him get by without noticing?"

"What room?" The woman behind the desk asked again. Jane's question seemed to have thrown a switch. The old woman's tone of voice changed in those two words.

"Twenty-seven, the honeymoon suite," Christine answered for Jane. Of their roles in their relationship, hers was never public relations unless it seemed like force was going to be necessary.

Something about this broad's aura told Christine that she was bigger and badder than Jane could handle. She'd scoffed slightly after Christine had mentioned the honeymoon suite. No doubt Daisy had been gossiping about the two lezzies fouling up the sheets.

"I've got one of our guest liaisons, our *maids*, in the kitchen right now making omelets, so I doubt she's been up to your room. Nobody would be entering your room before ten thirty, and even then they would knock and announce themselves to you. Are you sure that you didn't leave the door open yourselves? Did you check under the bed?"

"Can I speak to the manager please?" Christine said, tired of this woman. If calling a hotel maid a maid was considered crossing the line, she didn't want to live in this country anymore.

"I should have introduced myself before. My name is Victoria Brant." The woman seemed to straighten up as she said her own name. The hints of weakness and emotion that Christine had spotted when they'd first arrived at the front desk had been crushed, shored up behind the wall that was Victoria Brant. "I'm not only the manager, but the owner of the hotel. Please direct all questions to me."

Fuck, Christine thought.

"Could you at least tell your staff to be on the lookout for him?" Jane said, braver now, stepping in when Christine needed her for a change.

"If your dog is in this building, you have my word that he will be found and returned to you. You're welcome to look in the meantime, just please try to be mindful of other guests. Now if you'll please excuse me, I've got a lot on my plate."

"Thanks for your time," Christine said, trying to affect a voice that instead said *Thanks for nothin'* in a Brooklyn accent.

They did look through the hotel a second time, stopping back at the room to check to make sure that Bert hadn't been crawled up asleep under the drapes or snuggled into a closet. He was nowhere.

Jane looked out the window of the honeymoon suite and then opened the sliding glass door that opened onto a small balcony. Christine followed her out, the terrace so narrow that both of them could barely fit at the same time.

"What if he got out the back door?" she said, looking over the edge. Below them was a stretch of parking lot and beyond that was the woods. It was noon by the time they had put a hold on the search.

Christine had unpacked a bottle of Three Buck Chuck from their luggage and poured them both a glass of the wine. She sipped hers now, knowing that it would help her come up with whatever genius words of consolation she would say next.

"I don't think that's the most likely scenario," Christine said. She looked at Jane, following her gaze out into the woods. The tops of the trees swayed gently with the wind, the leaves making a sound like a dollar store rain stick.

"Not likely to turn out well for Bert," Jane said, a tear running down her chin into her wine. She lifted the glass and drank down the tear.

"There are plenty of guests, some of them with kids. They may have found Bert and decided that there'd be no harm in little Bobby and Suzy playing with him a bit before contacting the front desk about finding a dog."

"And if Bobby and Suzy decide they want to keep Bert forever? Those little fucking brats." Jane laughed, but she wasn't buying the fantasy. Christine could tell.

Jane's glass was empty. It was the hotel's glass, a crystal tumbler that had been placed next to the sink to be used for tap water. It was able to hold a lot more wine than most wineglasses.

Christine went back into the room for the bottle and topped both glasses back up.

"It's not even one o' clock," Jane said as she took the glass.

"You should rest now. It's been a long half a day," Christine said. "Today was supposed to be about R&R and wine anyway. I know it's a shitty situation, but maybe try to get some sleep."

"And you'll keep looking?" Jane asked, going to the duffel and unzipping it.

"I'll do my absolute best. If all else fails, I'll knock door to door. If Madam Brant has a problem with that, I'll knock on her too."

Jane giggled, the tic-tac sound of pills against plastic jostling as she took out her day planner pillbox. She opened up today and popped a Benadryl. She took Claritin for allergies, Benadryl for sleepy time and allergies.

They kissed until she fell asleep, the sun still spilling into the room through the glass door.

"Please find him," Jane said with her eyes still closed.

Christine waited until the sound of her breathing had changed before pulling her arm out from under her neck and setting to work.

How Bert got loose was a mystery that Christine planned to solve. As she opened the door to the hallway, the sound of the lock being thrown and the bolt retracting awakened something in her mind.

Was it the sound she'd heard and disregarded when she'd left this morning to work out, possibly leaving the door open? Or was it the sound from before that, from the dreams she'd had last night?

♦

Christine knocked on every door on the second floor since it seemed highly unlikely that Bert would brave the stairs or take a ride on the elevator.

Most of her knocks went unanswered, but the rooms that had been occupied had been sympathetic. There were a few pinched faces offering variations on "Aw, I hope you find him!" but no Bert sightings.

When she was done canvassing, she decided to up her detective game by seeking out members of the staff herself. Her first stop would be the front desk, the one place she was guaranteed to find someone to grill. She stopped at the top step before descending the staircase into the lobby.

A grown woman of forty-two years, she felt only slightly embarrassed to be peeking around the corner, checking that the coast was clear, but she'd much rather suffer a minor embarrassment than be forced to interact with Victoria Brant again.

There was an unfamiliar face behind the desk.

It was a younger, prettier face.

Young people could be assholes, but it was slightly less likely because the weight of the world's bullshit hadn't flattened them yet. Christine went unnoticed as she watched the girl, remaining still on the bottom step leading into the lobby.

She was pretty, with fair skin and chestnut hair that most people probably called red, but it wasn't really. The girl had dyed a silver streak in her hair that had started to grow back to marginally red. The streak was the best evidence that Christine had that the girl would be helpful, or at least tolerable.

The girl twisted one of the golden pens Christine had used to sign the guestbook, watching the ballpoint pen go in and out. Twenty-something and bored, Christine remembered what that was like.

Just as Christine had decided to stop watching her, the girl ducked under the entrance to the desk and walked towards the back door, the quickest way out to the parking lot.

Leaving the front desk unattended? This girl was tempting fate with her boss. Christine liked that.

She waited a few more moments, and then followed the girl out into the parking lot. As she opened the door, she tried to put a look of mild surprise on her face, not a look that gave away the fact that she'd been following her.

Walking through the door, she turned to see the girl lighting up a cigarette, a few inches from her. This did surprise her.

"Kids still smoke?" Christine asked. "Don't you all do Twitter and Facebook instead?"

"I don't smoke," the girl said, putting her lighter back into the pocket on her apron. She wore a uniform just like Daisy's, only it suited her better. The name Claire was embroidered above the left breast.

Christine looked at the cigarette in Claire's hand, then back at the girl.

"What I mean to say is that I don't smoke regularly," she said, seemingly mystified by her own statement. "Or I guess I only recently started smoking regularly. Sorry to sound so weird, but I kind of only just now realized that I've become a smoker."

"Well, it's good to know that it won't be too rough a transition when you start the patch."

"My friend used to smoke," the girl said, not even acknowledging Christine's lame joke. Not out of rudeness, but because she was so deep in thought that she hadn't heard it. "These were the kind too. Newports. I guess she got me into them. She hasn't called me the entire time I've been here."

"Sounds like a shitty friend, no offense," Christine said, adding the "no offense" as punctuation, as she often did.

"Not the best," Claire said, knocking some ash off with a tap of her finger. It was a practiced maneuver.

"Sorry to bother you on your smoke break, but have you seen our dog around?" Not my wife's dog, but *our* dog. Had the events of the afternoon forced Christine to take co-ownership of Bert?

"What's it look like?"

"Your boss didn't talk to you about him? Ask you to keep an eye out?"

"Sorry, no," Claire said, giving a frown like she meant it.

"Figures," Christine mumbled and then spoke up. "He's a min pin, black and brown."

"Didn't mean to ask a stupid question like that. I would have remembered seeing any dog. I didn't even know the hotel allowed them. That's probably something I should know."

"He went missing from our room and we're not quite sure how."

"What room are you in?" Claire asked, seeming to snap out of her initial fog and finally engage Christine.

"The honeymoon suite, second floor."

Claire made a sound to express deep thought, flipping the cigarette over between two fingers. "If he did get into the hallway, from the second floor he could take the stairs down into the lobby," she spoke just as much to herself as to Christine. "That means he could have gotten out the front door if we left it propped, which Daisy usually does on nice days, but it's unlikely that he'd get by without anyone seeing him."

Christine interrupted Claire's detective monologue. "Were you working the desk this morning before the manager?"

"No, I was burning orders of corn beef hash. Our chef didn't come into work this morning, so they had me step in. Before I started working here, I'd only ever cooked Pop Tarts and ramen.

"If your dog didn't leave the hotel, there're actually a few places on the first floor that he could have gotten into, some staff-only places and the dining room that we use for group functions. You said you talked to Ms. Brant about this?"

"Yeah, but she was less than helpful, kind of rude. She actually looked like she was having a rough time this morning. Puffy eyes."

"The kind of rude part sounds like her," Claire said and looked around the parking lot to make sure no one was around to hear, "but I don't think I've ever seen her show an emotion other than menopause."

Christine laughed.

"Is your husband out looking?" Claire asked.

"Wife, and no, she's upstairs sleeping it off. Bert's her dog."

"Oh, cool," Claire said. It was a much better response than she'd gotten from anyone else in Mission regarding their nuptials. "If he got out of the building, it's almost a certainty that he went out the front door, since this one," she indicated the door they were standing near, "is never propped open. If you wanted to take a few laps around the town to see if anyone picked him up, I could check the rest of the rooms on the first floor for you."

"Okay, thanks," Christine said.

The young girl bent at the knees and stubbed her smoke out against the gravel, then rose up.

"I really mean thanks," Christine continued, putting a hand on the girl's shoulder. "This was supposed to be a nice time, but it hasn't started out that way. If I can find Bert, maybe I can salvage it, but beyond that there's no way that this is going to go the way I wanted it to."

"He couldn't have gotten far. You'll find him. Traffic's minimal, so that shouldn't really be a concern," Claire said, not elaborating on that, the idea that Bert would snap and pop under the wheels of a car like a balloon tied to four twigs. Christine winced at the thought. "What was your name again?"

"Christine."

"Don't worry. And don't let Ms. Brant scare you off. The people around here are mostly quite nice. Even the cook isn't bad, and he's caused me all kinds of aggravation today. It's different from the city, better in some ways."

Christine thanked Claire again and then set off around the side of the building, walking up the driveway to the sidewalk. She walked up and down Main Street until it began to get dark. As she looked, she asked everyone that she came across, stopping into all of the businesses including the historic post office.

Nobody had seen Bert, but they had all been kinder and more encouraging than she'd expected.

The post office had been nice, all original, polished wood and small town charm. This didn't help alleviate the fact that as she walked back to the hotel, she still had no dog.

The streetlights were on as she stepped onto the long stretch of walkway that led to the hotel. In the distance, beyond The Brant, she could see the near total darkness of the woods, the shadows that in her mind were swallowing up Bert as she watched.

It made her want to scream.

Chapter Twenty

Victoria Brant replaced the bristle brush on the desk of her boudoir and looked at herself in the mirror. It felt odd, preparing for this meeting the same way a younger woman would to go see a gentleman suitor.

She was not a younger woman, though.

The bags under her eyes were not from lack of sleep. They'd just accumulated gradually over the years and never left, until the act of covering them with concealer felt as natural a part of waking up as brushing her teeth.

Facing the world had become a production.

It had been a long day, and reapplying her makeup and re-combing her hair was necessary for the walk she was about to take. Not only did she run the risk of running into guests or members of the community while she was on her way out, but she needed to look composed.

This wasn't makeup. It was war paint. She'd applied it with a heavier hand than usual, so that it could be noticed in only the moonlight, if that was what was required.

It had taken over an hour to have not a single hair astray, not a single eyelash bent or broken, not a single wrinkle or dark mark not spackled over. Usually she would ask Daisy to help her with such an exhaustive effort but tonight she needed to do this alone. She needed silence to think.

Whatever Daisy's virtues, silence was not one of them. Even when she wasn't talking, she liked talking. One of her favorite things was to use that whore-of-a-girl's cell phone to send text messages to Claire. It had gotten so bad that she'd begun sending texts without letting Victoria read over them first, so she'd had to take the phone away.

Victoria went to her closet and took down her boots. Using a tissue, she brushed off the fine layer of dust that had settled over them. It had been so long since she'd gone walking in the woods.

Was she afraid? Had the fissure become that deep and wide that she'd relinquished every acre of forest over to the children? It saddened her to think of these questions, frightened her to think of her answers.

Without Roy, they were outnumbered and without a guard dog.

Sitting down to put on the boots, she reminded herself that weakness was a state of mind, that they were not playing a numbers game.

Her feet had swollen throughout the day and the boots wouldn't slip on. She unlaced the boots all the way down to the second loop, the leather and fabric tongue hanging loose.

It had been a long time since she last looked at her feet critically. She seemed to have lost her ankles over the last few years. She weighed herself every day, and she'd only gained five pounds or so over the last decade. Victoria Brant wasn't getting fat. Age was just melting her body down.

Lacing up the boots, she wheezed with exertion as she pulled the strings tight. They hurt as she stood.

"When I get back I'm going to cut these off with scissors," she said. Talking to herself was not a habit, but it was not something that ashamed her. When praying, she was not addressing anyone in the room, so why should her mundane observations about her boots be any different?

The thought reminded her to pray. She didn't like the fact that she had to be prompted to pray. It should have been reflex.

Walking into the bedroom, she drew the curtains, laid out her mat, scratched a symbol into the air in front of her, and prayed.

Mouthing the words she knew so well, hymns that she had adapted, translated and added to herself, she could not get the image of Roy's white chef's outfit from her mind.

In her mind it was no longer white, though, not purely. It was streaked with mud, dirt and blood.

She couldn't tell if the image was a vision or a hallucination, or if it made much of a difference either way.

♦

Victoria Brant stood with the back door propped open, watching and listening to make sure that no one was in the parking lot. When she felt comfortable enough, she walked in a straight line from the back door to the edge of the woods.

She didn't carry a compass or a cell phone. She didn't own either. What she did carry was a pocket LED flashlight, the kind small enough to fit on a keychain.

There were no keys around the ring so she looped it around her middle finger to keep a firm grip on the two-inch chrome tube.

Every aspect of the woods felt foreign, even though she could still see the lights of the hotel behind her. That was her hotel and these used to be her woods.

Strange shadows crept across the forest floor as she walked. She'd catch the occasional blue-green glow of a pair of eyes watching her from the darkness. The first pair had startled her, but it wasn't animals that she was worried about.

She wondered if she was being watched. There was no way that she wouldn't hear any pursuers, but that didn't mean that David did not have some of his people lying in wait, watching her from behind the trees.

Patrick Dwyer knew that she was coming out here. He'd stopped by earlier this morning to deliver a box of groceries and hadn't found anyone to deliver them to. Roy always took in the orders, talked with Patrick for a while. The two of them were friends in the way that loners get to be.

"I don't mean to be bothering you, Ms. Brant," Patrick said after knocking on her office door.

Victoria put down the envelope she was holding and motioned him inside. When he shut the door behind him she knew that what he had to say was community business. Also that it was probably not good news.

"Did Roy call in sick this morning? Because he's not in the kitchen."

Patrick had stayed with her while they figured out their next course of action. There had even been a moment while they were discussing the possibility that Roy was dead that Pat had put his hand on her shoulder.

In retrospect, that was too informal a gesture, but she hadn't brushed him away or reprimanded him.

"I'm going to have to meet with him, alone." Her own words came back to her now, seeming to echo through the night, bouncing off of trees and scaring birds from their roosts.

It was not a much farther walk to the clearing. She lightly brushed the space under her eyes with her free hand. No tears. That was good.

The light from her keychain spread over the tall grass and settled on a black spot in the middle of it.

David waited for her there, sitting in the underbrush, his long legs folded under him.

"Thanks for coming," he said. Even though he was yards away, he spoke in an indoor voice that carried through the clearing to meet her.

Victoria could hear his joints crack as he got to his feet, his knees popping like muffled firecrackers. She thought of her own swollen ankles and took small solace in the fact that David seemed to be aging more rapidly than her. That was what happened when you drank yourself to sleep every morning and spent most of your time with people half your age.

She waited for him to come to her, not comfortable stepping out to meet him. If she gave up the cover of the trees, she would feel exposed.

"Right there is close enough," she said. He stood five feet from her, his hand out like she was going to shake it.

"Okay then, if that's what you want, Ms. Brant," David said. His beard was longer than she'd ever seen it, but his eyes were the same. They were the eyes of a child, even though the skin around them had grown bruised and slack with booze and time.

"Don't call me that. Don't use my name," she said.

He held up his hands, showing her that he understood and half-apologizing for the perceived insult.

"Where is Roy?"

"That's what you wanted to talk about? That's new business. Whatever happened to old business? I thought we should catch up first. How's the tourist murder industry? Booming?"

"Don't play with me, David," she said.

"You used to call me Davey. You're the one that started that.

I have everyone call me Davey. Am I going to have to switch back over now? People are going to be confused."

"This meeting is over. You're not going to tell me anything."

Victoria turned her back to him and took a step, returning to the woods, towards her hotel. His juvenile attitude had disarmed her. She didn't realize what a bad mistake turning her back to him was until she'd done it. He wasn't a little boy anymore.

"He's dead. Is that what you want to hear?"

She turned around to face him, slowly.

"Why? Tell me why you did it," she said. *Make me understand you*, she wanted to plead, but she couldn't say that. That was a question for the twelve-year-old David who'd marked up the walls with crayon, not the grown man who'd just admitted to killing one of her followers.

"Don't pretend like you didn't see the way things were going. Are going," he said. "Pat Dwyer's not allowed to sell us charcoal and frozen pizzas anymore? Are you kidding me? Do you think you're going to starve us out? We have cars, you know."

"Did I harm you? No. You and yours are fine."

"Oh, and the priest that you've got stashed away up there, what's he? The one that I guess you mail ordered from Vatican City or some shit, because I have no idea how one goes about acquiring something like that. He's just for show? He's voodoo bullshit," David said, not taking a step forward but leaning closer. He was so tall that she could feel the heat of his words. "It's a war of escalation."

She didn't want to talk about Father Hayden. This was his plan the whole time. He was not negotiating a surrender or peace—he was looking for information. She had to be careful not to give him any. She'd been sending him rumors for months, but they were the parts of the story she wanted to tell.

"When the town's gone, you're gone too. If you kill us, it will dry up and float away. You're smart, Davey, you have to know that. There's nothing out here for you. Come home." This may have been how she felt, but there was no harm in sharing it. It didn't tell him anything he wanted to know.

He wasn't coming home. It was too late for that. Too late for her to let him.

"I'm not going to wait tables and change bed sheets. I'm not anyone's servant," he said and paused. These pregnant pauses probably worked on his flock, his children, but Victoria saw them as the window dressing that they were. She had tricks of her own. What she was getting from David was a rehearsed speech, not a spontaneous monologue.

"That's where we've always disagreed. I mean, there are lots of differences in our ideologies, but that's the main one. You preach service and I extol self-reliance. You tell your people that we've all got to serve somebody, and that's what all the boring bits of your life are about. You use that to kill time between ceremonies. It's amateur hour," he said. "I tell my kids to live their lives. That's what He really teaches us. You don't bow to Him. You raise your fists and yell 'Right on!'"

"I've heard all this before. It hasn't changed much since you were sixteen," Victoria said. "Are we done, then? If you're not going to give me a reason why Roy is dead…"

He seemed hurt that his lecture had elicited no response, as if her counterargument would have given him pleasure, vindicated him somehow.

"He's dead because I wanted him to be," David said, his voice different now, more serious than she'd ever heard it. "Just like you're alive right now because I want you to be. If I killed you, what would they do? Would your priest protect you from this distance? Or does the magic work like a cell phone tower?" He took a step towards her. "Can you hear me now?"

Victoria felt her stomach tense and shifted her stance. The laces of her boots were cutting into her shins. She would be icing her feet when she got home.

"You're not going to kill me, David."

"I didn't say I was. I said I could."

"I used to love you," Victoria said. "It's strange to think about that now, looking at what you've let yourself become, but it's true."

"Yeah, I love you too," he said, pushing a strand of his long hair out of his eyes, his hand lingering on his beard. "We're done now."

He turned and began to walk back across the clearing. She could hear the crinkle of his beard as he scratched at his neck.

Victoria walked back to the hotel. It was close to two in the morning when she arrived. In the lobby, unconcerned with what her guests would think in the morning, she pried off her boots and left them on the corner of the front desk as she headed upstairs.

Chapter Twenty-One

Allison's mouth no longer hurt, but her teeth were still a mess.

She lay in bed, whipping her tongue in and out through the hole in her front teeth, tasting the air like one of the snakes she'd seen in the forest. Before coming to live here she'd never seen a snake in the wild. The ones she had seen in zoos and pet shops had frightened and disgusted her.

Now she loved them. Now she would trade her breasts and hair in order to be one.

Davey entered the trailer quietly, turning the knob and opening the door as gingerly as the old rusted frame would allow. He was sweet like that, always considerate when she was trying to sleep.

"You're up," he said. It sounded like a question even though it was a statement.

He took off his large hooded jacket and balled it up into the shelf above the doorway. The trailer was cramped, but Davey made the best of it by making sure that everything had its place.

Allison tried to be clean for him, re-taught herself the preschool lesson of using one thing and putting it away before you took out another toy.

She tried to stick to it, but she still didn't like to clean her own dishes. The ones she used and didn't scrub this afternoon were beginning to smell.

She was getting better at cleaning though, for Davey.

He pulled his shirt up over his head and she could see the lines of his muscles. He wasn't her type, spindly with prominent veins, but she'd learned to love it.

"How did it go?" she asked. Allison didn't know what the meeting was, but she knew it was important.

"Frustrating. Tiring. I'm beat," he said and crawled into bed next to her, his arms folding up around her. He smelled good.

He groaned and his hands glided from her belly to her breasts.

"When I say 'The Devil'," he said, whispering in her ear, "what image do you think of?"

Allison had to think for a moment. This was what it was like living with a genius. They asked you questions that never seemed to have anything to do with what was actually going on.

"Just the first thing that pops into your mind," he said. His hands moved behind her back and unhooked her bra. "Don't let me distract you."

That was a joke, had to be. He always distracted her. She'd learned to love the distractions.

"I think of a red guy with horns. Maybe kind of a cartoon, like on *The Simpsons*," she said. This seemed like a good enough answer.

"Now try and think of the second thing that comes to your mind," he said, "move down the list of images." His hands crept under the wire of her bra, touching the soft, pale flesh under her breasts. "When you think of the Devil, what do you see?"

"I see a man with horns and a goatee," she said. He brushed one of her nipples with the tip of his fingernail, as if he were urging her to say more.

"He's got red skin too. Maybe he's dressed in a nice suit, a martini in one hand."

His arms disentangled from around her, his hands retreated from her breasts and he sat up in bed. She could feel the skin of her chest dimple with gooseflesh as he retreated.

"Have you ever seen the image of Baphomet, the fellah with the goat head?"

Allison didn't have to think about what he meant. She'd never heard the figure called Baphomet before, but she saw him in her mind's eye all the same. He sat in the middle of a pentagram with two black candles burning at his sides, his cloven feet crossed under him.

Baphomet's eyes were split like a goat's and she could feel the heat of them surge through her imagination.

"Yeah, Satan on all the metal album covers." Allison said. "You should talk to my roommate. She likes that stuff."

She hadn't thought of Claire in a few days. Had she been working at The Brant Hotel all that time? She wondered how she was doing, if she liked working there.

One day she'd asked Davey if she could go and visit the hotel. He'd talked her out of it.

"So you think of three different figures, minimum, when you think of the Devil?" Davey asked. He'd turned towards her in bed. In the low light she could see the muscles of his chest, the raised scar tissue crisscrossing his heart.

"Yes. Why does it matter?" She was beginning to get bored with this conversation, but she knew better than to anger Davey, especially when he seemed preoccupied.

"It matters because they're all wrong. None of them come close to any of his forms."

"Well, what does he look like then?" Allison felt herself becoming more interested despite the dual allure of sleep and her libido.

"What I mean to say is that there is no one image, and all the ones that you mentioned are best guesses. None of them meant to seriously represent him. They're pop culture, even the oldest one. The image of Baphomet is millennia old, but even that one's relatively recent when we consider the age of the world. They're all equally right and wrong, because they're putting a picture on the unpicturable. He's an idea, not a person or a creature."

"Nobody knows or can know what he looks like, so we make up pictures. Do I have it right?"

"Close enough," he said. She could tell by his expression that he was moving on to his next subject. "What does the Devil represent? To you."

"He's evil incarnate, right? Like, the ultimate badass." She lisped on badass, her tongue poking through the hole in her front teeth. The lisp reminded her of Daisy. She didn't like Daisy but wondered what she was up to right now. Sleeping, most likely.

Allison's mind wandered more these days. Probably because she thought less about shoes. She hadn't worn hers in a week, even when she walked outside in the dirt.

"The ultimate badass? That one's less open to interpretation," Davey said and she felt like she'd gotten a quiz question wrong. She pointed her eyes down at the bedspread, but he took her chin in two fingers and raised her face back up gently.

"He's unpredictability," Davey said. They lay back down, his beard tickling the back of her neck, his voice hot in her ear. "He's the other golden rule: no matter how good life is, you can have it fucked up for you in an instant."

Davey snapped his fingers for effect before continuing. "Chaos isn't the same as evil because Chaos has got consistency. If there's order on one side and the Devil on the other, he's the element of life that introduces unpredictability."

"So he's a good guy?" Allison asked. She was into the conversation now, but Davey's strong hands held her down, trying to go back to the places they were before.

"No, I'm just saying there is no good and bad. Those labels come after. They're manmade. The universe hasn't got morality. We made that up in the Bible. Just like we make up cartoon faces so that sweet little girls like you can recognize the Devil."

He slid two fingers down the front of her panties.

Allison let out a tiny sound at his touch. She meant it to be a moan, but it had come out a soft half-squeak. It was an authentic sex sound, because it meant that she was losing control of the artifice that she used to project when getting with all the boys before Davey.

She bit back the sound and asked another question. "You don't study the Bible? Not even the Old Testament?"

"I'm not saying it's not a good story, that it doesn't have some universal truths peeking through the bullshit," Davey said.

There were two hands on her but they felt like five. She squeezed her eyes shut tight, flashes of light shooting through the blackness of her vision.

"We just shouldn't rely on it. We should recognize that it's manmade, that it's totally biased."

"Biased towards who?" She was cresting now. It was almost impossible to concentrate, but she wanted answers almost as bad as she wanted his hands to keep going.

She felt a bead of sweat drip down into her bellybutton.

"Biased towards order. To God," he said. "If you make the mistake of personifying order and chaos, suddenly order starts looking like the hero. Once you give both of the ideas human features."

Allison couldn't speak now, wasn't going to be able to get out her next question. She bit her lower lip. The seal was uneven because of her broken tooth and she could feel spittle dribble down her chin, but she didn't care.

Davey knew that she had come without being prompted. He

removed his hands and patted down her blonde hair.

In the silence of the trailer Allison could only hear her own breath, feel the last dredges of euphoria as they dissipated out her fingers and toes.

"It's time for people to realize the other side of that story and stop using images of red guys with horns and white guys with beards. It's time that chaos got its fans."

Allison lay in silent awe, the genius beside her in bed brushing her hair back over her ear and kissing her good night.

Chapter Twenty-Two

Shoeless, Victoria Brant shuffled through the hallway of the hotel that she'd named after herself.

The individual hairs on her head seemed to pull against her scalp and every third door she would touch the metal knob and discharge a blue spark. The tiny static shocks helped to keep her awake after her exhausting trek through the woods.

Davey used to do this as a boy. She'd catch him sneaking into the hotel at all hours of the night, charging himself up with wattage and shooting out sparks.

"What are you doing, Davey?" she'd ask.

"Just taking a walk, Ms. Brant," he'd say, holding his child-size sneakers clenched in one hand. She remembered him as he was. It was impossible to tell back then how tall he would one day be. "I'm sorry. I know that I'm not supposed to be here."

The neighborhood kids often hung around Main Street, but Davey was the only one who'd sneak out of his bed to do it at night. Looking back, there had always been something different about the boy.

He didn't dress like the rest of the children of the town, no neon dinosaurs on his shirts or Batman insignias on his socks. As a child Davey had dressed like he did now, an adult dressed for a night out in a country town: plain white undershirt, plaid button-down, slacks or corduroys, but never jeans.

That was back when the town was new and the population still on the climb. Davey's parents had been devout, active members of the church. They were true believers, not salon enthusiasts who came to town to play dress-up and spend a night or two as glorified swingers.

They'd moved on, though, as much of the town had, but they'd left their son behind, a parting gift for old Ms. Brant. He was in his late teens then, prepared to live on his own with his friends. Even in those early days he'd had friends out in the woods.

His parents packing up for the West Coast and leaving him behind had become an urban legend around Mission, like the one about people flushing baby alligators into the sewers.

Davey had been small and harmless then, unable to grow a full beard, with spots of acne on his cheeks. But now he was full-grown and dangerous, gnashing his teeth every time he was given a chance.

Victoria walked without thinking where she was going. She passed her own room and kept going, the phantom sound of little David's socks pulling her up one more flight of stairs. The air cracked as she received a big shock from the banister.

The handrails in the stairwells used to polish up so brightly that they were indistinguishable from gold, but now the metal was mottled and tarnished. They weren't ugly, just aged, like her.

Victoria was in front of the door before her conscious mind realized what her destination was. Sometimes, on nights like this when she felt defeated, she would end up in the subbasement, caressing the tiles of the ceremony room.

Tonight was different. Tonight she'd been ascending steps, bringing herself closer to heaven, as it were.

Out of habit, she knocked softly on the door to Room Thirty-one. She didn't need to. Father Hayden couldn't hear her, would never be able to hear her. Daisy insisted on talking to him when it was feeding time, but the girl also talked to the flowerbeds. It didn't mean they could hear her.

Taking the keycard out of the front pocket of her dress, she unlocked the door to the room and shut it softly behind her.

The blinds were completely drawn and they were on the third floor, far above the one light over the parking lot, so no light entered the room.

She stood there in the darkness and tried to slow her breathing so she couldn't hear the rise and fall of her own dress. She let the nothingness wash over her and imagined that this was what the world must be like for him all the time.

Complete emptiness.

It only took a moment for the illusion to be shattered by her own need to breathe. She exhaled and flipped the light switch that she knew was three feet to her right.

Victoria had designed the layout of the rooms herself. It may have been years ago that she'd told the electricians how to run the wiring and told the movers where to put the furniture, but the years had been kind to The Brant.

The switch connected to both the foyer lights and the overhead bulbs in the bedroom. Guests had to click the bedside lamps on themselves if they wanted extra light to read by, reducing electricity costs and providing effective mood lighting when couples were returning to their rooms.

Father Hayden was on his back in the bed, folded neatly between the sheets. Victoria wondered for a moment whether he'd tucked himself in like that or if Daisy had done it.

His eyes were half open, but he was asleep.

He snored, a thin line of drool running down one of the scars at the side of his mouth, a tiny river in the fleshy crags of his face.

Every morning Daisy would put in his eye drops to keep his eyes from drying up and falling out of his head. Victoria walked over to his nightstand, not trying to soften her tread because she knew that he wouldn't wake anyway.

Unscrewing the cap to the Visine bottle, she aimed the end over Hayden's left eye and gave it a light squirt. She could hear the stream of solution leave the bottle, bouncing off Father Hayden's dry, dead eye and spattering beads onto the smooth flesh where his eyebrows used to lay.

It wasn't until she'd put the drops into his right eye that he awoke, sucking in air like a drowning man. She wondered if she'd woken him from a dream or nightmare, if he was capable of having either.

♦

The old woman didn't think he could hear, but he could. Not well, but well enough to make out words when they were being whispered to him in the hole where his ear used to be.

"Hello, Father," the old woman said.

The old woman was the worst.

Even though she spoke to him like an infant, he took an odd kind of enjoyment in being visited by Daisy. In many ways she was right, he was an infant, but her daily routines kept him fed and comfortable. When she touched him it was gently, with the hands of a mother or nurse.

The old woman was there to do the opposite. She touched him like a lover, and not a particularly caring one.

She didn't speak for a long time, so he remained still and listened to the sounds of the room.

He couldn't hear much beyond the bubble that covered about a foot from his left ear. The rest was muffled by an inch of molten skin.

Conscious that he didn't want to appear frightened, he focused on lying still and disinterested. They believed him to be one step from catatonic and he wasn't going to let them think any differently.

Acting out brought swift punishment. He'd learned to stop thinking about it.

The surface of the mattress sank in as she climbed into bed next to him. It was going to be one of those nights. He wondered what time it was. It could have been late night or early morning. The world around him had dimmed when the sun stopped entering the room.

He could tell light from darkness. The world around him was either a soft shade of yellow gray or total blackness. Other than gradations of light, his blindness was complete.

The old woman lifted up his shirt and placed her hand on his abdomen. She chose to caress the grapefruit-sized patch of skin above his belly button that had remained untouched by the fire. He still had hair there and she picked at the wiry strands of lower chest hair that his wife, Hannah, had called his "happy trail".

He tried not to think about his wife as the old woman touched him.

They'd brought him at least two pairs of silk pajamas. He may have had more, but it was impossible and trivial to tell the difference.

The soft fabric allowed him mobility with minimal chaffing, not that he went many places.

The feel of the silk had been unnerving at first. Against his fire-smoothed skin it seemed cool and damp, so much so that he could never tell when he was wet in actuality. But he got used to it, learned to enjoy rubbing it between his fingers.

"What do you think about all day, Father?" the old woman whispered. "Do you think about protecting us or ruining us?"

She called him Father even when there was no one else around to hear her. She knew that he wasn't a priest, but she was the only one besides the strong man that knew.

She'd never called him Hugh, Mayland or even Mr. Mayland (like she had after he'd checked into her hotel), so in return he never thought of her as anything other than the old woman. She wasn't Victoria Brant: she was his jailer and abuser.

The old woman styled herself as his savior. She'd not only saved his life, becoming an overnight expert on caring for burn victims, but she also let him live in her hotel for free.

The nature of the hotel and of the separatist group that had killed his wife and burnt him to a cinder was hard to follow, but he'd picked up enough to have a rough understanding of it. Davey led a group of young people who got their kicks from undermining the leaders of the town at every turn. When they weren't performing sacrificial murders of their own, the kids were ripping off the general store, placing phone calls to local police and trampling the farmers' crops with their meaningless rituals.

None of that was particularly harmful to the hotel or her people. Brant had cops in her congregation who dealt with most of these problems, but somehow over the last twenty-four hours the cold war had gone hot.

Most of this information came from comparing what Daisy said to him during the day to what the old woman whispered in his non-ear at night.

The intel he gathered from Daisy not only had to be parsed from the never-ending stream of seeming bullshit that flowed from her mouth, but also had to be fact-checked against what little her boss let him know.

Although he was a prisoner, he was also a confidant for both of them.

The two women had different reasons as to why Hugh Mayland was now called Father Hayden. Daisy used this moniker unironically, although she knew that Brant's cover story of the old church fire was fabricated (there had never been a church in Mission). She and the rest of the town were under the impression that he was a powerful dark priest, outsourced from a small town in South England to help protect the people of Mission.

Why she kept the fact that he was from England, Hugh didn't know. His mouth was badly burned. He'd never be understood if he tried to speak, never mind his accent.

The old woman used the name to try to convince herself of

the lie. It had been the strong man who'd found him crawling through the woods, Mayland's skin charred and peeling as he tried to escape the monsters that had drugged and killed his wife.

Later, from Daisy, he'd learned that the strong man's name was Roy, but, like the old woman, he would remain the strong man to Hugh.

"You wouldn't believe the night that I've just had," the old woman said. He could not smell wine on her breath, which he took as a good sign. She would often get violent afterwards if she was drunk. "I've just had a meeting with an old acquaintance of yours, if you can remember Davey. Things are not looking good."

The old woman tugged at the drawstring of his pajama bottoms. He tried to ignore what her hands were doing, focus on the implications of what she was saying.

The top half of his body had gotten the worst of the flames, leaving his privates still functioning. This was cause for celebration when he considered how lucky he was to be able to use his bedpan to go to the bathroom himself, but when the old woman slid down his silk bottoms it made him embarrassed to be a man.

Embarrassed not only in the sense that he was too cowardly to fight back against her advances, but also that his body responded to them. It would sound selfish, but the old woman's visits to his room were worse for Hugh than his nights in the basement.

There he was surrounded by murderous lunatics but nothing happened to him. Those were the nights that he was thankful for his blindness and his inability to hear most things. He sat in his throne and was occasionally smeared with blood, but other than that the ceremonies were rather mundane. On good nights he didn't even hear the pleading screams of the offerings.

Objectively, within his conscious mind, Hugh knew that he had suffered a psychotic break to be able to remain unfazed by the horrors he endured on a daily basis, but he welcomed the numbness.

"Don't you have a hex or a blood rite that can destroy him?" the old woman asked. She'd said jokes like this before, but this time it didn't sound like she was mocking his lack of magical powers, but instead imploring him to develop some. "The rest of them would wither and die without him. I should have done it myself or at least I should have had Roy do it."

Her voice sounded different tonight, not the husky tone laden with innuendo that she usually took. She sounded sadder, two minutes away from either screaming or tears. Maybe both.

Sad or not, she kept on massaging his member. He felt the blood begin to flow, his body responding without his mind, and he felt the hollowness inside him fill to the brim with shame.

He tried to focus on understanding what she was saying. When his jailers spoke to him, they did so under the impression that he couldn't understand what they were saying, so they talked about people he'd never met and events he'd never witnessed without the courtesy of exposition.

"I can't order him around anymore, because Roy's dead," she said. She sounded more frustrated and angry about this than mournful. Hugh guessed that Roy was the strong man, as there didn't seem to be many more male staffers at The Brant. From what Daisy had said, Roy also prepared a wonderful Salisbury steak.

She didn't say anything more, but busied herself with undoing the buttons on his shirt.

Considering what he knew about the state of the town, Hugh doubted that Roy died peacefully in his sleep of natural causes.

He toyed with possible scenarios for Roy's death, imagining everything from dramatic Hollywood shootouts to a familiar bonfire that gave him an involuntary chill. While he passed the time with these scenes, he tried to ignore the dampness of his skin and the lewd sucking sounds that filled the room.

There were tears on his chest, left from when Brant had run her mouth across the lines of his scar tissue. It was good to know that, tonight at least, she wasn't enjoying this either.

Hugh tried to preoccupy himself with what Roy had looked like. He couldn't remember seeing him during his stay at the hotel. The implications of his death were what he needed to focus on, though.

Even blind and near-deaf, Hugh Mayland understood that there was a war coming to Mission. He also understood that he had a part to play in it.

He was not a firm believer in the hetero-normative view of manhood.

In his life before the hotel, he had enjoyed books and plays, not hunting, fighting or fishing, but his time at The Brant had caused him to value the idea of revenge. Not just an English revenge, not the plots and schemes of Hamlet, but an American revenge.

The Bard could be a fount of inspiration too, but not now. What Hugh craved now was the justice of the gun, the cold American iron of Clint Eastwood and Charles Bronson.

Coward or not, numb or not, Hugh Mayland knew that he needed to kill someone before he allowed himself to die.

His body filled with sickly warmth for a moment, then went cold as the sweat evaporated off of his smooth body and silken pajamas.

"Thank you for that, Father," the old woman said.

He wanted to speak so badly then, but settled for screaming the words in his mind instead. It was the same thought he had every night that she came to his room.

My name is Hugh Mayland and I'm going to kill you.

Part Three:

The Great Beast

Chapter Twenty-Three

Claire looked into his eyes, his little skinless neck bobbling up and down like it was a spring, and screamed.

She'd found Bert.

To prepare for the dinner rush, Claire had hunted down a Phillips screwdriver to take the lock off the second refrigerator. She'd been surprised how easy it had been to pry off. The metal hinge had ripped up through the screws holding it in place, the leverage allowing her to bend it like Supergirl.

She'd felt pretty good about herself and her handiwork before opening up the fridge.

It was inside that she found Bert, his skin removed and most of the meat cleaned off his two hind legs. He'd been split lengthwise from neck to tail, his legs flattened under him against the cutting board.

The civilized part of Claire wanted to retch, but couldn't because the chef inside of her could only see meat. She'd gotten so used to working with Roy and chopping up raw meat that the cleaned and prepped dog didn't look like a dog. Bert was completely alien from any pet she'd ever known. He looked more like an overgrown chicken. The thought that she could see Bert as meat horrified her more than his corpse did.

She closed the refrigerator and leaned against it for support.

Claire tried fitting the pieces together in ways that didn't mesh. She started with the prime suspect in Bert's murder: Roy. Then she worked backwards to the question on everyone else's lips: Where was Roy?

For that matter, why the fuck is he chopping up dogs and stashing them next to the cold cuts?

It was as if she were working on a jigsaw puzzle but had pieces from ten separate pictures.

After a moment, she looked at the screwdriver she'd tossed to the floor while screaming, then back at the lock that she'd felt so proud of breaking off just a minute earlier.

Had anyone heard her scream? Was someone coming to her rescue right now? Should she try to pretend like she didn't see Bert, especially if Roy was planning to come back in time for the dinner service? Too many questions, none of them helping to put skin back over Christine's dog.

What little she'd known of Christine, Claire had liked. She was funny and sarcastic in a way that the people here didn't seem to get.

As hot and sweet as he was, Tobin was still a country boy at heart. He wasn't synced up with her city-girl cynicism, probably never would be. The older lesbian had been. Cosmopolitism and acerbic humor seemed to go hand in hand.

Now Christine would have to tell her wife that Bert wasn't coming back for belly rubs. The thought made her sad, but not sad enough to push away the swirl of questions and connections being tried, broken and reformed in her mind.

She thought all the way back to that first night.

Not her first night sleeping at The Brant, her first night partying. The night that she'd seen things—or thought she'd seen things—that she couldn't explain. Horror movie images of ritual sacrifice or at least the aftermath of a murder scene.

Then she heard Tobin's words echo in her head, about how Davey had long suspected the hotel was a front for some kind of sinister activities.

As soon as the connections were made, she stepped back to see that they weren't connections at all, merely similarities in tone. They were tenuous, circumstantial links at best. They came from a place of fear and confusion, not facts.

She'd worked with Roy. Aside from some regrettable facial hair and a wax-agnostic worldview, he was an all right guy.

One half of the lock was still attached to the fridge, so she pressed the broken part down and hammered at it with the end of the screwdriver. She cut the edge of her hand on the frayed raised metal, but the result was worth it. It wasn't going to hold up to heavy scrutiny (or a light tug), but the lock was back on the refrigerator, sealing Bert up in his tomb.

"What now?" Claire asked. What should have been a thought became words spoken to the empty kitchen.

She needed help but she was still hours away from her normal hook-up time with Tobin. "Hook-up" here had two meanings.

The discovery of Bert seemed to grant her a clarity she hadn't felt in days (or was it weeks?). She had to count on her fingers the number of days she'd been seeing Tobin. When she got to her second pinky, she stopped counting. How had the two of them become so close without her noticing?

If she hadn't just found the mutilated corpse of a house pet, she would have been alarmed at how quickly she'd become dependent on Tobin, but now she was glad to have him.

How could she have him and still have no way of contacting him right now?

"Cell phones give you brain tumors," he'd said one morning while putting on his pants. Putting on his pants seemed to be when he did most of his talking, at least most of the talking that Claire could remember.

The shack didn't have a landline, either. Calling him was not happening.

Claire would either have to walk out to the shack, a place she wasn't sure he'd be or that she could find on foot, or wait until his truck pulled into the gas station parking lot.

She didn't even know what Tobin did with his days, where he spent most of his time.

Davey's camp was an option, but also somewhere she wasn't able to get on her own. She'd only seen it a handful of times in the daylight, and all of those times she'd been too hung over to get more than a hazy impression of the place.

There was also the question of how she was supposed to work around prepping all the food for dinner, all the food that was now locked back in the fridge with Bert's remains.

It came to her then, the one person at The Brant she could trust most, the one who'd already watched her back, not to mention the one person too vapid and dull to be involved in any sort of dog-murder conspiracy.

Claire needed to find Daisy.

♦

Daisy sobbed for five solid minutes after Claire showed her Bert's flayed corpse. Maybe showing her hadn't been the best idea.

"I know it's hard, but what do we do?" Claire said as the rolling sobs slowed to a trickle.

It was like she'd said the magic words, Daisy's face sobered and she wiped her eyes on the corner of her apron.

"We should put him somewhere safe and prepare dinner," Daisy said, rolling up her sleeves. Claire had always thought of that as an expression, but Daisy was actually doing it.

"If this gets out, Ms. Brant will be ruined. The hotel will be closed. It would devastate the town. Bert seemed like a good dog, but we can't let his death destroy Mission," Daisy said.

Stunned by not only the melodrama but the change in Daisy's attitude, Claire could only nod and offer a solemn "Yes, of course." Sometimes the only way weird situations could go was further into the surreal.

Daisy riffled through a cabinet that Claire had never used and came back with a thick black Hefty bag. In a few quick whips of her arms, she had the bag open and was sliding Bert, cutting board and all, into the bag.

Bert's body pressed against the outside of the bag, his four legs poking an outline in the bag as Daisy twisted up and knotted the end.

The impression Bert's body left in the plastic caused a flash in Claire's brain.

It was a dream image, or what she'd been telling herself was a dream image: the five fingers of a human hand pressing up against a black garbage bag, a dismembered arm trying to push its way out of the trash.

Claire shivered.

"Put this down in that cupboard," Daisy said, and pointed. "Don't worry. It's sealed." She then handed her the bag o' Bert, Claire having no choice but to take it.

For someone who had just been weeping over a dog she'd only met once, Daisy had regained composure very quickly. That was the attitude she took when her patron was threatened. The dedication Daisy showed to Brant and the hotel was fanatical. Claire only just now realized this, even though it had been staring her in the face since the first day.

Claire shoved Bert into the cupboard, touching him through the bag and wincing at the cold of his exposed flesh.

As she pulled her hand back, the chill still on it, she had to ask, "What do you think he did with the fur?"

Chapter Twenty-Four

Daisy turned out to be an even more demanding chef than Roy. By the time the last half-collapsing turkey club sandwich and fries had been delivered to the final table in the dining room, it was fifteen minutes past when Claire was supposed to meet Tobin.

Instead of rushing out to the truck, she took her time and washed her hands. The sensation of pressing burger patties and then touching cold Bert through the thick plastic bag mingled in her mind as she lathered up her hands for a fourth time.

She glanced at her phone and saw that she was a half hour late by the time she crossed the street and let herself into Tobin's truck.

He'd been dozing in the driver's seat and woke with a start when she slammed the door shut behind her.

"Planning on cleaning up the shack?" Tobin asked as he turned the key in the ignition.

"Huh?" Claire said.

Tobin pointed down at her chest. Claire looked to see that she was still wearing her uniform and apron.

"Want to go back and change? I don't mind waiting."

"No, just get us out of here. I need to rest," Claire said.

"Is everything okay?" he asked.

"Not really, but I want to get moving before we start talking about it. I can't look at that building anymore," Claire said, her eyes on the rearview mirror, as if Roy were going to burst from the front door of The Brant and hop into the truck bed, a chainsaw in tow.

It wasn't fear, really, just exhaustion, mental and physical exhaustion. Even though it hadn't been in the dozens, it felt as though she'd helped prepare a hundred meals and cleaned half as many rooms since waking up this morning, and that was before becoming party to the cover-up of a dog murder.

The cheap mattress in the shack was going to feel like a silken cloud. She wanted to fall asleep while being held by Tobin.

The pickup pulled out of the driveway, its wheels peeling out as Tobin jammed the accelerator.

"Fast enough?" he asked with a slight smile. He was still unsure how upset she was, and it looked like he was taking care not to make anything worse by saying something too jokey.

She reached over and squeezed his shoulder, the scarred skin underneath his shirt taut with tension, hands cinched over the wheel.

Her stomach dropped, like the sensation of remembering that you left the front door unlocked. She'd left the hotel without saying anything to Christine. But what was there to say?

"Your wife's dog is dead and the guy who killed it has gone missing. I think you ought to leave. No, don't bother with checking out. Just get in your car and go."

Claire groaned. She had no real reason to tell Christine any of that, only a deep feeling that she should.

"What do you know about Roy? The cook at the hotel?" Claire said. Her speaking after such a long silence had caused Tobin to jump out of his stupor. The car jerked suddenly to the median and then reset itself.

"He's not as bad as the rest of them, that's one thing," Tobin said. Over the last month, when they were driving and talking, he'd usually take his eyes off the road and look at her while he spoke. It was dangerous and it annoyed her, but he didn't do it now. He kept his stare on the pavement.

Either he was learning what made her happy or he wasn't telling her something. One option made her feel a schoolgirl flutter for him. The other frightened her. She could barely feel anything over the elastic pull of her eyelids trying to shut themselves.

"Why do you say that?" she asked.

"I don't know. It's not like we are close," Tobin said. "I just know that he's a roughneck, and he hasn't changed that to suit the hotel. Everyone else that has or has had a job there has changed in order to do their job."

"I'm pretty sure that he killed one of our guest's pets and was planning on serving it up as a meal." She'd just realized that last part as she spoke it. Then she thought about all the Roy-cooked meals that she'd eaten over the last month. If she weren't so tired, she would have vomited.

"What?" He sounded appropriately surprised.

"I found it in the fridge, skinned and cleaned. I showed it to Daisy and she didn't want to tell anyone about it. We moved it out of the fridge and prepared the rest of the meals like nothing had happened. I don't know what she's going to do with the body."

They reached the turnoff for the shack and blew past it. With Tobin's eyes on the road, it was unlikely that he missed the turn by accident.

"Where are we going?" Claire said, a fear rising up, a fear of Tobin for the first time ever. Her rational mind tried to calm the scared animal inside her.

"I'm sorry, but you've got to tell Davey about this."

"I'm so tired. I can't deal with all that right now. Let's go home please."

"Don't worry. There's no party tonight. You just have to tell him everything you saw and heard. Then you can come back to the shack with me. You shouldn't be sleeping at the hotel tonight."

"I wasn't planning on it. We're in agreement on that."

"As I said, there's no party, just you, me and Davey having a talk."

She wanted to ask why they were going to the woods, why it was so vital that Davey collect her statement for his little investigation, why there was no party tonight when it seemed like there was a party every night, but she couldn't muster the energy. She just frowned.

"As long as you don't mind hiking through the woods while giving me a piggyback ride. I'm not walking."

"That sounds like a deal to me."

♦

Tobin wasn't kidding. He carried Claire on his back for most of the trip. They both giggled at the absurdity of it, but it had been a relief. Not only was it nice not to walk, but the closeness helped to calm her. The muscles of his back pressed up against her breasts and belly and she could smell the earth on him. His scent was more comforting and rustic than the forest surrounding them.

As they approached the camp, she became self-conscious of

the situation. She'd forgotten that she was wearing her uniform until she'd climbed up onto his back, hiking up the dress so he could grab on to her stockinged thighs. She was going to look lame enough. Riding in on someone's back could only make it worse.

He set her down and she patted the fabric of her uniform back into order.

There was no party tonight, but there was still a gathering of sorts. A campfire burned in the fire pit, but it wasn't the large, billowing bonfires that accompanied their nightly ragers. It was the soft, homey crackling fireplace of a suburban living room.

Jeb sat closest to the flames, staring into them, calculating when the best time to toss another log on would be. Tending the fire seemed to be Jeb's only job.

The big boy spent most of the parties cracking logs with his ax and tossing them into the pit. Those were the only things that Claire had ever seen him do beyond molest Eden.

Eden sat next to him, her back pressed up against his side, leaning into him like you would a comfortable easy chair. Covering her legs was a white sheet. She snipped at the sheet with scissors, then placed the scissors on the ground beneath her and swapped them for a needle and thread.

There was a red-and-white plastic bag next to her, a stack of still-packaged sheets inside the bag. The red circles on the bag were instantly recognizable. Jeb and Eden must have driven into civilization and made a Target run.

Claire tried to picture Jeb's dirty overalls and Eden's soiled white dress anywhere but the forest and couldn't. Seeing the pair standing on the antiseptic white tile of a department store seemed even more impossible. The thought of Eden perusing the Martha Stewart Home Collection or Jeb trying on a pair of Levi's bordered on the surreal. They were forest people, not Target people. Walmart, maybe, but not Target.

Eden seemed to be making her own dress out of plain white bed sheets. Going to a fabric store or buying ready-made clothes seemed more cost effective, but Claire wasn't going to say anything to the girl about it.

Claire didn't talk to Eden much. It wasn't just the girl's shyness, her pulsing scar or her intimidating boyfriend, though those also helped to keep Claire away. It was the waves of concentrated hate and jealousy that seemed to roll off Eden every time Claire tried to make polite conversation.

Despite her cherub size and mousy voice, Eden was probably the second oldest member of the group. Her age seemed to give her seniority, but it also gave her a severe distrust of all the younger girls in the group. Tobin had told Claire on numerous occasions not to mind her, that she wasn't that bad, but that didn't help Claire like her any better.

Beyond the pair of Jeb and Eden was a group of kids. Two boys and a girl sat chatting and drinking beers at a flimsy card table. Claire recognized them but couldn't remember their names. Every time she tried to learn names, it seemed like there was a new group of people to meet. She'd stopped trying.

The group at the card table drank, but not in celebration. One of them caught Claire's eye, but quickly looked away. They appeared preoccupied and dialed down the decibel level of their conversation until it was whispers.

Barrel up, leaning against one side of the card table, was a bolt-action rifle. Claire told herself that maybe the group was tired after a long day of hunting, but that didn't do much to assuage the chill she got from looking at the gun.

"Wait here. I'll go get him," Tobin said, giving her hand a quick squeeze before leaving her by the fire.

She watched him bound up the steps to Davey's trailer. Shady as he was being, his ass still looked great in a pair of boot-cut jeans.

The inside of the trailer was the only place in camp she hadn't seen. Some nights would see her invited into Jeb and Eden's tent for bong hits. She'd taken a shower using the outdoor stall and used the outhouse on the edge of the camp. However, she'd never gotten one single look inside that trailer.

Tobin knocked and then entered. She couldn't see anything of note behind the open door before he closed it behind him.

It was possible that he'd be in there for a few minutes. Time had to get killed.

"How're you?" Claire asked, looking over at Eden. Having to choose between her or her gorilla of a boyfriend, she made the attempt at small talk with Eden.

"I'm hanging in there," Eden said, not looking up from her sewing. Her lines didn't look particularly straight, but Claire couldn't fault her. She'd never sewn anything in her life.

"Whatcha making?" Claire asked, only later realizing that she had lapsed into baby talk again with Eden. The girl was just too small, too precious looking to be addressed in any normal way.

"A dress," the girl replied, her voice full of disdain. Eden looked up then, gave Claire a once-over, her eyes lingering on the embroidered name over Claire's breast.

"I'm making one for everyone. If I have enough sheets when I'm done with all our girls', I could make one for you too. Do you want a new dress?" The last question seemed to hold meaning beyond the obvious.

Eden said she was making a dress for *our* girls. That was it. It was Claire's job at the hotel that made her different, distanced her from Eden and the rest of the camp. She was the other. "That sounds nice. Thanks."

The stilted conversation didn't have to last much longer. A few moments after he entered the trailer Tobin was walking across camp towards her, Davey in front of him. The people of the camp watched Davey as he passed, all except for Jeb who kept on staring into the flames.

Tobin was carrying an electric lamp that he hadn't had before.

"It's nice to see you, Claire," Davey said. Before she knew what was happening, his arms were around her in a hug. There was such a calculated Mr. Mayor-vibe to most of Davey's interactions, but that didn't stop him from remaining charming.

Post-hug, Davey was all business. He put a big hand on her shoulder. "I hear that you've got some disturbing news for me. We need to talk but not here. Do you mind if we take a walk to my office? The trailer's a mess right now. I can't invite you in."

"That's fine," Claire said.

Davey's "office" was just a clearing in the woods. It was a five-minute walk from camp, far enough that the glow of the fire was no longer visible. Once they'd walked beyond the corona of campfire light, Tobin flicked on the electric lantern and bathed the forest around them in its eerie blue glow.

Claire found herself completely turned off when Tobin became Davey's stoic lackey. His personality changed and he went bodyguard-silent whenever Davey was around.

"I know that it's late and everyone's tired, you especially so, but please begin your story. Rewind to the start of the day, if you don't mind," Davey said.

Tobin set down the lantern on the ground, its light becoming striped by the tall grass surrounding the bulb. He took off his jacket and laid it over Claire's shoulders. It was a nice gesture, but she wasn't cold.

"By the time I'd come downstairs to help Roy with prep, Ms. Brant had already noticed he hadn't come into work," Claire said, then added, "Roy is the house chef."

"I'm aware of Roy Parsons' position. I'm also aware that he's not the type to miss work because of a hangover. Roy's been clean for five years, doesn't seem likely that he'd fall off the wagon, but it's still," Davey paused, not to choose a word but to emphasize a word, "possible."

"How did Ms. Brant seem to be acting?" Tobin said. She wasn't aware that there were going to be two interviewers or that her boyfriend was going to turn interrogator.

Davey gave Tobin a look that could have meant anything, but Claire guessed that he was just as surprised as she was to hear Tobin asking his own line of questions.

"She was upset, more so than she usually is about setbacks. Which I found odd, because at that time, Roy couldn't have been more than an hour late. It was still possible that he'd show up before breakfast."

"Upset how?" Davey said. "And, again, I apologize for asking questions that may seem mundane. I trust that Tobin has told you about my investigation. It probably sounds crazy to you, and maybe it is, but I'm too far into it now."

"Ms. Brant seemed different. She's usually so in control, but there were tears in her eyes. She wasn't just sad, though. She seemed overwhelmed, stressed." Claire looked from Tobin and then back to Davey, who had the fingers of one hand wrapped up in his beard. "I thought your investigation was of Ms. Brant, what does Roy have to do with that?"

"You don't just investigate powerful people. You investigate their network."

"I'm in her network," Claire said, trying and failing to smile.

"Just barely," Davey said, his own smile wolfish but genuine.

This was a turning point, the first time she'd been around Davey and not been drawn into his act. It was the only time she'd been around him and wished that she wasn't.

"Continue, then we can all go home," Tobin said.

"Brant had me take over for breakfast. All of that food is in a different refrigerator, except for the beef, that was locked in the stand-up fridge with a padlock. So there was no steak and eggs, but everything else on the menu I could fudge."

"And he didn't return for dinner?" Davey asked.

"No, but in between lunch and dinner I had a conversation with a guest about her missing dog. That's how I knew what it was when I found it."

"He'd skinned the poor thing?" Davey asked. "That's what Tobin told me."

"Yes, that, but he'd also started to clean the meat from the bones. Daisy and I had found a small Tupperware container with the separated meat in it."

"There was always darkness in Roy. This is the way that it comes out now that he's clean. Nobody's ever really clean, I guess," Davey said, making a show to talk more to himself than anyone else present. He turned his attention back to Claire. "Now, I know you don't want to think about it, but please try and remember, were there any designs carved into the animal? Anything that looked vaguely pagan?"

"No. He'd just field-dressed it and peeled the skin off like Bert was a tiny deer. What is this?" Claire asked. "What are you investigating the hotel for?"

Davey clicked his tongue, knotted his brow in thought.

"If I tell you," he said, back to talking to himself again, "it's not only going to change the way you think about Ms. Brant, but the way you think about us," Davey said. Then he looked at Tobin with an expression that asked, "Should I do it?"

"Tell me," Claire said. Realizing that she'd voiced it as a demand, she added a "Please.

"You know those conspiracy theorists on the internet? 9/11 was an inside job? The president is a reptilian alien? It was Jackie O that shot her husband with a derringer concealed in her purse? All that stuff is crazy bullshit, so don't confuse me with any of those people after what I'm about to say."

"Okay," Claire said. This was precisely the preface that crazy bullshit seemed to accompany.

"For as long as it's been here, the town of Mission has been run by a Satanist cult. The community was started by old-school Satanists, not harmful, just armchair dabblers in the occult. Have you ever heard of a guy named Anton LaVey?"

"The bald guy? The one who looked like present-day Rob Halford?"

"Yeah," Davey said, looking over to Tobin, both of them surprised.

"I've got the Motörhead logo tattooed behind my calf, so don't act so shocked that I know who Anton LaVey is," Claire said. She expected more out of Tobin. He just shrugged.

"Anyway, he preached a kooky form of self-reliance and sold books. These people in Mission took some inspiration from him and set up the town because they wanted to live their dark hippie lifestyle in peace."

Davey told his story with gusto. "Sure they sacrificed a few goats, had sex with each other's wives and husbands, lit a few black candles, but that was the extent of it. The novelty of dancing around in velvet capes wore off eventually and folks started to leave the town in droves. They wanted to head back to suburbia, were done with rural commune life. This made Victoria Brant very unhappy."

"No townspeople means no town means no hotel, correct?"

"Who is telling the story here?" Davey said, but he didn't sound upset. In a way he looked delighted. "Yes, you're right. Brant had to up the ante, try to turn what remained of the population into true believers."

"If they were harmless New Age kooks, why the investigation?" Claire asked. Her fear dissolved as she found herself swept up in the romance of Davey's fantasy. She didn't believe it, but it made a great story, one that Silverfish yearned to play a part in. Silverfish, not Claire. Claire cashed checks and waited tables and cleaned hotel rooms. Silverfish would rather be skipping her first-period chemistry class because she'd attended a midnight screening of *Repo Man* or drawing up a *Dungeons & Dragons* campaign where all the characters names are taken from all the lineups of Black Sabbath.

"Because they aren't harmless. They're killers. She's started murdering people in her rituals and the town loves her for it," Davey said. No smile this time.

Just as quickly as she had pushed to the fore, Silverfish retreated back inside Claire, back to a high school existence that would never end. Davey's story was suddenly no longer fun.

"You have proof of that?" Claire asked.

"We've got a section of forest filled up with cars that belong to missing persons, a local population that is violently hostile towards me and my friends, a chef that carves up beloved house pets and—most convincingly—we've got an eyewitness account of a human sacrifice taking place in the basement of the hotel," Davey said, leaning closer with each item on his list.

"You're the eyewitness," Tobin said.

Claire didn't need to be reminded, she already knew. Her face felt hot and her throat was dry as she tried to swallow. She had to work to build up the moisture to ask her next question.

"What happens now?"

Chapter Twenty-Five

Claire was now a double agent.

That was the thought she had as she fell into Tobin's bed. This would be the last time she'd be sleeping under his roof for a while, so she told herself to enjoy it. Davey had told her that, after tonight, she'd have to stay at The Brant for the time being. So her absence didn't arouse suspicion.

According to Davey, Brant already knew that she was spending nights out in the woods, there was no fooling her. "Anything that Daisy knows, Victoria knows. So think carefully about what you've shared with her and where she sees you go. As sweet and naïve as she seems, don't trust her."

She considered her new life of espionage as she pulled the sheets up over her uniform. She realized that she was saturating the fabric in Tobin's musk and did not care one bit.

Tobin didn't take his clothes off, either. He slid into bed beside her, grabbing her from behind, but not in the way he usually did. There was no sex in his touch, only caring and softness.

With one arm around her midsection, he pulled the band out of her hair with his free hand and placed it on the nightstand (an upended milk crate). He then began to stroke her hair, his fingers occasionally taking a gentle dig in and scratching her scalp.

His touch was magic. Every time the tips of his fingers would dip into her vision, he'd wrap the half-silver strand of her hair around his finger before pulling back and brushing the rest of her head. He worked in order, making sure not to miss an area and giving her just enough of a scalp massage to be relaxing instead of erotic.

"What's that?" she asked, having to try to form the words through the heaviness of her lips. Her eyes focused and unfocused on the black cylinder on Tobin's nightstand. The object was smaller on one end than the other, matte black, and phallic.

Despite the pressures of the day, she felt herself get hot under her stockings.

"That's something I picked up for protection," Tobin whispered in her ear.

"From what?" Claire said feeling like this was a joke.

Tobin took his hand from her waist and reached over her to the nightstand. He picked up the cylinder, the muscles and veins in his forearm bulging. It must have been heavier than it looked.

With a quick motion of his wrist the cylinder transformed with a loud click like a gun being cocked. It sounded dangerous.

"Oh," Claire heard herself say, pulling closer to consciousness, no longer as tired.

The cylinder was no longer overtly sexual in appearance, but that didn't make the weapon any less of a turn-on.

"Can I hold it?"

"Sure," he said. "But be careful, it's heavy. I don't want you knocking any of those pretty teeth out." He gave her a small but audible kiss on the forehead and handed over the baton.

Even with his warning she'd nearly dropped it on her face. *How could something so small be so heavy?* She used two hands to lift it up, pointing it forward.

"How do I make it go down again?" she asked.

"This here," he said, gliding her thumb over the small switch on the side. The tip of the weapon dropped back into the segment behind it, everything collapsing back into the handle.

She whipped both hands forward and extended the baton again.

"This is the weapon of a Jedi warrior. Not as random or clumsy as a blaster," she said and then made the appropriate accompanying sounds.

Tobin laughed.

"Shouldn't I have one of these?" she asked. "If I'm supposed to be going undercover, don't I need a concealed weapon? What if they dragged me into Father Hayden's room and he put a spell on me? Turned me into a newt or some shit?"

Earlier in the night, she'd heard all about how Brant was using the crippled priest as her new figurehead for her regime. The townspeople were under the impression that he was a powerful black priest that she'd had shipped overseas.

Davey didn't believe that Brant or anyone else possessed demonic supernatural power. Claire considered this and asked why then was it her job to gather information about Father Crispy if Davey didn't believe in him?

Davey had responded that it didn't matter what he believed only what the people of Mission thought he was capable of.

It made a certain kind of sense, but still didn't sound like a good enough reason for Claire to start asking questions about Father Hayden. Everything about going back to work to be a spy scared her.

"And I'm not allowed to scare off any of the guests? Even Christine and her wife?" Claire had asked Davey.

"We'll try to protect everyone the best we can, but for your own safety, Brant can't suspect that you're trying to undermine her."

Tobin wrapped his hand around the baton, pressing his palm into the end and collapsing it. "If you like it so much, it's yours. Just don't let anyone see you with it. Keep it on you at all times, because Daisy probably goes through your draws when you're not in your room."

All this talk about being watched diminished her libido and the warmth she'd felt a few minutes ago was gone.

She slipped the baton into the front pocket of her apron. Even through the fabric she could feel the coolness of the metal.

After Davey had left them, Claire had asked Tobin about what had been going through her mind the entire conversation. "When can I leave?"

"We're going back right now," he'd answered.

"No, I mean, if I asked you to would you drive me back to Boston? Right now. If I didn't feel up to helping you and your friend."

Tobin had stopped walking and looked her in the eye, lowering the lantern so she could see his face without the glare. "Of course I would. If that's what you wanted. I've never been to Boston, it might be nice to visit."

That was all she'd needed to hear. "Just making sure."

She recalled all this from the bed in the shack, Tobin's arm around her, his hand playing with her hair, the cool of the baton pressing against her abdomen.

She felt a complete serenity that she couldn't remember having with Mickey.

It wasn't until her conscious mind spooled down and she fell toward sleep that the nightmares began. The coldness against her thigh became the chilled paw of Bert. As that refrigerator burn warmed, the paw transformed into the cold hand of Christine, bloodless and dead. From the hand materialized the rest of the woman's body. Christine's face melted and resolved itself into Allison's familiar half-smirk.

In her dreams Claire had discovered something, made a horrible connection that involved her friend that still wasn't strong enough to wake her.

She was so tired.

A world away, Tobin kissed her and tried to soothe her as she spoke gibberish in her sleep.

When Claire awoke to her alarm the next morning, she didn't remember anything about the nightmares.

Not even the part that so disturbed her while it was unfolding.

Chapter Twenty-Six

By the time Claire had stopped hitting the snooze on her alarm and returned to The Brant she was three hours late for work.

"Where have you been and what have you been doing? You've missed out on some major drama," Daisy said.

Any time anyone said the word drama aloud without describing the genre of a movie, Claire felt herself hating that person a little more.

Claire remembered her coaching. "I've been with Tobin, doing, you know." The plan was to hide her affiliation with Davey by playing up her sexual relationship with Tobin. "I'm only human."

"I've warned you about that, but…" Daisy threw up her arms, a blush evident on her fleshy face. It was working, Daisy didn't much care about whether Claire got cozy with Tobin or not, as long as she stayed away from Davey.

"Well. we've got a new cook," Daisy said. Changing the subject away from sex, a topic that appeared to both shame and intrigue Daisy. "You're no longer it."

Claire tried to look relieved. "Who is it?"

"Mr. Dwyer's wife. I'd forgotten that he had a wife until she showed up and asked to be let into the kitchen. She never comes to any of the hotel functions and doesn't help Pat mind the store."

Knowing what she knew now, "hotel function" in that context sounded like a euphemism for black mass.

Daisy had been taking care of Claire's route for her while she was gone, but now pushed the linen cart down the hallway towards Claire. "I took care of twenty-one and twenty-three for you already."

"Thanks. Does she seem nice?" Claire said. She was having trouble relating to Daisy in the way she used to before Bert. Now she looked at Daisy and wondered how much of the vacuous attitude was genuine and how much of it was a character she was playing.

"Pat's wife? She'll do until Roy turns up or Ms. Brant finds a professional to take his place."

Not that Claire remembered much more than dreamlike snapshots, but she tried to recall the masked female form that was helping to clean up the subbasement. Could that have been Daisy under that poncho, loading dismembered body parts of guests into a black garbage bag?

Claire felt a single bead of sweat glide down the back of her neck. She needed to get herself under control. Before this was all over, she would be speaking with much more intimidating people than Daisy. She chastised herself for letting Davey's ghost stories put a cinematic spin on the bad trip she'd had after that first party.

"Are you okay?" Daisy asked. "Are you sure you've just been with Tobin?"

"Yes, why?" Claire almost swore, felt cornered. She tried to think what she was supposed to do if she got caught, but they hadn't gone over that. In her moment of panic, she almost took the baton from her front pocket and rapped it against Daisy's thick skull.

"You look pale and sweaty is all, I just want to make sure you haven't been going to any more of those parties," Daisy said, fixing her mouth into a church-lady frown. "Last time that happened, I was scrubbing sick off the floor and changing your clothes for you. I told you I wouldn't do it again, remember?"

"I remember," Claire said, climbing back down from alarm. She hadn't been followed or found out. Daisy was just her mother hen.

"I didn't get much sleep last night. I'm living clean. Promise."

"*Not much sleep*? Ick! I don't need to hear the gruesome details of your personal life, Claire," Daisy said.

She was easily offended for a woman who'd just yesterday wrapped up a dead dog and just moments earlier was blushing at the same details from Claire's life. This was the bipolar duality of Daisy. "Please hurry up and clean the rest of these rooms."

Daisy collected up her keychain from the top of the cart as she passed and then walked down the stairs.

Claire found herself concerned that she'd offended Daisy in some way, but then steeled her nerves, reminding herself that she didn't have an ounce of pity left for Daisy.

There was Zen calmness in resuming her normal route and cleaning up after guests.

It was scary to realize that the exercise that had exhausted her a month ago now brought her a compulsive pleasure. She fluffed pillows, squared bed sheets, folded towels and let her mind go blank as she performed these menial tasks.

She let herself fill in details about guests' lives and vacations through their belongings. A brochure for cave formation combined with a flashlight to change her impression of an elderly couple into aging-but-still-brave explorers. A mound of condom wrappers in a young guest's trash bin told her that they would probably be returning to the room after breakfast. Cleaning was part detective game, part daydream.

It wasn't until she reached the honeymoon suite that the reality of the last twenty-four hours smacked her on the nose.

She remembered that she was not supposed to interfere with Christine and her wife, but was she really going to start taking exacting orders from a man who lived in a Winnebago parked in the woods?

The *Do Not Disturb* sign hung from the knob. That meant that they were probably in there. She fished her phone out of her front pocket, her fingers brushing against the foam-and-metal grip of the baton.

It was ten thirty. There were plenty of guests that slept that late. Protocol was to take note of doors with the sign out front and then try them again after all other rooms had been cleared.

Claire took a quick look around for any other guests or staff and then knocked softly on the door to the honeymoon suite.

There was no answer.

In for a penny, Claire started to think, but the aphorism came out in Daisy's voice so she stopped.

She knocked harder.

There were no sounds from behind the door, no groggy voices being woken from sleep, no gentle hiss of the shower, nothing.

They could have left for the day without removing the sign, Claire thought.

Or they could have been stabbed fifty times with ceremonial knives while Ms. Brant chanted "Hail Satan", Silverfish thought.

A woman that Claire didn't recognize opened the door, at the same time allaying her fears and scaring the shit out of her.

"Hello," the woman said. She looked terrible and her breath

stank of stale wine. "We've got the sign on," she said, glancing at the cart beyond Claire.

"Hi, I didn't mean to wake you," Claire said. "Is Christine there?"

"Excuse me?" The meek woman seemed to gain some fight when Claire mentioned Christine.

Christine came to the door, zipping up a sweatshirt over what looked like bare flesh. She put a hand on the woman's shoulder.

This must be her wife.

Even with no makeup and dark tearstained circles under the woman's eyes, Claire could see that Christine had married up. The dark-haired woman was a foot taller than Christine, all of it in the legs. She had smooth, delicate features and even though she was well over forty, was quite beautiful.

"Hello, Claire, this is Jane," Christine said, she lowered her voice to a whisper and addressed her wife, "go back to bed, okay?"

Jane nodded to Claire, then did a comatose about-face and shuffled back into the room. Christine closed the door behind herself and stepped into the hallway.

This was not the place to have a heart-to-heart and Claire felt herself getting nervous that Ms. Brant or Daisy was going to come bounding up the stairs. She couldn't think of a good reason for either of them to be patrolling the third floor at this time, but that didn't make her feel any better.

"We got the news last night from your friend Daisy, so Jane's having a lost weekend," Christine said. "I'm joining her." Her eyes were bloodshot and she looked like she'd been partying just as hard as anyone in the woods ever had.

"The news? What news?" Claire asked. Unsure what Daisy could have told Christine, but sure it wasn't the truth.

"That Bert had been found down the street. Squished to a pulp," Christine said. Her voice was flat, but Claire got the feeling that it was from exhaustion instead of callousness towards Jane.

Claire didn't speak, needed a moment to think. She was going to say something, she didn't know what. She took the same approach that one takes to pulling off a Band-Aid.

Claire said what she wanted to, as fast as she could.

"You and Jane need to leave. I can't give you a refund, but believe me, just get in your car and drive. Don't tell anyone else that you're going. Leaving your bags would be the best case scenario."

Christine's expression wasn't as confused as Claire had anticipated. She took a few deep breaths in with her nose.

Claire changed her appraisal of the woman from hungover to still-drunk. She wondered how much of this conversation she understood and how much she would retain after she'd crawled back into bed with her wife and a bottle of red.

Before Claire had a chance to elaborate any further, the older woman spoke.

"You're right. This is no place for us. We'll get out soon," Christine said. Claire was surprised. Even through the apparent haze of booze, there was a depth of knowledge to the answer.

But there was sadness to the understanding that Claire realized she could be misinterpreting.

Did Christine think that she and her wife were being run out of town by the bigoted manager of the hotel? It didn't matter. Let her think that Brant was hateful—she was—as long as it got them to safety.

"Now, not soon. Can Jane drive?"

"Don't worry, we'll be gone soon," Christine said, putting a reassuring hand on Claire's shoulder. It was unclear if the hand wasn't also there to stabilize Christine. She wavered slightly and Claire felt more weight than necessary press against her clavicle.

"You're not safe here," Claire whispered. She was unsure if Christine could hear her, even in the silent hallway. She spoke up, "Travel safe."

"We will," Christine said, removing her hand. Her eyelids drooped to three-quarters closed and then shot back open. "Thank you, Claire."

Christine turned and tried to open the door. Claire leaned in and used her keycard to unlock it for her. There was the sweaty rush of warm air and the subdued acidic stink of wine vomit in the room. Claire tried not to breathe through her nose, held the door and let Christine pass her.

The older woman grunted another thanks. Before letting the door swing past her hip, she'd unzipped her sweatshirt and let it fall to the floor.

The last Claire saw of Christine was her naked back, pale and fleshy in the shuttered half-light of the honeymoon suite.

Chapter Twenty-Seven

"Do you enjoy working here?"

The question seemed hand-picked to do maximum damage. It went so deep that Claire heard it hit bone.

It was a managerial line that Claire knew intimately. She'd heard it twice before: once while she was still in high school and once while she was working at Sunrise Cantina. Neither time had hearing it been a pleasurable experience.

When she was seventeen, she was asked this same question by a pudgy man wearing wrinkled khakis, three lanyards and a soul patch.

"If you're going to be an effective saleswoman, you're going to have to learn the art of the pre-sale," Greg, the manager of Funcosoft, had said. "What's not important is what game you're ringing up for a customer—they've already made that decision—but what game is going to get them back in the store."

He was speaking straight from the employee training video that she'd watched a week earlier.

Working at Funcosoft seemed like a natural fit for Claire. Silverfish had loved video games and found herself adored by the burnout boys for it.

Turned out that one week into her new job, she was receiving the then-unknown to her "Do you enjoy working here?" line. Greg with the soul patch was teaching her a valuable lesson, though not the one he thought. He had instilled upon her a healthy disgust of the question "Do you enjoy working here?"

Funcosoft was run more like a pawn shop than the breezy geek hangout she imagined it to be. Most of Claire's time was spent using a hot air gun to reapply shrink wrap to used games and sell unneeded game insurance to parents that didn't know any better.

She'd lost that job a week later. On her way out of the store for the last time, she stuffed a copy of *Ico* down the waistband of her own khakis.

It was a great game, so working at Funcosoft hadn't been a total loss.

After two years as a waitress, she'd been asked by the owner of Sunrise if she enjoyed working there. Unlike high school, Claire had an immediate Pavlovian response to the question. What began like a normal "how are things" time-killer of a conversation was suddenly a precursor to losing her job at Sunrise.

This was back when she was still attached to Mickey. Love, maybe. Young enough to buy his line of bull, but old enough to buy her own beer and know better.

"I love working here," Claire had said.

Paul, the owner of Sunrise and its three sister restaurants had given her an incredulous look.

Only later did she realize that their conversation had been Paul's way of gauging if Claire was a lifer.

This was the conversation he had when his employees were staring down the barrel of graduation. What he was tacitly asking was would you like to make this official? Did this romance have a future? Are you going to keep waiting tables for me 'til death do us part?

Paul was affable, but predatory. He'd bump your pay a bit, make you senior hostess, but he needed to know that he could depend on you.

She'd kept repeating how much she loved the job until it was three years after graduation. If Mickey hadn't burned the place down, she would still be slinging veggie burgers to Suffolk students. In a way, Mickey really was her Prince Charming. He'd broken the spell of Sunrise, released her with her deal with Paul, the fry-oil-spattered Mephistopheles.

Now she found herself confronted with the question for a third time.

Ms. Brant repeated herself, rephrasing the question slightly. "Do you like working here at the hotel?"

They sat in Ms. Brant's business office, somewhere Claire had never been before. The desk was almost tidy in its dishevelment. There were stacks of receipts and records that were tumbling over each other and knocked askew but still rubber-banded and paper clipped to their pertinent group.

Around the moulding of the room was a line of greeting cards pinned to the wall. Claire caught snippets of the personalized inscriptions in each card as her eyes flitted around, trying not to focus on Victoria Brant. Phrases like *The time of our lives* and *Thank you* and *The stay of a lifetime* stood out as she went around the room.

She wondered how many of the cards Ms. Brant or Daisy had filled out themselves.

"Of course I enjoy working here," Claire said, tired of answering this question. "Why do you ask?" This time she was taking the offensive, a route she hadn't employed with Greg or Paul.

Brant placed her hands on top of her desk, resting them next to a framed Ziggy cartoon. Did her knuckles really crack as she clenched and unclenched her fists, or was that just Claire's imagination?

"I've seen things," Brant said. As she spoke she kept her hands busy, closing up a folder on the left side of her desk and moving it into a plastic inbox at the right corner, "and heard things that make me think otherwise."

Daisy's face flashed into her mind. This was never a welcomed image, but especially not now.

Claire was stuck, unclear how she was supposed to be reacting. Was this pressure being applied for counter-intelligence purposes? Was she supposed to squeal?

Speaking from her gut had halfway worked with Christine, so she decided to go for it.

"Is this about Tobin?" she asked, letting a hint of attitude into her voice. Might as well sell it, she thought as she decided to go for indignant gusto. "What does my love life have to do with my employment at this hotel?"

She hated using Tobin like this, but talking about him also made the experience an easier one. She felt something for him, something she hadn't felt since the clumsy, romantic days when Mickey didn't seem like a complete loser.

Her heartbeat was now in her ears. She wasn't worried about keeping her job as a guest liaison. She was wondering just what the consequences for getting caught fraternizing with Davey's second-in-command would be.

"Your involvement with that boy does trouble me, makes me think less of you as a woman, but it's not the problem," Brant said.

"Nice try, though."

Claire wanted to read the Ziggy comic but it was at such an angle that she couldn't make out the words. She tried though, because she had the irrational feeling that a little levity would defuse all the tension in the room.

"What I want to know is why two of our guests decided to checkout of the honeymoon suite two nights early."

There it was, Christine had heeded her warning but hadn't followed her directions. Claire thought she'd understood and that she wouldn't try to checkout via traditional methods. Claire wanted her to put her wife in the car and drive.

"Their dog was found dead," she didn't add "by me, in the fridge."

"Last night. Why did they choose to leave this afternoon?"

"I'm not quite sure I understand the question," Claire said. She prepared to hit every range of emotion, her defense would be scattershot. "Ms. Brant, I don't know what I'm supposed to be apologizing for. Did they blame me in any way as they left? Because I didn't do anything!"

Her spray-and-pray sentiment that began as complete ignorance then progressed to whiny petulance and ended with an accusation. "Did they pay for the nights they booked at least?"

Brant didn't answer any of Claire's questions, just stared forward, hands crossed in front of her.

Claire could see them now, the cracks in the foundation. Brant's mask of composure was slipping. Frustration, fear or anger, maybe a combination of all three, whatever the old woman was feeling it was about to bubble forth.

Claire felt the sudden desire to push her seat away from the desk. Just a few inches would get her far enough away from Brant's concentrated hate that her hair wouldn't be singed, she was sure of it.

"You know full well why they left," Brant said, her voice nearing a tea kettle shriek.

Deny, deny, deny. There was no turning back. "I don't know why you're so upset, or why I'm in trouble right now, but all I can say is that I'm sorry."

Ms. Brant let out a breath that seemed to release all the built-up pressure, deflating her. The shoulders of her floral-pattern dress sank below the seatback before she pumped herself back up again. She not only changed her body language, but her expression as well. She'd lost it for a moment, but was now pulling the mask back up.

Claire watched the transformation in awe.

The lines of her face, the delicate curve of her smile, the streaks of gray in her hair: Victoria Brant had reconfigured herself back into a Norman Rockwell painting.

Although the words hit like a fastball, was completely at odds with the image she was projecting, Brant delivered what came next in monotone.

"Go clean up the honeymoon suite. It reeks of cheap wine and vaginal fluid."

Chapter Twenty-Eight

Cleaning the honeymoon suite was an endurance test.

The amassed trash and sweaty sheets were intimidating, but worse was the ticking of the clock. In an hour and a half she was leaving The Brant whether she was done cleaning or not. Neither Brant's cold-blooded reptile bitch attitude or Daisy's death-ray of sanctimoniousness was going to keep her in the hotel.

At six o'clock, Tobin was picking her up in front of the gas station and she was getting in the car and telling him to drive.

Not to the shack, but back to Boston. Civilization. She was resolved.

She only had to make it through this.

Unless they burst in here with their curvy knives and torches and bring you down into the basement, Silverfish said. *Hail Satan!*

The possibility seemed remote to Claire, but imminent to Silverfish.

Claire thanked herself for taking great pains to lose her imagination.

No matter how hard she'd tried to put away childish things, Silverfish persisted. So did her infantile flights of nerdy goth-girl fancy. The platinum streak was still there in front of her eyes, however faded it seemed now.

She may have sold all her kid stuff on eBay, but the baton proved that she was still capable of coveting a shiny new toy. The baton weighed down her front pocket and she put a hand to it to feel its hardness through the fabric.

There were few things more childish than a fear of the dark, but Claire still found herself switching on every light when she entered the honeymoon suite.

The lights removed all mystery from the room, but something about that was worse. The shadows would have been preferable.

Christine and Jane had left in a hurry, taking everything but Bert's leash and dog bed with them. The leash was looped neatly around the doorknob to the closet, Bert's tiny pillow of a bed sitting under it.

The placement of the dog's artifacts gave the impression of a deliberate marker. *In Memoriam: Bertrum Dog III.*

The room around Bert's belongings was less orderly. There were empty wine bottles sitting on every flat surface, the coffee table, both nightstands, and one under the TV. It was more wine than it seemed possible for two women to drink over the course of two days.

They hadn't been drinking from wineglasses either, Claire picked up a half-filled tumbler and held it up to the light. There was a ring of dried spittle on the top, the imprints left by a hundred different sips. She gathered up two bottles in her other hand and entered the bathroom, ready to toss the dregs into the sink.

The problem was that the sink was already occupied.

Claire stopped, the two bottles almost slipping out of her hand as she looked down. She used her foot to lay the toilet lid down and set the bottles on top of it.

With her hands free, she inspected the sink. There was a thick red line, the thick consistency of a splatter of chocolate syrup.

That's blood if I ever saw it, Silverfish said. But she'd never seen this much blood up close, only ever in movies. Before she knew what she was doing, drawn by some perverse desire, her fingertip was outstretched and ready to poke at the small viscous puddle. She drew up short before touching it.

That wouldn't be smart, Claire thought and decided to assume that the blood *felt* like blood.

She tried to piece together where the blood came from, her vision sweeping the room as if engaged in a life-or-death game of eye spy.

Something that begins with B. She looked back to the toilet, there was a broken tumbler set down on the tank. There was a ring of dried blood around the base of the glass. The bloody tumbler was staining a pink ring into the white porcelain that would be nearly impossible to wash away.

Christine or Jane had broken their glass while holding it, cut their hand,

and then drained the wound over the sink. The blood was still there either because they were too drunk to wash it away or left it to deliberately spite the hotel.

"I'll buy that," Claire said aloud. It beat every gory and fantastic explanation that Silverfish was hurrying to come up with.

There was a moment when it wasn't only Silverfish who thought they weren't getting out of the honeymoon suite alive.

But that moment passed.

After an hour of sweeping the room into passable order, Claire used her yellow dish gloves to heap a pile of blood- and wine-stained linens onto the cart.

She wheeled the towels and sheets down the hallway, growing bolder with each step. She'd always wanted to quit a job in a spectacular fashion and this was her chance.

She pulled the cart to a stop, put the brakes on the two rear wheels and left it in the middle of the third-floor hallway.

Claire estimated that it would take less than an hour for a guest to complain about the smell.

Fuck 'em, Silverfish said and Claire nodded along with her. Maybe the gross, bloody sheets left in the hallway would convince some guests to cut their stays short.

Although she would have liked to walk out of The Brant wearing her civilian clothes, Claire decided that she wasn't going to risk going back to her room to change.

She had her phone, her cigarettes and her baton, what more did she need?

Before descending the last flight of stairs into the lobby, Claire took the baton out of her pocket. She squeezed the padding, feeling the coolness of the steel underneath. Part of her wanted to be given a reason to use it. At least a reason to flick open the release button and extend it, just so she could hear that satisfying sound and be made braver by it.

She hadn't been given one, though. The front desk was unmanned: no Daisy or Brant.

Silverfish gave a sigh of disappointment, but Claire speedwalked through the front door and didn't look back.

With her hand that was not full of concealed baton, she woke up the screen of her phone. Five fifty. She was ten minutes early for her pick up.

She crossed Main Street and waited in front of the general

store for Tobin to arrive.

To preserve both the battery on her phone and an ounce of sanity, she counted a hundred Mississippis before checking the time on her phone again. Five fifty-two.

She scrunched down low against the general store window, trying to make herself small so she wouldn't be noticed by Pat Dwyer if he looked outside.

It was twenty-five Mississippis before Dwyer poked his head out the door. She heard the jingle of sleigh bells and looked over at him.

"Waiting for your fellah?" he asked. It was hard not to like him. Even after Davey had told her about the town's connection to Brant, she couldn't believe it when she looked at Pat.

Despite his age, his puppy-dog innocence and his white coat combined to create the image of a little boy playing dress up. *One day I'll be a real pharmacist. Then I'll help people feel better.*

Claire didn't respond, but noticed that she still had the baton in a kung fu grip and slipped it back into her pocket. The blood rushed back into her hand, she looked down to see that her fingertips were white.

"Why don't you come inside and have a Coke?" Pat said. "You never know how long a man's going to take. Believe me, I am one."

Claire smiled. "No thanks, Mr. Dwyer."

Pat just nodded and made an aw' go-on wave of his hand.

She looked back at the phone. Five fifty-six, less than twenty percent battery remaining. The calming presence of Patrick Dwyer did nothing to soothe the bubbles of anxiety popping and churning in her stomach.

The sleigh bells sounded again. Dwyer had stepped out in front of the store with her. He squinted into the orange of the setting sun. "Think we'll be lucky enough to have another nice one tomorrow?" he asked.

Claire watched the tops of the trees. They were a darkness that was reaching up to snuff out the sun.

"Yeah," she said, "seems like it'll be warm enough."

Dwyer took one small step towards her and then leaned against the window himself.

This close, she could smell him. His wasn't the smoky earth scent of Tobin or Davey, but the harsh chemical smell of a hospital, softened only by the gravy smell of country cooking. The smell made her uncomfortable.

She went back to counting Mississippis as he lapsed into silence and watched the sunset.

Claire tried to count as Silverfish observed and watched Main Street for Tobin's truck. There were only ever two or three people on Main Street at a time, all of them guests of The Brant stretching their legs after a day of striking out to the rest of the Berkshires.

Pat was close to her, eyes on the trees and the sunset.

He's not watching the sunset, silly. He's watching you.

It was the first thing her inner teenager said that she believed immediately.

They both waited for twenty more minutes and three cigarettes in silence. Dwyer only left twice to ring up a customer, coming back outside after each time.

When the clock on her phone read six thirty, she began walking down Main Street towards Tobin's shack.

She turned back only once. Pat Dwyer was still leaning against the storefront, watching her as she walked away down the road.

He gave her a quick wave.

She started walking faster, until she could no longer see the gas station. Then she broke into a run.

Chapter Twenty-Nine

Not being able to change before leaving the hotel turned out to be a blessing in disguise. The white running shoes of Claire's uniform were much easier on her feet.

Easier, not perfect. They were still doing some damage to her feet as they smacked against the uneven ground.

She ran for a couple of minutes at a time, taking frequent breaks walking the side of the road in order to catch her breath.

Neither Claire nor Silverfish had been much for exercise, it was one of the few things they still had in common.

In Tobin's truck, the shack was only a ten-minute drive up the street and down a dirt road. On foot—in the quickly darkening summer night—it was a journey and a half.

She reached the turnoff of the dirt road while the sky above her was still purple. No sun, but enough twilight to see by. Instead of sticking to one side, she walked down the middle of the trail where it was at its flattest. She had no desire to twist an ankle tripping over a root or stone.

By the time she reached the shack, it was almost completely dark. The world took on that weird two-dimensional feel it does when you're outside for the day-to-night transition. Grabbing for the knob to the front door, Claire missed the first time she went to grip on to it.

She got it on her second attempt, but the door was locked. Claire went to her tiptoes and took the spare key from above the doorframe.

The shack was small enough and well-insulated enough that a few hours of body heat was enough to keep the temperature warm for the rest of the day.

Tonight the shack was cold inside.

She flipped the light switch and the two low-wattage bulbs coughed to life.

The one feature of the room, the bed, was askew, as if someone had tossed the mattress over looking for something and made a halfhearted attempt to return it to its original position. Nothing else seemed out of place, but somehow that made the slightly off bed even worse.

Claire used her knees and shins to press the mattress back into place, moving it flush to the corner of the room.

Sitting down on the bed, she checked her phone for a text message or missed call. Tobin didn't have a phone, so this was beyond wishful thinking. Checking for texts seemed like an artifact of her life back in Boston, that magical time when she could send messages through the air to her boyfriend.

He's your boyfriend now? Silverfish asked. It was a valid question, but not one to try and answer at this exact moment.

The clock on the phone read quarter past seven.

She untied the white sneakers and pulled them off. Removing the pressure of the laces opened them up like a wound. First a chill washed over each toe, then pain replaced the numbness as blood pumped back into her chafed, sweaty feet.

If she wanted to check how bad the blisters were going to be, she could have peeled off her socks, but she kept them on to preserve the mystery.

Instead of her mangled feet, she focused on where Tobin could be and where he wasn't. It would have been impossible to miss his truck between the shack and the gas station, so that explanation didn't work. There was the possibility that he would be coming to pick her up from the south. She'd never seen him use that route to pick her up before, but she still didn't know how he spent most of his days. He could have, but he probably didn't.

They got him, Silverfish said.

Or he was caught up somewhere, Claire shot back, trying to push images of hooded cultists out of her mind. It was barely over an hour since he was meant to pick her up.

"I should have stayed at the station," she said to no one.

I'm acting crazy.

No, you're acting like a survivor, Silverfish said. *You got out of there because you knew it was no good, wasn't safe. You stayed visible and made it hard for them to do anything to you without another visitor of Mission seeing you.*

Her inner sixteen-year-old had a point. Maybe she had played it smart. Sitting on the edge of the bed, she considered her options.

Now that she was at the shack, it was about a ten-minute hike to camp. That was if she didn't get lost. Without Tobin to guide her through the darkness, that seemed unlikely.

She wasn't going back to the hotel. Besides Davey's claim that the town was home to a secret satanic society seeming more compelling with each passing second, it was now full dark. A two-mile trek in total darkness did not appeal to her.

The only smart option was to play the waiting game.

She laid her head back on Tobin's pillow and the motion cemented her decision. It took considerable effort to heft her legs up onto the mattress, but as she set them down she was hit with a blast of exhaustion.

I'll never be able to sleep, was her last thought before dipping into semiconsciousness.

It may have been a minute or an hour, but she was awoken by the crackling of underbrush outside the shack. At first, she thought the sounds could have been a deer, but after a moment it became clear that it was a human, their footfalls slow and deliberate, but still too heavy to be considered stealthy.

He's back! Was her first thought accompanied by white-hot warmth that bloomed in her chest and made her smile.

Or it's Roy, Silverfish offered. She tossed the idea out casually, an underhanded lob, but with the knowledge that what she was throwing was a live grenade.

Claire's hand went to the light switch, but paused before turning out the lights. Whoever was out there, they might not know that she was in here, but if she hit the lights, they sure would.

With the lights on, there was no use taking a look out the window. She'd be completely night-blind *and* on display for whoever was out there.

In some ways, this was the scenario that she'd been looking forward to the whole night. Pushing herself into the corner of the room behind the door, she took the baton out of her pocket. With a quick thrust of her forearm down to her side, the weapon extended.

The click felt great.

The footsteps got closer, stopping at the back of the shack and then working their way around to the front window. There was a soft knock, a knuckle on glass and a moment later the doorknob began to turn.

Claire cursed herself for not locking it.

"Claire?" the voice crossing the threshold asked. Not Roy, but not Tobin either.

It was Davey, his bearded face peeking behind the door, as if he had known where she was the entire time. His eyes darted down to the baton and then back to her face.

"It's okay, you can put that away," he said. His voice had the quiet calm of a hostage negotiator.

He showed her his hands, one filled with a large flashlight, and closed the door behind himself.

"Where's Tobin?" she asked.

"You may want to sit down," Davey said, "the situation has escalated, as I bet you've guessed."

He looked down at her feet and so did she. Her white socks were mottled with red and yellow spots where the blood and pus had seeped through.

"Are you okay?" Davey asked, but didn't wait for an answer. He knelt and brought a plastic container out from under Tobin's bed. He handed her a thicker pair of socks and she put them on without taking off her old ones.

"Thanks," she said. "Now tell me."

"He's been taken."

What he said didn't surprise Claire, Silverfish even less so.

"Where? By who?" she asked.

"Roy. That would be my first guess. Tobin's a strong guy, but if Roy got the drop on him, Roy's going to win. I mean, it's clearly not Roy pulling the strings, but to answer your question literally, Roy took him."

Davey was shaken, if she couldn't tell from the sweat and dirt on his cheeks, she'd be able to pick up on the fact that his speech was rambling and inarticulate. It was the opposite of what she'd come to expect from him and it scared her worse than anything else she'd seen so far this night.

"And to answer my question figuratively?" Claire asked. "You mean that Brant had him taken?"

Davey nodded, using his free hand to pat down his long hair, clicking the flashlight on and off with his other. "People like her…they don't get their hands bloody. Not when they've got a staff, followers."

Seeing a Davey who was no longer cool and collected was like watching while a magician pulls a dead rabbit out of his hat. The trick was not only ruined, it was *so* ruined that it would soon accrue therapy bills.

"There's something else, but I don't know if I should show it to you," Davey said.

"What? I can handle it," she said, but she wasn't so sure.

"We'd have to walk to it, are you able to?"

"I'll be fine," she said.

"Not after you see this you won't be," he said.

She stuffed her oversized socks into her shoes and they went on a walk through the woods.

Chapter Thirty

Davey had offered to carry her, but she'd declined. That was something she and Tobin did together. She would walk.

Her white stockings were beginning to rip around her shins, small holes started by the occasional prick from burrs and thorns expanded with each step. In the areas where flesh wasn't visible through the fabric yet, pinpoints of blood were.

She couldn't tell if her legs felt better or worse when the light wasn't pointed towards them.

In the radiance of the flashlight and the moon, Claire could see that Davey had a pistol tucked into his pants. It was wedged in the space below his spine and above his ass crack. The weight of it changed his gait, adding to the overall impression that this was the least comfortable Davey had ever allowed himself to be.

It seemed an awkward place to hide a gun and told Claire that Davey didn't wear one often.

"We're here," Davey said, casting the flashlight over the dark green fiberglass of a car. What make and model Claire couldn't tell, she could only see part of the fender and a bit of one door. The rest was covered in broken branches and dead leaves, buried the way a toddler might hide his Tyco trucks in the backyard.

They walked a few yards beyond the car mound until they came to a hill of upturned dirt.

Davey covered the beam of the flashlight with his hand and looked over at her. His hand glowed orange and she imagined him holding a ball of fire.

"You're sure you want to look?" he asked. "It's gruesome."

"Yes," Claire said before thinking about it.

The hole was rectangular, taller than it was wide, and not deep enough to be an effective grave.

"I found this on my way out here to find you," Davey said. "I didn't hear anyone working on the hole or leaving as I approached, so I think they were left like this for us to find. Are these the women you told us about?"

Claire looked away to be sick. She couldn't control herself and was splattering her hands and knees because she felt dizzy, the act of gagging the only thing that kept her from fainting.

When she was done she kept retching until the taste of blood had removed some of the acid sting of the vomit.

Davey placed a hand flat on her back, but she tried to dive away from it and shake it off, his touch worse than isolation.

She'd only looked into the hole for a second, but that had been long enough.

Christine's bare back stuck in her mind. It was the last part of the woman Claire had seen when she was alive. There had been something intimate about that glimpse of skin she'd been allowed in the hotel room, but now the same skin was pointed up in the night sky for anyone to see.

Jane and her wife were naked except for the clear plastic bags pulled down over their heads and zip-tied around their necks. Each bag had a dime-sized hole in the back of it. Blood pooled at the bottom of each bag, making it impossible to see their faces.

Claire sat against a tree, her back to the hole. They stayed quiet for a long time. They would have stayed like that longer, but Claire broke the silence.

"Give me that gun you've got," she said and placed her hand out flat. She then wiggled her fingers for emphasis.

Davey stood gawking at her for a moment before reaching around his back, his long arms made the motion almost comical.

"What do you need it for?" he asked. He looked at the chamber of the gun, not at Claire.

"You think that they've got him down in the basement? In the room that I told you about?"

"I don't know. It's been a long time since I've been welcome at the hotel, and I've never been invited down there."

"But if you had to take a best guess," Claire said. It felt strange to be the more in control party here. Davey was cracking.

"I'd say you're right."

"Then give me the gun and I'll go get him back."

"How? That's reckless," Davey said.

"He's going to be dead soon. Give me the gun," she said. "Since you shouldn't do it, they hate you."

Hate must have been the magic word, because he handed it over.

She was used to the weight of the baton so it wasn't the heaviness of the pistol that surprised her, but the lightness.

"What kind of gun did that?" Claire asked, motioning at Christine and Jane but not looking at them. If she saw them again she'd lose all resolve.

"Nine millimeter, I'd guess," he said. "I'm not an expert in these things."

"No but your followers are, right?" Claire said. She leveled the gun at him. That one movement of her arm seemed to flip a switch and turn the world into unreality. She'd never held a gun in her life, but hoped that every movie and video game she'd ever played was lending some credibility to her grip and stance.

"What are you doing?" Davey asked with real panic in his voice. If anxiousness had made him a different person, then fear had made him a different, pitiful species.

"Tell me that you had nothing to do with this," Claire said. "Tell me that you didn't kill them."

"Of course," Davey said. He placed his free hand in front of the barrel. It would not be an effective shield for his face. "It was her! She did it because this is what she does! I'm sorry, please put the gun down."

She did.

There was no proof that he was lying, not even a hint of evidence that she could think of. Putting the gun on him had just felt like the thing to do, so she did. Claire recognized that she was running on impulse now, sometimes with Silverfish pushing the buttons. It felt good to give up a bit of control in one area to take more back in another.

"Can you tell me how to fire this thing," Claire said and smiled.

Davey huffed, looked like he was regaining some amount of his former composure, and showed her how to click off the safety.

"Why were you so afraid? The safety was on."

"You looked like you knew what you were doing."

She laughed at this and then started off back towards Mission.

Chapter Thirty-One

The sky had already started to perceptibly lighten as she walked up the front path of The Brant.

Claire must have spent more time asleep at the shack than she thought. If the time was at all important, she would have checked her phone, but it wasn't so she had no desire to.

It was early enough that the sun would be up in an hour or two. That was enough information.

The grip of the gun was heavy against her breasts. She had no other safe place to hold it but her front apron pocket. To be safe, she moved her phone and baton to the elastic of her stockings. As she walked she hoped that they wouldn't slip down the band and become bulges against her legs.

She took a deep breath and pushed open the glass door. The sleigh bells chimed. They wouldn't have been a problem if she'd gone around back, but it was too late now.

At first it appeared that there was no one in the lobby, but then Daisy picked her head up from the front desk, hair tousled.

"Are you okay?" Daisy said. There was a thin stream of drool running over her chin and a red indentation where she'd fallen asleep on one of the guestbook's golden pens.

"I'm fine," Claire said. She wasn't, of course. Even the dull, half-asleep Daisy would be able to see that. Her stockings were torn and dotted with blood, her knees stained with dirt and vomit. She didn't need a mirror to know that her eyes were sunken and bloodshot. All over her body and face it felt as though the oily grime on her skin was a centimeter thick.

She kept moving forward, headed for the stairs. To get to the service stairwell she'd have to walk one flight up, head all the way down the hallway and then begin her descent down to the basement.

"Go back to sleep," Claire said, not bothering to speak to Daisy anymore and taking the first step up the stairs. Daisy was the only person left in Mission that Claire no longer felt intimidated by. She was comfortable enough to turn her back on her, but still took the steps two at a time.

She turned the corner at the top of the stairs and could hear the front desk phone being picked up off of its cradle.

"She just walked right in. I think something is wrong with her," Daisy said into the phone.

Et tu, Daisy?

It hurt to run, but she padded down the hallway carpet in double time.

At the top of the service stairwell she stopped and listened. It was unclear what she was supposed to be listening for but she'd know it if she heard it.

There was silence. The Brant had all the activity she'd become accustomed to when she first woke up for work: none.

At the basement door, she drew the gun out from her pocket and clicked off the safety like Davey had shown her. He hadn't shown her the rest, but she hoped that it was as simple as pulling back the hammer to point and shoot.

She wondered what Davey had done after she left him in the woods. Had he gone back to his camp to join the party that was probably still in progress? Had he stayed the night in the shack, ashamed that Claire had seen another side of him, the side he tried so hard to hide from his young fan club?

Her fatigue was catching up to her. She'd lost a minute daydreaming about Davey when what she needed to be was flying high on adrenaline.

It was possible that a few yards from where she was standing, Tobin's lifeblood was spiraling down the drain of Brant's kill room.

That was the image she needed to see to spur her on and she thanked Silverfish for presenting it to her.

Don't mention it, her teenage persona said in a voice made small with the weight of high school anxiety.

Claire's hand went so tight on the grip that she was worried she was going to inadvertently pull the trigger and send a bullet into a guest's room above her.

She opened the first door, undoing the latch before swinging it open as quickly as she could.

Even in the lowlight coming from the stairwell, she could tell that there was nothing in the basement but surplus tables, pool chairs and umbrellas covered with tarps. She propped open the door for its light and then walked into the basement.

This was the first time she was seeing this room sober and it felt at once foreign and familiar. It was the same sensation she had when she woke up after dreaming of Tokyo. Claire had never been to Tokyo, but there still felt like there was a certain authenticity to the dreams.

She moved through the room, careful to mind the chair legs, remembering the bruised shins she ended up with after tripping last time.

The sliding doors that last time had emanated that blue fluorescent light stood open, nothing but gloom and emptiness inside them. The tile kill room was empty. Not even Father Hayden's chair there to furnish it.

Claire stepped into the room, looked to all four corners, knelt down and nudged the drain with the muzzle of the pistol. Rust-red flakes flew up as steel scraped iron, but they were just that: rust, not blood.

Where is he? she asked herself, keeping the words in her mind, confident that if she spoke aloud someone or something would materialize to answer.

Tiled to look like a high school locker-room or not, the space had a power to it that Claire couldn't deny.

She asked herself if Christine and Jane had died here, and if they hadn't, whether they would still be dead if Claire hadn't interfered.

No, there's no time for that.

The guilt could crush her later, now she had to do the best she could to stop anyone else from dying.

"What do you think it is you're doing down here?"

For an older woman, Victoria Brant moved with frightening stealth.

Claire was not a violent person, but she'd never had occasion. Ms. Brant's *caught you with your hand in the cookie jar* tone made her want to plug the self-righteous old lady then and there.

Turning, Claire leveled the pistol at Brant's chest.

The woman was silhouetted in the doorway, backlit so that her shadowed face was unreadable.

Claire wanted to believe that Brant's nostrils were flared in surprise and that her lower lip trembled in abject fear, but she knew that Victoria Brant was stone-faced, implacable.

Would bullets even harm her, or would she spit them out like watermelon seeds before lifting up Claire's skirt and giving her the spanking of a lifetime?

Claire thumbed back the hammer, hoping that that was how it was done.

"We're going to room thirty-one," she said. "Now."

"Whatever Davey's put you up to, convinced you that I'm responsible for…"

"Did I say that we were holding a conversation before we went?" Claire interrupted her. She had to stop the words from coming out of Brant's mouth. Short of shooting her, yelling at her like a TV bank robber seemed like the second-best plan.

"He sent you to kill Father Hayden?" Brant said and then added a word, lower, for herself, "Coward."

"No, I sent myself to kill *you*. Now where's Tobin?"

"So that's it," Brant said, there was no fear in her voice, only moderate amusement. "Do you want to check every room on the way to thirty-one? Or should we start there and work our way down?"

"Let's start there, check out your priest first."

"We don't have your boy. You do know that, don't you? Why would we take him?"

Claire was done talking, she stepped forward, gun outstretched and Brant matched her steps backwards.

She wasn't completely unafraid, that was good.

"You take out your keycard," Claire said. "Slowly! And have it ready for when we get up there."

♦

Room thirty-one was identical to every other guest room only it smelled of shit and Lysol.

Brant entered the room in front of Claire.

To reduce the risk of a guest seeing the owner of the hotel being led upstairs at gunpoint, Claire had put the gun under her apron, keeping it trained on Brant's back. The result was a peculiar resemblance to Napoleon, but better than keeping the gun in the open.

She took her right hand out from behind the apron and switched the pistol to her left. Her right wrist was sore from keeping it cocked at such an awkward angle under the fabric.

"Here you go," Brant said. She lifted both hands. "Just an invalid man of God and an empty room, are you satisfied?"

Claire checked the closet and then moved on to the bathroom, taking one step in to make sure that there was nothing in the tub. Except for Father Hayden, the room was empty.

In the full light, Hayden looked even worse than he had in her drunken stupor. He was pitiful only up to the point where it was still possible for him to be unbearably grotesque.

Claire felt the conflicting impulses to both protect him and never lay eyes on him again.

His milk eyes seemed to fix on her as she studied him, his head tilted to the side as if to hear them better.

"What's he doing?" Claire asked. Brant looked over to the bed where Hayden lay propped up on a mound of pillows. Father Hayden pushed both of his hands flat against the top sheet and pushed himself up with what looked like incredible effort.

"Stay," Brant yelled. Her command went unheeded as Hayden disentangled one leg from the comforter and placed it flat on the carpet. "Can you hear me?" She was screaming, as if trying to be heard in a windstorm. "What are you doing? Don't get up. Stay!"

His knee shook as he tried to get up from the bed.

Brant crossed to his side of the bed and pushed him back down with two fingers from each hand. He crumpled back down onto the mattress as if she'd hit with a crowbar.

He must have been so weak.

That sympathy she felt towards Hayden rose up again, only to be quashed by the burnt man's high-pitched keening noise. The yelp lasted for only a second and sounded like a wordless attempt to dress down Ms. Brant for pushing him. He stopped for a coughing fit that ended after producing several brown globs into the fresh-looking bed sheet, using it like a tissue.

"Don't do that," Brant said, smacking Hayden's ruined hands.

He latched on to her as she came closer, one hand on each of her wrists. His melted fingers looked like tentacles wrapped around her liver-spotted skin. He must have had more strength in his hand than in his arms or legs because Brant struggled to detach him.

"What is he doing?" Claire asked, suddenly unsure where her sympathies were supposed to lie in this struggle. Was Hayden dangerous?

"He's never been like this," Brant said, dislodging one hand only to have it reattach itself to her throat.

"Get off of her!"

Hayden ignored Claire's shouts.

She stepped to the edge of the bed, far enough away from Brant that she wasn't going to be tackled by the bigger woman.

Brant's face was red, her cheeks puffed out. Hayden had her by the throat, but not firmly enough. She was able to inhale as he repositioned his hand, trying to fight off her defenses with his other one.

"Hey," Claire said and pressed the cool muzzle into Hayden's neck. The shiny, scarred flesh there wrinkled and grew taut around the end of the gun.

He stopped for a moment before turning to face Claire. *Can he see and hear me?* The question was irrelevant as he released Brant's throat and lunged forward towards Claire.

The gunshot echoed throughout the room, the sound waves seeming to punch Claire in the sides of the head. Her hand ached from where the recoil had jolted her and the smell of cordite reached her nose.

She hadn't meant to pull the trigger, it just happened.

Hayden was propelled back into his tower of pillows. The band of flesh that connected his neck and his shoulder was now incomplete and he was gushing blood onto the quilted comforter.

"No!" Brant shouted and dived to Hayden, applying pressure to the wound and hugging him to her in the same motion.

Rage, stress, stoicism and feigned sweetness were the only modes Claire had ever seen Brant in, but now she witnessed the woman in panicked grief. "Please," she whispered into Hayden's hairless head.

There was the sound like the backfiring of a car from the street outside the hotel.

Brant looked up at Claire, her hands trying to staunch the flow of blood as Hayden flailed against her grip, not wanting to be held.

"What have you done to us?" Brant asked, tears in her eyes. The old woman jumped as another bang sounded, this one inside the hotel itself.

The gunshot was followed by another and another. They echoed through the hills of Mission, Massachusetts, Claire entirely unsure of their meaning.

Chapter Thirty-Two

From the woods on the opposite side of Main Street, Eden watched Claire walk into The Brant Hotel.

Once the sleigh bells had tinkled and she watched the door close and stay closed, she walked out of the woods and into the gas station parking lot.

She wore her new gown, the shoulders tied and the corners sewed just enough to keep the dress on. As she walked she could feel the breeze against her naked body, the white gown fluttering up and then floating back down to rest against her bare skin. Her scar felt cold like drying putty, but the rest of her was warm enough.

Behind and in front of her, more white figures exited the tree line. Some of them were so far away that their gowns were just white specks that seemed to levitate above the ground, approaching the few houses that rested on the hills.

They had planned for this for weeks and no one would dare miss their cue.

Everyone wore their gown as they had been instructed.

Everyone except Jeb, who'd ripped his trying it on and would not let her fix it. He'd torn off a corner of the sheet and wrapped it around his waist.

The loincloth did little to hide his manhood. It bobbed and jumped in time as he walked.

Jeb was making a mockery of the ceremony. She knew that she was supposed to love him, but if someone had to die because something went wrong, she hoped it was him.

Most of the figures who made their way down Main Street carried some kind of firearm. The majority of them were hunting equipment, rifles and shotguns, but there was the occasional handgun as well. Rarer still were the cutting weapons, the machetes and the hatchets, but they were there too.

Jeb carried an ax and a gun. He held the rifle aloft by its stock, useless as anything but a cudgel. His arms flexed as he swung at the air with his ax, letting out a growl as he did so.

She shushed him.

Eden and Jeb broke from the flow of the group, approaching the back door of the general store while the four others continued onto the rest of Main.

Pat Dwyer and his wife lived in the apartment above the store. The plan was to wait for the signal before Jeb broke down the door and they both rushed inside.

Eden knew that convincing Jeb to wait for the signal would be the most difficult part of the operation, but she had a plan for that, too.

They stood facing each other on opposite sides of the door, Jeb's enthusiasm apparent in the twitch of his muscles. His scars danced and jumped with every small, excitable movement he made.

Eden allowed the shoulder of her gown to slip, felt the cool pre-morning air on her nipple.

Jeb laughed and then used the end of his ax to put the strap back in place.

She let it fall again. This time was her turn to giggle. She watched the loincloth rise as Jeb became excited. She knew that she would have no problem getting him to wait for the signal.

Jeb propped both his weapons against the brick wall.

Eden began to peel off her gown.

Before she could lift it up over her head, there was movement behind the door of the general store. She let the fabric drop back down and listened.

Without warning, the door swung outward, Pat Dwyer propping it open while holding a bushel of groceries. They must have caught him making an early morning delivery to the kitchen across the street.

The old man gasped, but that was the only sound he was able to get out before Jeb had both hands wrapped around his mouth.

Eden picked up the gun from against the wall and leveled it against Dwyer's heart.

She looked at Jeb, hearing teeth crack as he tightened his grip. Jeb bumped Dwyer's head against the wall with a soft smack.

"Don't," Eden said with a hiss. "You've got to wait!"

Before she could get the words out, there was the unmistakable sound of a gunshot from inside the hotel.

Jeb smiled and nodded at her.

Dwyer's eyes went wild like he knew what came next.

Eden pulled the trigger.

♦

Allison was going to be a queen and a queen needed a crown with crown jewels to accompany it.

While Davey was off preparing for the morning, she'd assembled her crown and garland. She'd worked so hard to make her accessories that her fingers had bled.

Now in the morning light she could see the blood that dotted her new gown. Eden had been so nice to make it for her and she'd made a mess of it.

She frowned but only for a moment, until she realized how nice her jewelry must have looked.

The best building material she could find had also been the most problematic.

The branches she used had thorns. The pain and blood had been worth it, though, because the ensemble had worked out brilliantly.

Allison used the thorns to hold the flowers in place.

She stood by the fire, pirouetting along with the embers to music that she imagined.

There was no one left in camp, so she danced with abandon. Her necklace and crown infrequently caught on the fabric of her gown or her flesh and tore a small hole.

She could hear Davey's footfalls before she saw him.

Allison stopped dancing and watched him enter the camp. His tall shoulders were stooped, but even slouching he was handsome.

He straightened up and smiled when he saw her.

"You look beautiful," he said and gave her a dry, light kiss on the mouth.

"Do you really like it?" she asked and gave him a quick spin. It was a motion she'd remembered doing for her then-boyfriend after her first spray tan. She might have been paler now, but she felt so much better to be away from all that stuff.

"I love it," Davey said, checking his watch. He was just being silly to amuse her, because he didn't wear a watch. "Is it about time to go, you think?"

"Oh yes," she said only just able to contain her excitement.

He offered her one long arm and she took it.

"Your kingdom awaits, my queen."

Her blush must have outshone the bright droplets of blood dribbling from her scalp.

◆

Tobin and his Chosen Few stayed low and wove through the cars as they crossed the parking lot and entered the back door of The Brant.

The four of them waited in the hallway that led to the lobby for a minute and waited for the signal to sound.

Tobin had been allowed to put together his own group for the overthrow of the hotel. Davey had suggested Jeb, but Tobin did not want to be outshone by the big bastard. He'd taken Sissy, John and Billy, all good soldiers who could follow orders and shoot straight.

They stood in a rough semicircle, holding their breaths. The boys watched the lobby in front of them, Sissy kept her eyes on the parking lot through the glass door.

Tobin had opted not to wear the gown and wore his plain clothes. The other three were dressed in their white gowns, makeshift duct tape bandoliers around their shoulders to hold their ammunition.

The first shot sounded from upstairs, followed almost immediately by one outside.

Jeb, Tobin guessed. Recklessness. That was another reason why he hadn't brought him along.

Tobin took the lead down the hallway and peeked around the corner before waving the rest of them towards him. Daisy was seated at the front desk, her brow knit with worry, her hand on the telephone.

"Start on the rooms," he said to John, "I'll deal with her."

Tobin walked into the lobby, bringing the Winchester up and shooting Daisy low and in the side. She fell off her chair as she screamed.

The shot might have been enough to kill her, might not have.

Sissy and Billy made their way up the stairs to the second floor, not stopping to look at Daisy crumpled behind the desk.

"Move," John yelled, from behind them, "don't let anyone get by you." Tobin imagined that the teen was relishing the opportunity to be the second-in-command, the illusion of power.

Tobin knelt over Daisy. She moaned as he dug a card key out of her front pocket and tossed it to John over the desk. The teenager wiped the key against his gown, cleaning the blood off it, and then followed the rest of his strike team upstairs.

Tobin stayed behind with Daisy.

"You were always so sweet Daisy," he said. "Why?"

She just breathed and whimpered in response, so he made his question more specific.

"Why did you choose to stay here? You're not much older than me, you've got nothing in common with them," he said. "Why do it? You must have known that it was going to come to this. Your team losing."

She swallowed hard, it sounded like there was more than saliva and mucus in her breath, probably some blood.

"You haven't won anything," she said. Moments from death, it seemed like her lisp had finally been fixed.

There were screams and the sound of gunshots from upstairs.

"Hear that?" he asked. "That's victory. By any means necessary."

"Fuck you," Daisy said. It was the first time he'd ever heard her curse, it sounded so unnatural that it may have been the first time she'd *ever* cursed.

He glanced at her wound and then noted that the puddle under her was so dark and deep it was almost black.

"Are you going to kill that girl?" Daisy asked, launching into her own set of questions. Her voice was so weak that it sounded like she was fighting off sleep. "Did she know anything about this? Does she know what you are?"

Tobin ignored her questions, just stared at her and waited for her to stop.

"She doesn't," Daisy said, sounding confident that she'd guessed the right answer.

"Sorry, but don't want to waste the bullet on you," he said. "These are expensive. But I can't leave you here like this."

Tobin stood, sucked on his upper lip in frustration, and kicked

Daisy's face in with the heel of his boot.

Chapter Thirty-Three

Hugh Mayland was not going to be able to kill the old woman. Not only that, but he was going to die while cradled in her arms, her tears dripping off his head like a baptism.

These realizations seemed to make the blood pump faster out of the hole in his neck.

He would also die without ever knowing who shot him.

"Where's Tobin?" the voice shouted. The girl must be closer now, hovering over Brant and Hugh. He imagined that she was still brandishing the gun, possibly pushing it into the old woman's skull the way she'd put the tip to Hugh's neck.

Who the fuck is Tobin? Hugh thought. There was an entire drama that he was not privy to. He tried to construct a narrative that could have lead to this point.

"I told you that I don't have him," Brant said. "They're killing everyone, don't you understand? Can't you hear?"

Hugh was unclear on what that last part meant. He couldn't hear anything outside of this room. It could have been a made-you-look feint on the old woman's part. He hoped that the girl wouldn't fall for it.

Shoot her, he thought. *Please!*

Even though she'd shot him, Hugh had nothing but love for the girl.

He even had the time and concentration to make up a story about her. In his version of events, she and her husband, Tobin, had been staying at the hotel. Something had happened to Tobin and this girl had figured out that Brant was responsible.

In his mind, the girl was an avenging angel, the gun-toting vigilante that Hugh Mayland had often dreamed of becoming himself since his stay here began.

If she'd also been instrumental in putting Hugh out of his misery, so be it. As long as he got to hear her put a bullet in the old woman, he would die happy.

"This is your last chance, tell me where Tobin is," the girl said to the old woman.

"He's with David! This is all David's work! Don't you understand that, you thick little—" The old woman's words were cut off by another gunshot, this one sounding like it came from the opposite end of the room, but that could have just been a trick played by Hugh's near-deafness.

The old woman's arms twitched and then disengaged themselves from Hugh. He fell back against his pillows and into a pond of his own wetness.

"Why did you do that," the girl cried out. Hugh thanked God that she was still alive, but he was still confused as to what had happened, who had shot who.

He put his hand out in front of him and reached over the bed. Hugh tried to exercise them every day, but still his arms and legs were weak. He was beyond tired, but the adrenaline pushed him forward.

Slipping in his silk pajamas and blood, he slid onto the floor, hitting a familiar softness that wasn't the carpet.

There was muffled conversation elsewhere in the room, but he couldn't make out the words and probably would have been too excited to focus.

He moved his hands around the shape on the floor, trying to make an image in his mind, wanting to savor this moment before he lost consciousness.

It was Brant's body, all right.

Even though the familiarity shamed him, he knew every wrinkle and contour.

When he reached her face, he couldn't stop himself from giggling, the childlike joy flowing up from his throat. He coughed and felt blood try and fail to clear out of his lungs.

One side of her head was missing, the skull jagged like a broken terracotta pot.

He pressed both hands into Brant's face, feeling the warmth leaving her body.

He'd outlived her.

Hugh Mayland felt comfortable enough to slump back against

the bed and allow himself to be done.
He hoped that the afterlife looked like London.
He couldn't wait to see Hannah again.
He embraced the blackness, hoping that later there would be light.

Chapter Thirty-Four

Claire's father had taught her not to lie, but if she was going to lie, he'd said, make sure to stick with it.

Brant was sticking to her lie.

"I told you that I don't have him! They're killing everyone, don't you understand? Can't you hear?"

Claire held the gun tight. Each gunshot caused her to spiral deeper into confusion, so she held on to the one thread that still made sense.

"This is your last chance, tell me where Tobin is," she said. She was no longer afraid to get close to Brant. If the woman tried to attack her, the woman was going to die. That was the decision Claire had made.

As Ms. Brant started to speak again, saying something about how this had been all David's fault, there was the familiar beep of the electric lock at the hotel door.

Claire spun just in time to see Tobin enter the room, his rifle raised.

He fired and the top corner of Brant's head exploded. Claire's right side was covered in warm gore as Brant slumped to her knees and fell backwards against the nightstand. Father Hayden's water pitcher fell to the floor but didn't break.

"Why did you do that?" Claire asked, the question coming out in more of a yell than she wanted it to. The gunshot still rang in her ears.

Tobin lowered the rifle, letting it swing around his shoulder, the strap drawing it to his back. He held out both hands for her and even though she was confused and scared, she went to him.

His arms wrapped around her tightly. Disregarding the mess

of blood and specks of bone, he kissed her.

His fingers wrapped around her free hand while the other's worked to disarm her. She let him take the pistol, only feeling a slight postpartum chill when she no longer had the familiar weight in her hand.

"Where were you?" she asked, her voice a whisper. He held both of her hands tighter to stop them from trembling.

"They had me locked in one of the second-floor rooms," he said. "I have no idea why they didn't bring me downstairs and end it. Their mistake, I guess."

"Who let you out? What are those shots?"

"The revolution, baby," he said. "That's the answer to both questions."

The blood on her face was beginning to cool and become sticky, she had to get it off or she was going to vomit like she had in the woods.

"I need to wash my face," she said and pushed Tobin away. She hoped that the push hadn't been too rough, whether he was able to tell how disgusted she was.

She left bloody handprints on every bathroom fixture she touched. The embossed gold faucet knobs were tarnished with blood, the brown red giving definition to the leaping rabbits etched into the metal.

The water felt good, cleansing not only her skin but her clogged mind.

"It's been quite a long day," Tobin yelled from the bedroom, filling the silence between gunshots. The sounds were infrequent now. The revolution must have been winding down.

There was suddenly something she wanted to know. She thought how to phrase the question as she toweled off her face. Tobin's answer would change the course of the next few minutes.

She yelled through the bathroom door, listening for Tobin's answers.

"How many guests has Brant killed? Do they always use the same place?"

"Don't think about that right now."

"I want to know," she said while pulling at the elastic of her stockings. The baton had left a divot in her skin and the blood rushed back into it with pins and needles.

"It's a ceremony. Part of ceremony is tradition, so yeah. I guess they use that room for," he paused and added some weight to his voice, "everything."

She unlatched the door, then flushed the toilet to hide the sound that the baton made.

She thought of the way that Christine and Jane had been left in the woods, thought of the way that Davey had described the scene. *I think they were left like this for us to find*, he'd said.

She opened the door, walked straight at Tobin and swung.

Her first hit had been crucial and she didn't miss, bringing the bulb of the baton down on his nose, flesh and cartilage buckling and folding like wet cardboard. There was no blood yet, but there would be.

She wound up again with her backhand before he had a chance to bring his arms up to defend himself. Her next hit wasn't as clean but there was still a satisfying smack as she clipped him on the left ear.

There was no pain in Tobin's eyes only confusion and anger.

"No," he said, falling to the floor. He brought his right hand up to block her while his left fumbled with the strap of his rifle.

With one swing, the three outermost fingers on his left hand broke outward, the webbing between the pinky and ring finger tearing, blood rising up from the wound.

He was never able to get the gun up after she went back to working on his head. She didn't stop hitting him until she could no longer lift the baton.

Before leaving, she took Tobin's rifle and looked around at the three bodies in the room.

Father Hayden had stopped breathing, his hands covered in Brant's blood. Even without lips, she could see that he'd died with a slight smile on his face.

◆

After everything that had transpired in room thirty-one, The Brant Hotel was silent. Outside there were no more gunshots.

Claire walked to the end of the hallway, unable to see much out the window other than a small swath of the empty Main Street going out of town.

Descending the service staircase, she stopped at the second

floor, hearing voices. In the hallway, there stood three teenagers dressed in white bed sheets. She recognized them from camp, but couldn't place their names.

Around them the carpet of the second floor hallway was covered in bloody footprints, the doors to all the rooms ajar.

Claire knew what had happened without being told. These three young people, kids, had killed everyone on the second floor and were now having a cigarette break before moving upstairs.

You should kill them, a voice inside her said. It wasn't Silverfish anymore, but it wasn't Claire, either. It was a new voice, forged and tempered in room thirty-one.

She didn't kill them. There were too many of them and they were too used to killing. She may have gotten one or two with the element of surprise, but she'd never survive. Instead she stayed out of sight and waited for them to head upstairs before creeping down the hallway and towards the lobby.

She didn't look behind the front desk, didn't want to know where the blood that seeped under the wood was coming from.

"I'm sorry, Daisy," she said to the empty lobby.

Through the glass double doors she could see the familiar glisten of a fire.

Slip out the back, you can try and escape through the woods.

"No," she said aloud, not entirely sure why other than that she was tired and that Mission seemed too big, too populous for her to escape on foot. She approached the front door and pushed through, listening to the sound of the sleigh bells announce her exit to the outside world.

There was a bonfire on the front lawn of The Brant. Most of the kindling was made up of The Brant's green-and-gold sign, but a portion of the burning material wasn't wood.

Claire smelled the cooking meat and was ashamed of herself for feeling hungry.

She went unnoticed for a longer time than seemed possible. As she stood there, she watched Jeb throw Pat Dwyer's naked body onto the fire while everyone watched and sang songs.

Davey stood with his back to her, hand in hand with a new member of the congregation, one that Claire didn't recognize from the back. The girl turned around to look at her.

As she turned, Allison became the first of the gowned figures to notice Claire.

"There she is," Allison said and pointed. Her friend opened her mouth wide enough so Claire could see the space in her teeth.

What have they done to you? Claire thought, a tear running down her face.

Everyone else turned, some of them still singing, some of them becoming silent.

Davey stood next to Allison, his hand resting across her shoulders. Allison was bleeding from the head where she wore a crown of thorns and flowers, but the pain didn't seem to bother her. She just smiled an empty, unknowing smile.

A member of the crowd, his name was Josh, Claire thought, looked to Davey.

"Can we?" Josh asked Davey. The boys and girls around Josh looked at Davey too, hands tight around their weapons.

"Yes."

Davey nodded and a moment later the bullets tore through Claire's body.

Next Summer

Allison's fingers glided over the keyboard. There had not been a computer in David's Airstream, so she had not touched computer keys in what felt like forever.

Her fingers still bore the scars from when she'd made her ceremonial crown and garland, even though the wounds were long healed.

She looked up at the message she'd typed into the text entry window.

Recently under new management, The Second Chance Hotel is on the lookout for a dedicated, hard-working and friendly guest liaison to join our staff for the summer. Experience is encouraged but not required. Serious inquiries only.

There were times like these, when she was reminded of an aspect of her life before, that she would get a touch of sadness. A brief, deep loneliness when she thought about Claire. Then she remembered how the others had shot her down like that, only to laugh about it later.

But then she remembered all she had now, how lucky she was to be growing up and growing *into* a community, and all the parts of her old life that she did not need any longer.

She stood up from her seat, stretched and hit the *Post* button.

Out in the lobby, she could hear Sissy helping a guest to check-in. As Allison left the office, the girl briefly paused in helping the customer to greet her.

"Good morning, Ms. Pomero. How are you today?"

She felt great.

Acknowledgments (2014)

After I finished this book, I stood over my better half's shoulder and watched her as she read the entire thing. It was three in the morning by the time we were finished. I love you, Jen.

My other pre-reader, Josh, did some heavy lifting, too.

Huge thanks to these people who have read my work and said nice things about it publicly. This includes Brandon St. Pierre, Jennifer Francis, Jesse Lawrence, Anita Eva, Tod Clark, Mike Antonio, Andrew Kasch and anyone else who was kind enough to take the time and review or tell a friend about *Tribesmen* or *Video Night*.

I'm in the blessed position to know some tremendously talented writers who've influenced both my work and career. Eternal thanks to Stephen Graham Jones, John Skipp, Matt Serafini, Ed Kurtz, Lynne Hansen, Jeff Strand, Gabino Iglesias, Cameron Pierce, J. David Osborne, Shane McKenzie, Bracken MacLeod, David Bernstein, Alan Spencer, Aaron Dries, Nate Kenyon and last (but not least) my friends and vocal supporters John Boden, Mercedes Yardley, Ken & Sarah Wood and the rest of the *Shock Totem* crew.

Big ups to Sam McCanna for turning my books into gorgeous T-shirts for his company Skurvy Ink (skurvyink.com) and Justin Coons and Nick Gucker for their art.

Final thanks to Don D'Auria, who's not only my editor, but a fount of 1960s and '70s Euro-horror knowledge and quality conversation.

Apologies to anyone I didn't mention above, not the least of which seems to be my mother and father, the people I owe the most. I love you.

Author's Afterword

I don't have kids, but I've been told that it's not cool to favor one kid over the others.

I don't have kids, but I *do* have a backlist of novels. But since it would be grossly inappropriate to compare novels to children, I feel like I'm on firm moral ground when I declare that *The Summer Job* is my favorite novel on that backlist.

Between school and work I spent a little over seven years living in the city of Boston, and even while most of the book takes place in the fictional(?) Mission, MA: this is a book that serves to remind me of a place I love.

Though I was born a New Yorker and am currently a proud Philadelphian, there is something about New England.

I mean, we have Dunkin Donuts here in Philly, but I rarely visit them, preferring to keep Dunks a treat for Boston visits. Like the smell of dead leaves in the Commons, or the taste of the fish and chips at my favorite Irish pub: it's one more piece of sense memory that I want to remain special.

And speaking of Boston visits: I still get up to town once a year. I do it on business, vending my books at the Rock and Shock convention in Worcester (Woostahhh), MA. When I call that business, it's more of a mix of business and pleasure, because I've been going to Rock and Shock long before I was published, would gladly travel to it if I didn't sell a single book at the con.

But I do sell books there and *The Summer Job* is usually the one I try to sell the hardest to people who come up to the table and seem hesitant to pick up a "har-u-rah" book.

It's mellower than my other stuff, it's more feminine, it's more (I think) literary. At least, that's what I'd thought it was before going back over it to prepare this new edition. But there's also a fierceness that I didn't remember it having. There are also a few characters who I must have blocked from my memory, they were just too unpleasant. And those aren't bad things: if anything I'm surprised that I can be surprised by something I wrote.

Don't worry: I'm going to end this extended pat on the back very soon, but before I do I have a few pieces of housekeeping (or "guest liaisoning" if we can borrow a term):

Those acknowledgements preceding this afterword are from the first paperback edition, since then the book has been released as a beautiful limited edition from Sinister Grin Press, who I must thank (Tristan Thorne, Matt Worthington, Frank Walls) and with a cover by the supremely talented Sasha Yosselani, who I must also thank. This new mass market edition sports a cover by Fredrick Richardson. Who did a spectacular job, I think. Justin Coons designed a T-shirt and then was cool enough to print me out a gorgeous poster of the same design in color.

Thank you so much for taking the time to read *The Summer Job*. If you liked it, I sincerely hope you consider leaving a review (both Amazon and Goodreads help immensely) and check out some of my other work.

If you didn't like it: I still hope you leave that review and check out some of my other work (it's TOTES different, I promise).

Until next time. I'll see you in the New England of my dreams.

Warmest wishes,
Adam Cesare
1/26/2017

Want More Cesare? Read on to get your fix:

THE BLACKEST EYES
ADAM CESARE
AUTHOR OF *EXPONENTIAL*

Download a FREE exclusive ebook
by visiting www.adamcesare.com

The Blackest Eyes is a mini collection of two short stories. This ebook is free for everyone who signs up for *Adam Cesare's Mailing List of Terror*.

What are you Waiting for? Go to AdamCesare.com and sign up today!

THE LOW SEASON

ADAM CESARE

Also Available:

The Con Season

Horror movie starlet Clarissa Lee is beautiful, internationally known, and…completely broke.

To cap off years of questionable financial and personal decisions, Clarissa accepts an invitation to participate in a "fully immersive" fan convention. She arrives at an off-season summer camp and finds what was supposed to be a quick buck has become a real-life slasher movie.

Deep in the woods of Kentucky with a supporting cast of B-level celebrities, Clarissa must fight to survive the deadly game that the con's organizers have rigged against her.

A demented, funny, bloody, and strangely-poignant horror novel.

**Available now in ebook,
paperback, and audiobook.**

THE ITALIAN CANNIBAL HORROR CLASSIC!

WARNING! BANNED IN 28 COUNTRIES

ADAM CESARE'S
TRIBESMEN

Also Available:

Tribesmen

"Sick and sardonic and just plain brilliant." **- Duane Swierczynski, author of *Fun & Games* and *Canary***

"The best new writer I've read in years. Wonderfully lean prose and edge-of-your-seat thrills. Drop everything else and start reading *Tribesmen*." **- Nate Kenyon, author of *Day One* and *Sparrow Rock***

"A cunning, cinematic redmeat feast for weird film lovers and horror freaks, Adam Cesare's *Tribesmen* is a first-rate literary midnight movie, and a blistering debut. BRING YOUR FRIENDS!" **- John Skipp**

"*Tribesmen* is a gory and clever homage to those Italian cannibal flicks that we all love so dearly, but without the real-life animal cruelty! Highly recommended." **- Jeff Strand, author of *Pressure* and *Wolf Hunt***

"Sometimes everything goes wrong, in the best possible way. Think *Snuff* and *Cannibal Holocaust* meeting at a midnight movie. And then give one of them a camera, the other a knife."
- Stephen Graham Jones, author of *It Came from Del Rio*, *The Gospel of Z* and *Demon Theory*

This novella is available in ebook, audiobook, and paperback.

VIDEO NIGHT

ADAM CESARE

Also Available:

Video Night

"If you put together the gore, action, monsters, and sense of excitement that made '80s horror movies so great, you'll only have about half of what makes *Video Night a must-read tome for horror fans."* –**Horrortalk**

"The momentum keeps building. The stakes keep escalating. The monsters just keep getting worse and worse, the catastrophic mayhem more juicy and hopeless. Best of all, the writing moves like a greased torpedo, compulsively readable as it rockets through your brain [...] Adam Cesare's gonna be a Fango superstar." – ***Fangoria***

"Video Night is a sharp, smart, energetic novel which pays tribute to all the brilliantly gross horror comedies of the VHS era, even as it carves out its own corners of shock literature." -***Daily Grindhouse***

Check out this novel in ebook and paperback.

THE FIRST ONE YOU EXPECT

ADAM CESARE

Also Available:

The First One You Expect

"The First One You Expect is a fast, sexy, fun, dangerous read, and enough of a taste to make me hope Cesare ventures into crime fiction regularly." **-Spinetingler Magazine**

"An engaging, contemporary thriller with a cutting-edge narrative, and characters so real they could live next door." **-Rio Youers, author of *Westlake Soul* and *Point Hollow***

"[A] hugely entertaining parable of the be-careful-what-you-wish-for kind." **-Crime Fiction Lover on their "Top 5 Books of 2014" list**

This novel is available in ebook and paperback.

MERCY HOUSE

ADAM CESARE

Also Available:

Mercy House

"Adam Cesare's *Mercy House* is a rowdy, gory, blood-soaked horror tale guaranteed to keep you up at night. And if that was all it was, I'd have been a happy reader. But Cesare has a maturity far and away beyond his years. His characters are treated with a surprising capacity for understanding and empathy, giving them an unexpected depth rarely seen among the nightmare crowd. *Mercy House* is the kind of novel you sprint through, eating up the pages as fast as you can turn them, and yet it lingers in the mind like a haunting memory, or the ghost of a smell. Cesare is poised to take the reins of the new generation. Looking for the new face of horror? This is it right here."—**Joe McKinney, Bram Stoker Award–winning author of *The Dead Won't Die* and *Dead City***

"*Mercy House* is 100% distilled nightmare juice. Adam Cesare notches up the horror to nigh-unbearable levels. Even my skin was screaming by the end of this book."—**Nick Cutter, author of *The Troop***

"Adam Cesare makes his presence felt with *Mercy House*. A no-holds-barred combo of survival horror and the occult."—**Laird Barron, author of *The Beautiful Thing That Awaits Us All***

"This is extreme horror at its best, so don't step into this book with an uneasy stomach. You must wait sixty minutes after eating before opening up *Mercy House*."—***LitReactor***

This novel is available as an ebook from Random House Hydra.

EXPONENTIAL

ADAM CESARE

Also Available:

Exponential

Five strangers drawn together at a roadside bar on the outskirts of Las Vegas. One rampaging monster absorbing victims and accumulating biomass as it stalks northward from Arizona. The miles separating them rapidly dwindling.

No: this is not the world's weirdest math problem, it's Exponential the rollicking, brutal, and weirdly inspirational horror novel from Adam Cesare.

Criminals and screw-ups need to face down a monster borne from science run amok in this literary tribute to creature features like Tremors and The Blob.

"*Exponential* is an excellent novel, one of the best creature features I've read in years..."
-Horror After Dark

"Adam Cesare's mix of grim violence and old school horror movie references make for a great read."
-Rue Morgue

Check out this novel in ebook, audiobook or paperback.

THE ARCADE SCENE
ISN'T DEAD...IT'S ALIVE!
ZERO
LIVES REMAINING
ADAM CESARE

Also Available:

Zero Lives Remaining

"The victims in *Zero Lives Remaining* are different--far from being the typical lost, wide-eyed fodder, these outcasts and obsessives quickly catch on to the truth of their awful situation and come to battle armed in their own strange ways...enough to leave every joystick of the arcade drenched in blood." **–RUE MORGUE**

"While *Video Night* is an exceptional novel, the wistfulness in Cesare's latest, *Zero Lives Remaining*, is twice as thick, the monsters a tad more gooey and intelligent, and the pacing even more insane. The result is a narrative that oozes a bizarre kind of melancholy while celebrating the classic video games and music of a different era while crushing bodies with more speed, creativity, and ease than most current best-selling horror authors put together." **–HORRORTALK**

"Cesare is on the top of his game and delivers possibly his best story yet by unleashing a fountain of energy to keep you turning pages and enough horror to make you think twice about touching another arcade game." **–SPLATTERPUNK MAGAZINE**

"I've yet to read an Adam Cesare novel that didn't A) immediately reach up from the page, grab me by the Dennis Rodman lapels, and pull me facefirst into the story, or B) get me to fall head over heels for this world before I'm even a quarter of the way through the book." **–STEPHEN GRAHAM JONES,** *Mongrels* **and** *The Last Final Girl*

This novella is available in ebook, paperback, and audiobook.

♦

For more titles and news about upcoming work be sure to visit AdamCesare.com to sign up for the mailing list or find Adam on Amazon

About the Author

Adam Cesare is a New Yorker who lives in Philadelphia.

His work has been featured in numerous magazines and anthologies. His nonfiction has appeared in *Paracinema*, *The LA Review of Books* and other venues. He also writes a monthly column about the intersection of horror fiction and film for *Cemetery Dance Online*.

His novels and novellas are available in ebook and paperback from Amazon, Barnes & Noble, and all other fine retailers.

Please visit his website adamcesare.com to learn more. Author photo by John Urbancik.